Isabella's Painting

by Ellen Butler

A
Karina Cardinal
Novel

K.C.

Power to the Pen

Power to the Pen
PO Box 1474
Woodbridge, VA 22195
PowertothePen@ellenbutler.net

Trade Paperback ISBN 13: 978-0-9984193-3-6
Digital ISBN 13: 978-0-9984193-2-9

Categories: Fiction, Thriller & Suspense, Mystery, Women
Sleuths

Cover Art by: SelfPubBookCovers.com/RLSather

Dedication

To Mimi.

Chapter One

The Nantucket style mini-mansion loomed in front of me like a bad dream, its glittering twinkle-lights and festive greenery seeming to mock my utter lack of holiday cheer. I rose from the BMW and straightened the wrinkles out of my black silk cocktail dress, better known as "Old Faithful"—my go-to outfit for work parties, rubber-chicken dinner fundraisers, and trips to the theater. Purchased over a year ago, its lines cascaded beautifully over my curves while hiding flaws and gave me the confidence I needed to get through tonight's party.

"You look stunning." Patrick, looking tall and handsome in a gray suit and red Christmas tie, closed the passenger door and kissed my cheek. He took my hand as we ascended the flight of steps, and I eyed the two life-sized Nutcrackers standing sentry on either side of the front door. "Your hands are cold. Are you nervous?"

"Maybe a little."

"Don't be. You'll fit right in."

We were in the midst of the Fort Hunt neighborhood, a wealthy Virginia suburb outside Washington, D.C., filled with rolling hills, private schools, and million-dollar waterfront homes. The house belonged to Patrick's parents. Needless to say, my current boyfriend had never really known the life of living paycheck to paycheck. Don't get me wrong, I certainly didn't grow up in a life of poverty either. But my parents, a school teacher and federal government employee, had three children to raise in pricey Northern Virginia. I had my fair share of law school loans, and though I made a decent wage working in the government regulatory affairs division for a medical association, I'd never known the luxury of not having to worry about what things cost.

However, it was neither Patrick's opulent childhood home nor his parents' money that had me wearing Old Faithful. It was the fact that this was the third time I'd met his mother and father, and the fact that I'd been hearing about the Dunne's annual Christmas bash for weeks, setting high expectations. Not only would I have to be on my game to impress his parents, but also 300 of their closest friends and business associates, as well. Tonight, I was to be paraded out publicly for the first time as "Patrick's Girlfriend," which meant going light on the wine, staying away from politics, and keeping an upbeat attitude when what I'd really like to do is kick off my stilettos and binge watch my favorite new addiction, *The Man in the High Castle,* on my comfy couch.

Not that I didn't enjoy a good party—only it was Friday and the end of a brutally long week that I'd spent attending one breakfast, lunch, or cocktail fundraiser after another, along with trotting all over Capitol Hill, trying to convince stubborn Representatives or their legal aides why H.R. 246 wouldn't ruin the healthcare community and was good for both doctors and patients. The bill was stuck in committee and needed two more impossible votes to move it forward to the floor before Congress went on break. I was tired and discouraged. The timing of the big Dunne shindig couldn't be worse. I'd thought about begging off, but in the end, I didn't want to let Patrick down. This was one of his holiday highlights. He'd been talking it up since Thanksgiving, and I'd been told the night wouldn't be complete without my presence.

Patrick opened the door and I followed his lead. My heels clacked against the marble floor as we entered a two-story foyer with a dramatic circular sweeping front staircase, also encased in greenery dotted with red bows along the posts, and what must have been a twelve-foot Christmas tree magnificently glowing in multicolored lights, red ribbons, and gold ornaments. The front hall looked like the cover of a decorator's magazine.

"Mom?" Patrick called as he dropped our overnight duffle bags. "Mom? We're here."

A brindle-colored greyhound loped up and nuzzled Patrick's hand. "Hey, Ivan, how are you, old boy?" Patrick said.

"He's a pretty one." I held out my hand. Ivan's long snout sniffed once, twice, then he leaned his head into it. "You never told me your parents had a dog."

"He's a race track rescue. Full name, Ivana Win."

"And did he?"

"Not once."

"That's okay. I bet you're happier here anyway, aren't you?" I cooed, scratching behind his ears. Ivan groaned at my ministrations.

"Patrick, is that you?" Mrs. Dunne, or Molly as she'd insisted I call her, bustled into the formal living room wearing slacks and a red sweater. Her dark blonde stacked bob, normally sleek and straight, was tousled as though she'd been running frustrated fingers through it. "And Karina. How handsome you two look." She pulled Patrick down to kiss his cheek. "Karina, I adore those shoes."

I almost embarrassed myself by sticking out my hand until I remembered Molly was a hugger. She opened her arms, and I bent down for the squeeze, inhaling the light flowery scent of her perfume. With me in heels, Molly only came up to my chin.

"Mom, you're not dressed yet."

"I know. There was a problem with the caterer, they showed up half an hour late and I've only now finished telling them what to do." She checked her watch. "It's alright, I've still got an hour, and everyone arrives fashionably late anyway, so really I have about an hour and a half. I was about to head up the back stairs when I heard you."

"Is there anything I can do to help?" I offered.

"As a matter of fact, I am going to put you two to work. Patrick, you know how we like things, and your father had a meeting run late and hasn't returned home yet. Can you oversee the caterers? Just make sure everything fits properly on the dining table. They should also be taking some of the hors d'oeuvres down to the sideboard in the lower level. Make sure they don't forget. The bartenders are in their usual places, and your father's already selected the wines."

"No problem. You go up and get dressed. Karina and I will take care of the caterers."

"Actually, I want Karina to come up with me. I'm waffling between two dresses and I want another woman's opinion, especially one with taste as good as hers."

Co-opted into helping Molly, I followed in her wake up the front stairs, down a long hallway, and into a master bedroom larger than the apartment in which I currently lived.

"Why don't you sit there on the loveseat and I'll bring out the two dresses."

Ivan had followed Molly as well and, after a few circles, he settled into his own red and green fleece bed next to the loveseat.

The first dress was a shiny gold potato sack. I wasn't sure if Molly was serious as she held the hanger up to her body.

I frowned and tilted my head. "Hmm, okay, let's see the other one."

She pulled forward a red dress that would hang off her middle-aged curves in the right places and dropped into a shallow V around her décolletage. Paired with a set of pearl earrings and necklace, it would be perfect for the event.

"The red. No doubt." I gave it a thumbs-up and rose to leave her to it.

"Oh, don't go just yet. I wanted to have a moment for some girl time."

Grimacing on the inside, but smiling on the out, I returned to my seat where Molly joined me.

"I just wanted to say that I know you've had a horrible week."

"How did you…"

"Patrick called. He told me about the trouble you're having with your bill on the Hill, and I know you'd probably rather be curled up in your robe and slippers on the couch—"

Is she psychic?

"—but I wanted to say thank you for mustering the effort to come. The party means so much to Patrick's father, and since Jonathan is deployed this holiday season, we all appreciate having as many loved ones as possible around this time of year." Her eyes misted as she spoke.

All my petty thoughts about Patrick's parents and their opulent party shriveled and died. It must be terrible having a child thousands of miles away, in danger, and during the holidays. I cleared my throat. "Well … it's my pleasure. Thank you for inviting me."

"Of course." She wiped away the dampness from her eyes.

"And, Molly, if you ever need … well … anything, don't hesitate to call. It must be hard with Jonathan deployed. You know, if you need to talk or …." My unformed thought faded out.

"Thank you, dear. You've already done so much by lifting Patrick's spirits around the holidays. I knew you were a good egg the first time we met." She patted my hand. "Now, I'd better go put on my glad rags."

By nine o'clock, the house overflowed with holiday revelers. Waiters roved through the crowds carrying trays of chicken satay, mini-eggrolls, and bacon-wrapped scallops while the caterers continually refilled empty trays on the dining table. The lower level was only slightly less crowded than the main level. A group of children gathered around the enormous flat screen, watching Christmas cartoons, while clusters of adults made idle chit-chat and drank the Dunne's booze.

Patrick slipped his arm around my waist, and I took a moment to lean against him, fully regretting my decision to wear the beautiful but deadly four-inch red heels. I had expected to find a comfy chair to claim as my own and engage in conversation with whatever guest was nearby while fading into the woodwork. However, between Molly and Patrick, I'd not had a chance to sit since my little tête-à-tête in Molly's room. She had insisted on introducing me to any person that came within a ten-foot radius, and when Molly wasn't introducing me, Patrick was insisting I meet this person or that person who had been a major influence in his life at one time or another.

My smile never faltered, I answered intelligently enough, and I enjoyed meeting many of the guests. However, Patrick and Mr. McDavis, an economics professor at George Washington University who was wearing a blinking Christmas tree tie, had moved into discussing the derivatives market, an area well out of any sphere of my expertise. I watched the bartender pour a martini and caught my breath when a stool opened in front of him. Shifting my weight, I waited for Mr. McDavis to finish his longwinded thought, so I could courteously excuse myself from the discussion and make a beeline for the seat.

McDavis paused to drink. I opened my mouth. Before I could speak, a light hand touched my arm.

"Excuse me, has anyone seen Marty?" Molly joined our threesome.

"Why, you're looking festive." McDavis lifted his glass in salute. "Smashing party as usual, Molly. You've outdone yourself."

"Thank you, Professor. We're so glad you could make it. I'm on the hunt for my husband. Councilman Olsen has just arrived, and I know Marty specifically wanted to speak with him."

"I think I saw him heading toward the library about fifteen minutes ago," Patrick said.

A gray-haired black man in a navy suit slid into my coveted bar stool, and I held back a sigh.

"Would you fetch him for me please, Patrick?" Molly asked.

"I'll get him. You stay here and visit with the professor," I volunteered, seizing the opportunity to escape McDavis and his derivatives.

"You're a darling, Karina. Do you know where the library is?"

"Yes, Patrick showed me around before the party started. Main floor, down the hall, past the kitchen. Where should I tell him to find the councilman?"

Molly glanced over my shoulder. "It looks like he's settled in at the bar." She indicated the navy suit.

I leisurely ambled up the stairs, through the bustling kitchen, and down the hall to be met with a closed library door. I knocked against the ornate wooden door and heard a voice, but the background noise from the party kept me from distinguishing what it said. Tentatively, I pushed it open.

"Hello? Marty?"

Patrick's father jerked, banging his hand on the underside of the large mahogany desk, and out of my periphery I could have sworn something at the fireplace on my right moved with a slight hissing noise. A white-haired gentleman wearing a smart black suit and red paisley cravat rose from the high-backed chair perpendicular to the desk.

Marty's bushy salt and pepper brows knit and the striking pale blue eyes he shared with his son narrowed as he said rather sharply, "Karina, what are you doing here?"

"I'm terribly sorry to interrupt, but Molly sent me to find

you." I gave a sheepish smile to diffuse his annoyance, realizing he'd probably told me to wait a moment. "Councilman Olsen arrived and is camped out at the bar in the basement … your wife seemed to be under the impression you needed to speak with him."

Marty's stance and face relaxed as I spoke, and he shoved his hands into his pockets. "I do indeed."

The white-haired gentleman shifted. He was a few inches shorter than Marty's six-foot frame and, even though Marty wore a festive red vest with a white dress shirt, the cravat gave off an effeminate air compared to his host.

"O'Brien, let me introduce my son's girlfriend, Karina Cardinal. Karina, this is a … business acquaintance of mine, Christoph O'Brien."

I stepped further into the room and held out my hand. "Nice to meet you, Mr. O'Brien."

"*Bonjour, belle.*" Instead of shaking my hand as I'd expected, the dapper gentleman bowed, his lips hovering over the skin before releasing it. "The pleasure is mine."

His old-fashioned manners charmed me, and I found my brittle smile softening into appreciation.

"O'Brien, I believe we'll have to finish this tomorrow. I need to speak with the councilman before he leaves."

"Of course, there's no hurry. I'm in town for a few days. Tomorrow it is."

The two men shared a look and a silent discussion passed, leaving me feeling left out.

"In the meantime, why don't you join the party? You must be thirsty. Karina, would you be so kind as to show O'Brien to the bar?"

Both men patently ignored the full brandy glasses sitting on the desk between them.

"Absolutely. Mr. O'Brien, if you'll follow me."

"Thank you, my dear, and call me Chris."

When I turned, my gaze darted to the fireplace to find nothing out of the ordinary. A large oil painting of a hunting scene I'd seen earlier in the evening when Patrick showed me the room hung still and silent over the mantel. A wooden crate I didn't recall from earlier leaned against the bookshelves on the far side of the fireplace.

I led Chris to the dining room table, which held considerably fewer platters, but still a fair amount of food, and was now sparse of partygoers. "Have you eaten? Why don't you fix a plate while I get you a drink? What's your poison?"

"Scotch on the rocks."

A pair of velvet wing chairs and drum table at the far side of the dining room, next to the fireplace, sat vacant. "I'll bring it back here. Would you like to sit while you eat?" I indicated the empty chairs.

"Indeed. Can I make a plate for you?"

"Oh, no thank you. I've already eaten. I'll only be a moment."

Minutes later, my aching feet finally got needed relief as I settled into the soft chair.

Chris sat opposite to me and picked up the lowball glass I'd placed before him. *"Sláinte."*

"Cheers." My wine glass clinked against his crystal. The Tempranillo warmed my belly as I relaxed quietly in my chair, allowing Chris time to eat.

"How long have you been with Patrick?" He finally spoke after finishing off the prime rib.

"We began dating at the end of September."

He swallowed an olive. "And the all-important question, how did you meet?"

"We met at a winery. Through Events and Adventures."

"Events and Adventures? What is that? One of those online dating sites?"

"No, it's a social singles meetup group. You pay to join the club and they organize different events around the area—hiking, biking, golf outings, tours. They even arranged for a skydiving adventure. You go on the ones that interest you, and everyone who attends is single."

His brows rose. "Fascinating. So, you've gone skydiving?"

"Heavens, no. I'm more of a winery-tour-and-horse-racing-adventure type of gal. I did one hike, but I'm not super outdoorsy. Half a mile down the trail, I twisted my ankle and two guys helped me limp back to the parking lot. Neither one asked for my phone number."

"I see. And is everyone looking for their significant other?"

"Not necessarily, many do it for fun and to meet other single people in the area with similar interests. Obviously, others are searching for something more."

"And you? What were you looking for?"

"A little of both. I enjoyed participating in organized activities and knowing, as a single person, I wouldn't end up being the third wheel. I'd been doing it for a few months when I met Patrick at the winery."

"Patrick was a member of the group?"

I shook my head. "I arrived late for our group's tour. But since I'd already paid, they bumped me to the next one where I met Patrick. He was there with his brother. One last hurrah before Jonathan was deployed. You know about Jonathan?"

"Of course." He dug into the potato salad.

I had a feeling he'd no idea who Jonathan was, but I didn't bother to explain further. "After the winery tour, they invited me to join them in the tasting room."

"Two gentlemen? How did you end up with Patrick?"

"I don't know." I shrugged and sipped the wine.

My mind went back to that fateful day. Jonathan and Patrick were both six feet tall with athletic builds and dark hair.

Jonathan's close-cropped military cut and upright bearing
bespoke his position in the Marines and serious nature, while
Patrick's slight slouch suggested his more easygoing and
approachable personality. Both men resembled their father with
prominent brows over deep-set eyes, but whereas Patrick had his
father's blue eyes, Jonathan shared his mother's soulful brown
ones. Both men intrigued me, but it was Patrick's humor and
intense gaze that sent tingles down my spine from the start. It
wasn't until later that I discovered his father was the Dunne in
Dunne and Jenkins Building and Real Estate—a large commercial
developer in the D.C. metro area. However, neither son had
followed in their father's footsteps.

Chris laid the fork and knife together on the empty plate and
stretched his legs out, reclining against the seat with the scotch
cupped between his hands.

"Enough about me. What do you do?" One of my shoulder-
length curls fell forward, and I tucked it back behind my ear.

"I work in the import-export business."

"I see," I said, not seeing at all. "And what types of things do
you import-export?"

"All sorts of goods and materials."

His replies were evasive, and my mind immediately jumped
to drugs. "From any country in particular? Mexico, perhaps?"

He chuckled as if enjoying a private joke. "No, not much
comes from Mexico. Italy, France, occasionally Spain."

"France? What does the U.S. import from France?"

"What does France export?" He stroked his glass. "Let me
think ... machinery, oil ... pharmaceuticals."

An undercurrent of secrecy seemed to surround his answers,
which I found odd. I didn't ask another question, instead waiting
for him to continue. He seemed to be enjoying the mystery he
was creating, and I wondered if he was simply an eccentric old
man yanking my chain.

Isabella's Painting ♦ 12

He clanked the ice in his glass and swallowed the last of the scotch. "But … my dealings with France are in wine."

"Yes, of course, French wines." My shoulders relaxed. "I had a fabulous full-bodied glass of Bordeaux earlier this evening. Quite possibly one of the best reds I've ever tasted. So smooth. Is that your business with Marty, then? Are you his French wine connection?"

O'Brien's faded blue eyes caught mine, then darted away. "No, afraid not. Our transaction has to do with his art collection."

"I see." Indeed, I did. Before the party, on my tour of the house, Patrick had taken to pointing out paintings by famous artists, some I knew, many I didn't. A Degas pencil drawing stuck out in my mind. But it wasn't simply artwork that his father collected. Throughout the house, there were shelves of glass cases housing antique statues, a Tang Dynasty vase, an Erté mirror, what I guessed to be hundreds of thousands of dollars worth of art and antiquities. When I mentioned this to Patrick, he explained to me his father had invested in state-of-the-art security. The glass cases were wired with pressure plates, and the exterior of the house was monitored with cameras.

"Are you buying or selling?"

Chris held up the tumbler and gazed at the melting cubes.

"Or would it be indiscreet to disclose such information?"

"Mm..."

The man roused my curiosity, but before I could ply him for additional information, Patrick came around the corner and spotted me. "I've been looking for you." He reached out his hand.

Giving an internal sigh, I took it and rose to my sore feet. "I've been keeping Mr. O'Brien company."

"Hello, I don't believe we've met."

This surprised me. I'd assumed Patrick would have met his father's art dealer, but perhaps there were many. I introduced the two.

"I've been enjoying this beautiful lady's company," O'Brien said.

"I'm sorry to take her away, but Mom's been wanting you to meet one of her friends from Junior League."

I turned to Chris and held out my hand. "Please, excuse me. It's been nice talking with you."

He took my hand, sandwiching it between his own. "Again, the pleasure was all mine. I am aware quiet corners should be left to old men. Lovely young ladies, such as yourself, should not have their lights dimmed by dark corners, but rather be the centerpiece, the belle of the ball."

I bit my lip and held back an eyeroll at his heavy-handed compliments. "I hope your business transaction comes to an effective conclusion."

"I have no doubt it will. I wish you a Happy Christmas."

"And to you."

"Happy Holidays." Patrick nodded at Chris, then slid his hand across my lower back and guided me toward the front of the house. "What the hell was that all about? Who was that old guy?" he asked, speaking out of the side of his mouth.

"I believe he and your father are discussing some art."

Patrick paused and glanced over his shoulder, but we'd gone out of Chris's line of sight. He shrugged, and we powered through the clumps of guests until I heard Molly's ringing voice. "Ah, Patrick, you've found her."

Chapter Two

Moonlight drifted through the gauzy curtains, and I stared at the unmoving fan blades above the unfamiliar bed. I rolled to my side. The glowing clock numbers read 3:24, and I scrunched my eyes closed, but it was no use. The pain wouldn't go away on its own. I needed to take something for it. This happened occasionally—one too many glasses of red wine and the tannins would attack my poor little brain, giving me a whopper of a headache. My limit was two glasses, and I'd pushed the limit tonight. Slipping out of bed, I pulled a pair of socks and a green hoodie out of my duffle bag and donned them.

The hallway was silent, but I could see well enough—tiny nightlights plugged into outlets intermittently lit the way to the grand staircase. My socked feet barely made a sound as I drifted down the steps. The tick of the grandfather clock in the front hall sounded loud to my ears, and I nearly jumped out of my skin as it struck the half hour with a sing-song chime. I stopped in my tracks with a hand to my chest. Finally, the last echo of the bells ended, and I carried on to the kitchen. It took but a moment to find a clean glass, fill it with water, and slug back the two little pills that would bring relief.

When Patrick told me his mother had invited us to spend the night following the party, I'd originally thought it a fine idea. It allowed both of us to drink and not have to worry about driving home or getting a cab. Now, I wished for the comforts of my own bed. As I swallowed the last of the liquid, I glanced around the kitchen, also lit by nightlights, and found little sign of the party that had just finished a few hours ago. No glassware or dishes lined the sink, and the counters were wiped clean. The catering staff did their job well. I ran my hand along the quartz and saw a green light in the corner, near the ceiling, turn to red. It was one of the motion sensors Patrick had pointed out earlier. He'd said the motion sensors were only turned on when the house was empty. The light turned green again. I waved my hand, and the light went red. I guessed the sensors were always on by default, just not armed to trigger the alarm.

Gently, I laid the glass on the counter. Something else came to mind that Patrick had mentioned. There were no cameras inside the house. Molly had put her foot down, and refused to allow Marty to install interior cameras, because she "didn't like the feeling of being spied on in her own home." His father relied on the pressure plates beneath the sculptures and artwork to keep them safe. When I'd asked Patrick about the hunting scene above the fireplace in the library, he laughed and said it was practically worthless. His mother had picked it up at a flea market when they were a young couple, struggling to make ends meet. It held more sentimental value than a monetary one.

The knob twisted beneath my fingers, and the low glow of the lamp came to life. Somehow my feet had drawn me down the hall to the library, and now I stood staring at the "worthless" painting. Though I valued the beauty and importance in historical culture, I knew very little about art. Living in the D.C. area, I had trotted through the art museums on the Mall for class field trips, and occasionally played tour guide for out-of-town guests. I could differentiate between a Picasso and Degas, but that's where my expertise ended.

The hunting scene looked good to me. The brush strokes were fine, and the bright red paint colors of the hunter's coats drew me into the picture. Black and white hounds, their tails up and ears perked, seemed ready to dart off into the fields to find their fox. However, the painting wasn't the reason I stood in the library now. Brazen curiosity could be the only explanation.

My fingers pushed and prodded decorative pieces of trim surrounding the mantel, the fluted plinth, the center of a carved flower, the pineapple in the middle of the frieze. Nothing. I couldn't shake the feeling something had moved in this area, and Marty had definitely been irritated by my barging in. Was there a hidey hole in the fireplace, or possibly a passage to a secret room? The residence was large enough to house a hidden chamber. I remembered reading an old gothic novel about an art collector who kept high-value artwork in a concealed room off the study. I felt like Miss Marple searching for a clue.

But a clue to what?

When the fireplace yielded nothing, I turned in a circle. Floor-to-ceiling bookshelves lined both sides of the long walls of the rectangular room. A library ladder on rails stood midway down on the left side. It would take hours for me to test the books and knick-knacks filling the shelves. Besides, my instincts told me the books were the wrong track.

The opposite end of the room from the fireplace revealed a pair of French doors leading out onto the back patio and pool area. Marty's antique desk sat closer to the doors than the fireplace. On it was a desk blotter, pencil holder, a few framed photos of family, and various bric-a-brac. The cleanup crew must not have visited this room because the brandy snifters from earlier remained. Chris's still held liquid in the bulbous glass, however, Marty's had been emptied.

The leather chair creaked as I lowered myself onto the seat. Ahead of me rose the magnificent fireplace. The bottom drawer was locked, but the other drawers opened and closed with little effort and were filled with nothing unusual—files, paperclips, pens, a stapler. What had Marty been reaching for? I closed my eyes and allowed my fingers to feel under the lip of the desktop. Sure enough, some sort of catch met my searching touch. I pressed. There was a click. The hunting scene disappeared upward to reveal another smaller painting.

The grandfather clock began its chime, startling me. I jumped, pressing the hidden button, and the painting disappeared. In between the tolling, I heard a new sound—the creak of a floor board. My fingers shook so much it took an extra few seconds to twist off the light before darting back to safety. The last bong of the clock, striking four, echoed through the house as I entered the kitchen.

When Patrick discovered me, I was innocently perusing the leftovers in the subzero refrigerator.

"What are you doing up?" he asked in a soft voice.

I pulled out a leftover meat and cheese platter and prayed he wouldn't notice my uneven breathing, flushed countenance, or hear the pounding of my heart. "Woke up with a red wine headache. I thought some protein might help. Your mother won't mind, will she?"

"Not at all. I've a bit of a headache, too. I guess everyone overindulged. Wouldn't be the first time."

"How did you know where I was?" I pulled the plastic off the tray.

"I thought you might be cold, so I snuck into your room to warm you up." He leered at me before snatching up a cheddar square and popping it in his mouth.

Since we were an unmarried couple, Molly had seen fit to give us separate rooms, even though I was thirty and her son thirty-two, and I was pretty sure she knew we spent our weekends together. However, the house was hers, and if she wished to observe the proprieties, who was I to argue?

"Naughty boy. What would your mom say?" I bit into a slice of summer sausage.

He pulled down a glass from the cabinet and stuck it in the refrigerator water dispenser. "She'd probably tell me I was honor bound to make an honest woman out of you."

I snorted. "She does know that we spend the weekends together. Hell, she phoned my apartment looking for you at six in the morning last Saturday."

"Oh, she knows. She just turns a blind eye." He took a long drink. "My mother would like life to be one of her historical romances, where all the women are virginal innocents that reform the rakish Duke and are the making of the man."

My brows rose, and I leaned against the counter folding my arms across my chest. "Uh-huh, and you would be the rakish Duke in this scenario?"

He put down the glass with an audible clink and wrapped his arms around my waist. I caught the faint scent of his spicy cologne and allowed my hands to creep up to his shoulders. "No, in my scenario you are already a fallen woman since you were no innocent when we met. I am the lord who will take the hussy, peddling her body to make a living, off the streets—"

My palms planted themselves against the soft green T-shirt on his chest. "Did you just call me a prostitute?"

"Shh. I'd take her as my mistress, giving her a home and a safe environment. Eventually, I'd fall in love and make an honest woman out of her."

"I see ... and you would be what ... Baron of Baloney? The Marquis of Malarkey?" His teeth flashed, and I bit my lip to keep from laughing. "I do believe you've been reading too many of your mother's smutty novels," I said in my best Scarlett O'Hara accent.

He didn't answer, and in the dim light I watched his face turn from playful to solemn. His grin slid into a straight line. His light eyes bored into me; serious thoughts seemed to swirl behind them.

My own smile disappeared; I touched his cheek. "What?"

"You were pretty amazing tonight."

"You're pretty great yourself. I've no idea how you kept up with the Professor's derivatives discussion."

"I kept my eye on you the whole night."

"Stalker." I gave a breathy laugh.

"Do you know how many people came up to me and complimented you?"

"How many?"

"Dozens."

"So, I pass inspection amongst the Dunne elite?" I wiggled my brows.

"You more than pass. Everybody loves you. You seem to have outdone any girlfriend Jonathan or I have ever brought home."

"Of which, I'm sure there were many."

"Less than you'd think."

"Why so serious?" I ran a finger along his jawline. "Isn't it a good thing that I didn't embarrass your family, or myself for that matter?"

"It's just that ..." His lips pursed, and I watched an internal debate wage.

"Oh, for heaven's sakes, stop thinking and just kiss me already."

So, he did.

It was a lovely soft kiss that warmed my body through. He pulled me close, and his hands slid beneath my hoodie, rubbing up and down my silky pajamas, then descended to cup my derriere. I do believe I would have wantonly allowed him further indiscretions ... if the lights hadn't flashed on, practically blinding me.

In a nanosecond, we were a foot apart from one another.

"Hello."

"Dad?"

"Patrick, Karina." Marty came around the corner, pulling the sash tight on his red and black plaid robe. "What's going on?"

"Karina had a headache … and … I was hungry. What are *you* doing up?"

"Same as you. Hungry. I never seem to have time to eat at these damn affairs. What are we having? Um … salami, wonderful." Marty plucked up a piece of meat, wrapped it around a chunk of gouda and took a bite. "Don't tell your mother, she's been restricting my sandwich meats. Something to do with nitrates."

My face blazed with embarrassment. I couldn't believe I—a thirty-year-old woman— almost got caught making out with my boyfriend by his dad. In the kitchen, no less. How demoralizing. Then I remembered my snooping mission, and it burned for a different reason that had nothing to do with my carnal thoughts about his son.

"Well, I think I'll leave you boys to it. My headache is feeling better and I could use a few more hours of shut-eye. Any time in particular we need to leave in the morning?"

Patrick grabbed my hand and gave me a quick peck. "I'm in no hurry. Go ahead and sleep in."

Marty bade me goodnight as he scooped up a stuffed olive. I escaped back to my room where I stared at the ceiling fan for another hour before finally falling asleep.

Chapter Three

The cursor blinked inside the little Google search box. It had
been over a week since the Dunne's holiday bash, and I simply
hadn't had time to explore the barely glimpsed painting. Okay,
maybe that wasn't exactly true. I'd been wrestling with the fact
that it was none of my business to know why Marty was hiding a
two-by-two-foot painting behind his fireplace. However, my
overwhelming curiosity kept tugging at me like a whiny toddler.
On more than one occasion, I'd almost asked Patrick about it.
Most recently, during dinner on Tuesday night.

We'd met up at an Italian restaurant close to my office in Old
Town Alexandria. Patrick had been telling me about a new client
his firm landed when my gaze fell upon a painting of Venice on
the wall behind him. His words became a distorted buzz as my
thoughts were drawn back to his father's dim library.

"Hello?" Patrick's hand waved in front of my eyes. "Earth to
Karina."

The restaurant noises interrupted my daydream, and Patrick
came back into focus.

"You zoned out on me and had this queer look on your face.
What happened?" Patrick grinned.

I opened my mouth to tell him what I'd seen above the
fireplace, but the waiter arrived with our food. By the time he left,
I'd reconsidered and instead diverted Patrick onto a discussion
about our plans for New Year's Eve.

The cursor blinked. I'd glimpsed the painting so quickly, I
wasn't even sure I knew what to search for. My fingers moved to
type in the only thing that stood out to me—black and white

floor. The image search yielded nothing but some wild striped floors and techniques for laying black and white tile. I then tried—famous painting black and white checked floor—which also yielded nothing but a forty-minute diversion down a rabbit hole and a new desire to repaint my kitchen floors. The chair creaked as I shifted. Rotating my stiff shoulders, I wondered for a moment if I sought in vain.

However, I knew I'd prevaricated with the first two searches. I forced my fingers to type the words I'd been fearing from the beginning—stolen painting, black and white checkerboard floor. More of the same. The mouse scrolled through images until, midway down, I paused. There it was, the distinctive black-and-white checked floor. One lady sat in profile at a pianoforte, while another stood singing with sheet music in her hand. In between the two women sat a man on an orange chair wearing a brown coat and sash, his back toward the viewer. The foreground revealed a tall counter covered in a blue and red Turkish rug with a mandolin resting upon it. A forgotten cello lay on the floor partially obscured by the carpet. I clicked the image and read a headline by the *UK Daily Mail* about a Boston mobster and a five-hundred-million-dollar art heist from the Isabella Stewart Gardner Museum.

Before I could read further, a staff meeting reminder popped up in front of the article at the exact moment Stacey, one of my coworkers, appeared in my doorway.

"Are you coming?" She waved a packet of paper at me. "It's an all-staff meeting."

"Yes, of course." With a few clicks of the mouse, I dismissed the reminder and bookmarked the webpage before closing out of the internet browser.

****

The pinot grigio slipping down my throat tasted of honeyed pear, and I welcomed the refreshing flavor as my sensible heels skittered across the floor. I flopped down on the couch with a sigh. The day had been so busy I'd not had time to return to the article, and now the little black laptop on my coffee table mocked me. On my way home, Patrick texted to tell me he was running late for dinner. I'd turned the stewing crockpot down to warm, and the crusty boule bread I'd picked up from Panera during lunch sat on the cutting board. There was nothing else I needed to prepare for our meal. With a sigh, I put down the wine and opened the computer.

The Isabella Stewart Gardner Museum heist happened early in the morning on the eighteenth of March in 1990. Two thieves dressed as police officers gained access to the museum, tied up the two security guards in the basement, and spent over an hour robbing the museum of thirteen works of art, including Rembrandts, a couple of Degas, a Flinck, a Manet, a Chinese vase, and *The Concert*, by Dutch painter Johannes Vermeer.

After twenty-seven years, not one piece of artwork had been recovered and, as I followed links and delved deeper into the robbery, bizarre stories and theories regarding the reason for the theft and location of the artwork reigned supreme. One *Boston Globe* investigative reporter, who must have spent years of his life following the trail, was thought to have been shown one of the stolen Rembrandts during a shady late-night visit to a Boston warehouse. On more than one occasion, it sounded as though there had been a possibility of a negotiated recovery of the artwork, only to have those chances lost, either because something had spooked the negotiator into becoming tightlipped, or it turned out to be a false lead.

Another article revealed the FBI dug up a famous mobster's Connecticut yard—twice—to come out empty handed. There were countless different theories as to where the art currently resided. Through all of them ran two consistent themes. First, the Boston mafia was somehow involved in planning the original theft. And second, the artwork had not been burned, as sometimes happened when paintings had been stolen, to cover a thief's tracks. The art heist had been investigated by the FBI, reporters, professional art recovery agents, multiple Gardner Museum heads of security, and dilettantes, such as myself. The FBI and attorney general remained on the case and continued to actively follow legitimate leads. The Gardner museum dedicated a portion of their website to the stolen artwork, posting a ten-million-dollar reward for information that led to the recovery of the masterpieces.

"Dinner smells delicious."

I slammed my laptop shut and shoved it away as if it had bitten me.

Patrick entered the living room, loosening his tie. "Sorry I'm so late. I found your phone sitting on the dash and your car unlocked." He held it up before tossing it to me. "I assume you didn't get my text to go ahead and eat without me?"

"Thanks, I forgot to bring it up." I checked for messages. "Did you lock the car?"

"Yes. You know, that's the second time I've found your car unlocked."

"Subconsciously, I'm hoping someone will steal it." I laughed. My ten-year-old silver Chevy sedan had over one hundred thousand miles on it, multiple door dings, and had done battle in two fender benders. The last was so minor, I never bothered to get the baseball sized dent out of my bumper. I figured the dent made it easy for me to identify the car in a parking lot.

"It doesn't matter. I was doing some work too." I scooped up my half-drunk glass of wine as I rose.

Patrick leaned over and kissed me. "Mm, tasty. What are you drinking?"

"A pinot grigio. Pull up a chair. Shall I fix you a glass?"

"Absolutely." He followed my suggestion, sliding onto one of the bar stools at the kitchen island.

"Tell me about your day. Did you finish preparing the presentation?" I asked.

Patrick prattled on about his prospective client while I retrieved the silverware and bowls and sliced the bread. I tried to focus on what my boyfriend was saying to keep my mind occupied and my eyes from straying to the laptop, which held a surfeit of opened browser tabs on the Gardner heist. I placed two steaming bowls of stew on the counter, poured a glass of wine for Patrick, topped off my own, and joined him.

"So, what do you think?" he asked.

Crap. What did I miss? What's he talking about? Divert! "Well … I'm not sure, what do you think?" I raised a spoonful of stew to my lips, blowing on it before taking a bite

A look of confusion crossed his features. "I thought this was a no brainer. You love the theater."

"Yes … I" —*What show? Where? When?*— "think, of course…"

"And box seats."

"Yes, wow. Well, box seats—"

"Look." Patrick put down his spoon. "I know you haven't met the Graysons. They couldn't make it to the party this year, but Tom Grayson is one of my dad's oldest friends. And Phyllis, his wife, is as sweet as southern pie. I'll be there, and my parents will, too. I'm not sure who else will be invited…"

"Yes, yes." I held up a hand. "No need to say anymore. What night again?" I lifted my phone off the counter and scrolled to the calendar app.

"Next Thursday, the twenty-second. The show is at eight."

Normally I took a yoga class on Thursdays, but there was no way I'd bypass box seats to a show. "Okay…" I typed in the event. "Theater on Thursday it is. You said the Kennedy Center, right?"

"Are they showing the Nutcracker anywhere else?"

I snickered at his naiveté. "It's Christmas. The Nutcracker is probably showing at fifty different venues between here and Baltimore."

He paused and tugged his ear, one of his more endearing traits. "I think it's the Kennedy Center, but I'll double check. Oh, and my parents invited everyone to cocktails and hors d'oeuvres at their house. Six thirty. We'd have to bug out of the city before six to make it. Do you want to? Or should we just meet them at the theater?"

I looked at my calendar for Thursday. I had a five o'clock meeting on the Hill. It would make my life a whole lot easier if we stayed in the city. Nevertheless, come hell or high water, I wanted another crack at that painting. How I'd make it happen with a gaggle of cocktail drinkers and Marty in my way, I'd no idea.

"Cocktails are great. I'll metro to your office. We can leave from there."

Chapter Four

The midweek afternoon sun shone bright with high, light fluffy clouds, no breeze, and temperatures hovering around the mid-forties—a perfect winter day. My ten thirty meeting ended early, and I wasn't expected back in the office for another hour. I pulled on my gloves as I stood in front of the American Indian Museum, contemplating the columned building across the vast expanse of grass separating the Smithsonian museums. Flicking the scarf around my neck, I strode across the gravelly pathway, determinedly heading toward the National Gallery of Art.

The National Gallery of Art comprised of two buildings. The East building, on my right, was designed by famous Chinese-American architect, I.M. Pei, on a trapezoid footprint with sharp angles. The architecture reflected the modern art collections it housed. However, my feet walked to the left toward the classical lines of architect John Russell Pope's West building, completed sometime in the early '40s. Having visited in the past, I knew all the ancient masters were housed in the West building.

Five minutes later, I approached the marble information desk. A pair of German tourists moved aside and a short-haired African-American woman wearing a cranberry blazer greeted me. "How can I help you?"

"I was wondering if you have anything by Vermeer on display?"

"I believe so, let me check." Her long, lacquered nails tip-tapped across the computer keys.

My research had revealed the number of paintings attributed to Vermeer were limited to either thirty-five or thirty-six, depending upon the source. It's one of the reasons why art lovers argued a price couldn't be placed on the missing Vermeer, because there were so few in existence. The *Girl with the Pearl Earring*, due to the 2003 movie of the same name, was probably Vermeer's most well-known painting in modern day, but if I recalled correctly, it was displayed somewhere in Europe.

"It looks like we currently have two on display: *Girl with a Red Hat* and *Girl with a Flute.*"

"Wonderful. Can you tell me how to find them?"

She pulled out a map and provided directions to the Dutch rooms, circling the chamber where the two paintings hung.

My favorite of the two had to be the slightly larger *Girl with a Red Hat.* I say slightly larger because the two paintings weren't any bigger than nine or ten inches tall. The facial features of the models—high arched eyebrows, straight nose, narrow bone structure, and wistful mouth—were so similar they could have been the same model. But it was the brightly contrasting red hat and blue coat that won my vote. The plaque gave minimal information about the piece, revealing nothing new that would help me with my own recent interaction with another possible Vermeer.

Honestly, I don't know what I sought to gain by coming here.

My stomach grumbled, and I checked my watch. I only had about twenty-five minutes to get back to the office, which would allow time for a hotdog-cart lunch that I could eat on the way to the Metro. I found a food truck close to the museum's Constitution Avenue exit and stood in line behind a woman and two small children. Both looked to be of preschool age and debated which soda flavor would go with the hotdog lunch. The time on my phone indicated that I was down to twenty minutes. *Nuts, I'm going to be late for the meeting.*

"K.C.!"

Only one person used that nickname. I turned to find a tall

figure I knew well striding toward me. "Michael Finnegan!" I exclaimed with genuine affection.

"It's good to see you." He enclosed me in a brief hug.

I grinned at the dark-haired man with the smiling mocha eyes. "How is life at the FBI treating you?"

He wore a black trench coat over the requisite dark suit and white shirt. A green striped tie was the only color to break up his monochromatic appearance. "Same, same. I haven't seen you since…"

"That alumni mixer at the Torpedo Factory. Gosh that was what … May, June?" Mike and I had met in college at UVA. I was a Political Policy and Law major while Mike majored in Government Affairs. We met in a Constitutional Law class our sophomore year and joined the same study group where we spent hours in heated debate over Supreme court cases of yore. A friendship based on mutual respect was born. I'll admit there had also been an undercurrent of sexual attraction, but it seemed the timing never worked out for us. I was dating a junior when we met, and by the time that fiasco ended, he was dating a freshman. After we graduated, I stayed on to get a law degree while he moved up to Northern Virginia. He became a Capitol police officer, worked nights to get his Cyber Security Certification, and afterward was recruited to work for the FBI.

"Beginning of June. You never showed up to happy hour at the Capitol Grille when I texted you at the end of summer … even though you said you'd come," he admonished.

"Ugh, I know. I'm sorry, it just didn't work out. Text me the next time you go, and I promise I'll do my best to make it happen."

"Sure, sure. I remember you were telling me about joining that Events and Adventures group. How's that working out?"

I blushed and grinned. "Well…"

"Don't tell me, you're engaged." He grabbed my left hand.

"Lord, no." I pulled out of his grasp. "But, I've been seeing this guy for a few months that I met through one of the events."

"What's his name?" He grinned. "Should I run a background check on him?"

The Vermeer flashed in my mind's eye, and I gasped, "*No.*" Mike's smile faded at my abrupt refusal and I forced my face to relax into pleasantness. "I mean, I don't need a background check. His name is Patrick Dunne. His father is *the* Dunne in Dunne and Jenkins Commercial Real Estate. Anything I might need—I can find on Google."

Mike's smile returned. "Oh-ho, like that, is it? So, what's it like living high on the hog? Is he a kinky rich guy? Do you call him Mister Grey?" His eyebrows waggled.

"Get outta here." I shoved his shoulder. "Patrick lives in a modest apartment in D.C., I'll have you know. He doesn't work for Daddy's company. It's not like I'm taking helicopter rides to New York, or living in a Watergate penthouse."

"How disappointing."

"You always did have a weird sense of humor."

The family in front finally moved on and I stepped forward. "Can I buy you lunch?"

"Sure, you owe me for ditching on the happy hour."

I motioned to the truncated sandwich board menu. "Go ahead and order while I send a quick text to my boss."

On Hill, running late. Will miss department meeting. Sorry.

"One dog with kraut and a Pepsi," Mike said to the Middle-Eastern food truck attendant.

"I'll have a dog, ketchup and mustard, Diet Pepsi." While our hotdogs were being prepared, I did some quick thinking and decided I might be able to pump Mike for information.

"It's not too cold out, why don't we see if we can find a bench in the sculpture garden?" I indicated the park next to the National

Gallery of Art, which housed large modern art sculptures and a skating rink.

"Lead the way."

It didn't take long to find a place. We situated ourselves on a sun-drenched bench near the Constitution Avenue exit.

"So," I said between bites, "I was thinking about you just the other day."

Mike stopped mid-bite, his brows rising.

"I stumbled upon this interesting article in *Time* magazine— 'The Five Best Museum Heists in History.' Does your division work on anything like that?" I nonchalantly bit into my own dog and waited for him to finish chewing.

"Not my department. But, for a time, I worked with a guy who was a part of the Art Crimes division. He oversaw the team investigating the Gardner Museum heist."

Bingo. "Yes, I read about that one." I made a moue with my mouth. "Quite an interesting tale. Weren't the paintings stolen in the '90s?"

"As a matter of fact, 1990. That's the Art Crimes Team, and I can tell you it's a real thorn in their butt that the stuff has never been recovered."

"I'm not surprised." I whistled. "If I recall, the paintings are valued at a cool five hundred mil. I would hope they are looking for it. So…" I leaned in closer and lowered my voice. "Do you think the mafia still has it buried in some basement or warehouse? And what do you think about that Connor guy who was in jail and claimed to have masterminded the theft a year before it happened? Do you think it still exists, or was it burned?"

He shrugged and sipped his soda.

"Goodness, I'd love to talk with one of the investigators. Get the *real* scoop on how much the FBI knows about it. I imagine there's only so much that can be fit to print."

"Oh, no, not you?"

"What? Not me, what?" I made my eyes go wide and innocent.

"You're one of those. You come across the story and become the latest in a long line of … Nancy Drews. Amateur sleuths hot on the trail of a twenty-five-year-old art heist."

"Twenty-eight," I corrected, "and compared to that one in Stockholm or the gig in Amsterdam, the Gardner heist is really the most interesting. They got away with so much stuff."

He rolled his eyes and finished the last bite of kraut dog, then wiped his hands with the thin, useless napkin it came with. "Listen, do you know how many false leads that team has to deal with on a regular basis? Every time a new article pops up on the internet, it's days of quack calls from Aunt Hilda who thinks she saw one of the paintings in her husband's friend's nephew's basement back in 1998. And that poor team has to follow up on any possible lead."

"Okay, I get it. But come on, it's all rather glamorous. You've got to have some theory."

"My theory is that it's been split up, sold on the black market, and is currently residing across the world. Or it's being used as currency among various mafia families. They'll never find the artwork together. Any art collector that has it knows it's stolen. The best we can hope for is eventually their conscience will get the better of them and it'll be returned to the rightful owners."

"I read the FBI believes the original perpetrators are dead."

"That's the theory."

"Is it theory or fact?"

He sighed and took another sip. "Fact, as far as I know."

"So…" I looked across the pathway at the large red metal sculpture that read AMOR. "What would happen to anyone who bought or currently housed a painting? Would they still be prosecuted? After all, the statute of limitations is far gone."

"Anyone dealing in stolen art can be prosecuted for

something. Taking stolen works across state or international lines is illegal. Possessing stolen art from any museum is a felony. Often the acquisition of the art is shady. It's not like someone's going to stumble across a Rembrandt at a flea market."

"They might. How do you know?" I bit my cheek.

He shot me a derisive look. "That's not how it works. Not with this kind of art. First, it's too well known. Second, if the mob is involved, they know exactly what they've got in their possession."

"There does seem to be a lot of deaths revolving around the people involved. Do you think any of them are related to the art?"

He shrugged. "It could be. On the other hand, it could be one low level guy skimming off the drug money collections. The boss found out and the next thing you know the skimmer's decapitated body is found in the trunk of his own car."

I shivered. Indeed, one of the suspected perpetrators was found beaten and stabbed in the trunk of his car.

"One theory is that the theft was done to make an exchange. Get a mobster out of jail," I said.

"Yes, I've heard that one," Mike replied.

"But that didn't happen."

He shook his head and leaned back. "They stole too much. Maybe it would have worked out if they'd taken a single piece. It's been done in the past." He gave me a deadpan look. "I think once it blew up in the papers, everyone involved realized it was too much. The attorney general was never going to make an exchange or let the original thieves slide."

"Now it seems as though the museum just wants their stuff back. One article I read indicated that the FBI screwed up a possible return after the museum curator paid ten thousand in good faith."

A guitar riff sounded and Mike fished a phone out of his inside pocket. "I don't know anything about that," he said in a distracted tone as he read something on his cell. His brow furrowed as he typed a response.

"Something wrong?"

"It's nothing." He finished and slid the phone back into his coat. "However, I've got to get back to the office." Rising, he held out a hand.

"Yes, me too." I allowed him to pull me to my feet. "It was great catching up with you. Oh, wait, I never did ask, are you still seeing that blonde accountant you had with you at the mixer?"

"No." His gaze held mine and a slight jolt went down my spine. "It fizzled out."

I swallowed. "I'm sorry to hear that." Another thought occurred to me and I couldn't help asking, "At the Capitol Grille happy hour, were you … was she?"

A rueful expression crossed his features. "Done."

"Oh, I see." Once again, we were ships passing in the night. He was free, and I wasn't.

"Thanks for lunch."

"Anytime." We hugged.

Mike's cell rang; he waved as he strode through the gate, putting the phone to his ear. I watched him leave and stared at the empty opening for a long time after he'd gone.

Chapter Five

Thursday arrived with both excitement and trepidation. Ever since my visit to the museum, my discussion with Mike, and subsequent research, I'd debated with myself about Marty's painting. Stories abounded of scandalous art forgeries discovered throughout history, and the likelihood that Marty's painting was the lost Vermeer from the Gardner Museum seemed farfetched.

First, how did he come by it, and where did he get the money to pay for such a thing? Even if he acquired such a piece on the black market, the seller would surely know its high value and that they could get millions out of a dirty, willing buyer. The last time a Vermeer was auctioned, it sold to a private collector at Sotheby's for a cool thirty million. I didn't know much about black market prices of stolen paintings, but even a measly ten percent would mean three million. Granted, Marty was rich, but I wasn't so sure he was spend-three-million-on-a-painting rich. He seemed to be more the tens-of-thousands-artwork rich. On the other hand, the painting was still a hot item and someone desperate for money might be foolish enough to let it go for a song. Nevertheless, what bothered me the most was Marty didn't strike me as the type of major player you'd see on the black-market-art-collection scene.

One could conclude the painting was a forgery. Initially, I assumed Marty would have any painting authenticated. My research revealed part of the authentication process was determining the provenance of the art. But that would be indeterminate when purchasing stolen artwork. Also, finding an authenticator of questionable morals might not be as easy to locate for a legitimate art collector.

These questions and more ran around in my head most of the week like a squirrel searching for buried nuts. I hadn't slept well in days and to be honest, it'd come to the point where I wasn't even sure I wanted to see the damn thing again. I mean really, who cares if Marty had some hidden artwork, forged or real? Who was I to intervene? If it was forged, then the laugh would be on him. If it was real …

"You're awfully quiet." Patrick, once again, interrupted my scattered thoughts.

The windshield wipers swiped back and forth as bright red tail lights lit up the car and made prisms of the rivulets of rain running down the side of the windshield. Patrick drew the BMW to a halt again in the heavy rush hour traffic.

I yawned and adjusted the seat belt at my shoulder. "Just a little tired. I'm sure once I have something to eat and drink, I'll feel better."

"Tomorrow is your last day. Congress goes on break and you get some vacation time." He rubbed a hand along my stockinged knee.

"Halleluiah." I grinned.

"I'm looking forward to spending down time with you. I've missed you. You've been so busy these past few weeks, we've hardly seen each other."

"Yeah, me too," I mumbled and sunk lower in my seat. I had told Patrick nothing about the Vermeer or my stolen art investigation. Nothing. The omission and white lies weighed on me, but for some reason I didn't feel as though I could just blurt out what I'd seen. How do you tell your boyfriend you snooped through his father's office, in the middle of the night, and found a stolen painting? Worse, not only had I been secretly researching the painting, yesterday after work, I spent an hour googling Marty, his business, and anything that had to do with art. Not one negative article did I find. There were a few Better Business

Bureau complaints against his company, but considering it was a $200 million corporation, there was nothing unusual about that.

It occurred to me I could try a different tactic. "Hon, are all your father's artworks on display around the house, or does he have more of his collection secreted away?"

"Secreted away?" His gaze didn't stray from the busy traffic, but I could tell by his profile his mouth had turned down.

"Yeah, like in a … warehouse or something? I read recently that some people only collect art as an investment and put it away in climate controlled storage units. Waiting for it to become even more valuable."

"Oh, no. Dad would hate that. He feels that art *should* be displayed. I'll admit, part of it is an ego boost for him—showing people a *real* Degas—but he's a true appreciator of art. I'd go so far to say it's a passion for him. Every piece in his collection is rather personal. Whenever he purchases a new painting, there's always a big to-do. He hasn't purchased anything in about two years. But the last time, when he acquired the Tang Vase, he held a catered party in honor of it, and he jawed anyone's ear off who came within a five-foot radius. It's like the art was his honored guest, he introduced people to it."

I laughed, and Patrick joined me. "I'm not kidding. After a few months, he seems to get used to having it around, and he's not so little-kid-with-a-new-toy."

"Hm."

"Still, I've seen him occasionally turn off the pressure plates and wander around the house touching … picking up the sculptures. Almost in reverence."

"What about you? Has the arts and antiquities bug rubbed off on you?"

"Not like Dad. Don't get me wrong, I have a sense of the importance of the pieces he purchases and art as a whole. But I haven't studied and researched it like my father. He's got an eye for it that I lack. As a matter of fact, he called into question a Wyeth painting that a dealer in D.C. was trying to sell. It was later identified as a forgery."

So, Marty was no bird for the plucking.

"What brought this up?" Patrick asked.

"Oh … well … you showed me all that stuff at your parents' holiday party. I guess it stuck with me. I've never been an art connoisseur, but your Dad's collection has piqued my interest."

"We didn't even have time to see all of Dad's collection."

"No?"

He shook his head. "There's an upstairs den where he's got some more paintings and even a fossil."

"A fossil! Seriously? Like from a T-rex?"

He laughed. "Nothing so dramatic. It's like a toe-bone or something from a Troodon. If we have time tonight, I'll show it to you."

"That would be great. If you don't think your father will mind."

Patrick snorted. "No way. Like I said, Dad feels art should be admired. Just don't let on that you're *too* interested."

"Really, why?"

"If he finds out, he'll cozy up to you and keep a running monologue about all his favorites and why they should be yours as well. Christ!" Patrick slammed on the brakes as some fool cut us off. Our seat belts locked. Someone behind us blared their horn. "Jackass." Patrick mumbled under his breath as traffic started moving again.

"That idiot has the life expectancy of a mayfly."

He huffed. "No kidding. What were we talking about?"

"Your dad and his art obsession."

"Right, if you show too much interest, you'll never be able to get rid of him, and I don't want to have to share you with him tonight." He shot me a look.

I joined Patrick's laughter. "Okay, I'll keep my interest at a minimum."

Traffic slowed to a crawl again and Patrick sighed. "I don't know what I was thinking. We should have stayed in the city and gotten a bite to eat."

Guilt tapped my shoulder. The only reason we were sitting in this horrible rainy traffic was because of me. Patrick was a people pleaser, it's part of what made him a successful marketer. Even though his mother offered the invitation, Patrick would have begged off had I not insisted we accept it. Now, we'd be arriving late and would probably have ten or fifteen minutes before we'd have to get back in the car and return to the city for the play. We crept past a disabled car on the side of the road, and traffic in front of us finally started moving the speed limit.

We arrived at the Dunnes' home only ten minutes late, which would give us about half an hour to have drinks and visit. Patrick's parents, along with Tom and Phyllis Grayson, gathered around the kitchen island. Hugs, kisses, introductions, and drinks had already been handled, and Patrick stood next to me, his arm resting against the small of my back. I'd opted for a glass of Chardonnay and munched on a carrot while listening to Phyllis talk about her oldest son, a soon-to-be Duke law school graduate. Phyllis, a sixtyish woman, wore a simple black dress with a chunky necklace in bold blues and greens that complemented her shoulder-length brown hairstyle. She spoke with a southern accent, punctuating her sentences with hand movements.

"Karina, you're a lawyer, right?" Molly asked.

"I am, yes."

Phyllis's gaze turned to me and, for the first time since I'd arrived, she seemed interested in something I had to say. "Really? And where did you go to school?"

"UVA."

Her brows rose. "Impressive. I believe it's ranked in the top ten in the nation." She tapped a pink lacquered nail against the counter for emphasis.

"If you say so. It's where I went as an undergrad. They offered me scholarship money to stay for law school." I shrugged and gave an embarrassed smile. "Money talks."

"What kind of law do you practice?" Tom asked.

I glanced at Phyllis's husband. He wore a plaid sport coat, slacks, and no tie, but it wasn't the outfit that fascinated me—he'd groomed his facial hair into a curly handlebar mustache that wiggled as he chewed on a radish.

"I work for a medical association in federal governmental affairs," I told him.

"So, are you their in-house counsel?" Phyllis asked.

"No, I'm an advocate for the members."

Phyllis pursed her lips in confusion.

"She's a lobbyist," Molly clarified.

Ugh, I hate using that moniker. Most people thought D.C. lobbyists were manipulative, slimy characters oozing around the Hill, lining representatives' and senators' slush funds for pork belly legislation. Sometimes that was true. In reality, a large portion of us worked for nonprofit organizations that were simply trying to better our laws for humanity. Organizations, like the one I worked for, didn't have deep pocket money to buy congressional votes.

"I see." From Phyllis's fake smile, I could tell she thought the worst.

"Karina is an advocate for the physician assistant profession and patient care. Right now, she's working on a bill that will improve medical care access to rural, mostly poor, communities," Patrick explained.

I goggled at him.

"What?" He stared back. "I listen when you talk. I even watched the C-SPAN footage when you testified last month."

I laughed. "You didn't?"

He frowned. "Of course. I like to keep an eye on you."

"I had no idea. You have some perseverance to get through one of those boring committee meetings."

Patrick winked and sipped his wine.

"How did you end up in that job?" Tom asked.

"I spent a summer interning on the Hill for a senator during my undergraduate years. When I got out, I was hired on the team and spent a few years on the Hill as a legislative assistant. You see, I thought I'd run for office one day."

"Ah, we have a budding politician in our midst," Tom teased.

I tried not to stare at the mustache as I spoke, but it was so mesmerizing I found it difficult to peel my eyes away. "I was … until I realized Congress spends half their time in office raising funds for the next election instead of doing their damn job. Let's just say the rosy glasses came off and I became jaded to the political campaign B.S.," I said with asperity.

My comments dropped anvil-like onto the conversation. Patrick sucked in a breath and the comfort of his hand disappeared from its perch at my back. *Damn.* I knew politics were a no-no with new people, they were so divisive. Moreover, this couple, much like Patrick's parents, likely contributed to politicians' fundraising coffers. Hell, they were probably friends with a pile of congressmen. I blamed the 'stache for distracting my good sense.

Phyllis sipped her Manhattan, Tom grabbed a celery stick and crunched down on it. Nobody made eye contact with me. I sucked half my wine in one gulp.

Finally, Marty stepped into the breach. "You know, I have a set of antique leather-bound law books that might interest you."

"Really?" I set the glass down. "I'd *love* to see them."

My overly excited response was due to both the embarrassment I caused with my harsh comments and the fact that antique books were likely stored in Marty's library—the *exact* location I'd been racking my brain to come up with an excuse to get into. We had less than ten minutes before we needed to leave, and mentally I'd thrown in the towel on that operation, yet here was Marty laying it at my feet.

"Sure, anyone else?" Marty asked, scooping up a cracker with cream cheese, salmon, and dill.

"No thanks, I'll pass on the moldy old law books." Phyllis giggled at her tacky remark.

Everyone else shook their heads. Molly asked if anyone had seen the latest Egyptian exhibit at the Natural History Museum, and Phyllis launched into her opinion of it.

Marty shrugged. "Looks like it's just you and me, kid."

I followed him down the hall to the library. He flicked a switch and recessed lighting flooded the room.

"They're over here along the far wall. I have twenty-eight in total." He indicated a set of rich tan leather-bound books with black and red accents.

I reached out, then stopped myself before touching one. "May I?"

"Hold on, let me get you a pair of gloves." He rummaged around in one of his desk drawers before presenting me with a pair of thin, white cotton gloves. "My antique book seller would have a heart attack if I allowed anyone to touch them without the gloves. Apparently, the oils in our hands break down the bindings and paper."

I slipped on the gloves and pulled forth one of the tomes. The inside cover listed the manufacturers date as 1902. The paper was as thin as bible paper, and the font, so small, made it difficult to read the passages. "Wow, these are fantastic."

"Here, I've got a magnifying glass you can use. The type is so close together I don't know how anyone can read them." He pulled out the leather chair, shoved his laptop aside, and indicated

I take a seat at his desk.

The glass helped, and I got caught up reading an ancient law regarding the illegal sale of livestock. Marty leaned over my shoulder to read along with me. The entire time my fingers itched, knowing the catch I sought rested inches away.

I decided I would drop one of my earrings and use it as an excuse to return to the room when Molly's voice called, "Marty— you got a text."

"I'll be right back."

There would only be a minute or two, even less if Marty simply retrieved his phone and returned to the library. I found the switch under the desk and—w*hoosh*—the hunting painting disappeared. It took a few seconds to register. I stared unbelievingly at the empty space. Gone.

Had I imagined it? Did I make up the late night, barely-glimpsed-at-painting in my head?

A footfall in the hallway alerted me; I pressed the button and returned my attention to the book.

"I'm sorry, Karina. We have to cut this short," Marty said as he entered the room. "Molly informs me it's time to leave or we'll be late for the play."

I rose and returned the book to its proper place before removing the gloves. "Thank you for allowing me to see them. They are fantastic."

He tapped on his phone, and I thanked the heavens the distraction kept him from noticing my burning cheeks and shaking hands.

"Over the Christmas break there'll be time for you to look at them longer."

"I would adore that."

"Come on, slow pokes." Patrick entered the room with my coat and purse in hand. "Mom's going to have a fit if we don't get moving." He helped me into the long red overcoat, and Marty followed us out of the library, flipping the lights off as we exited.

The rest of the evening went off without a hitch. Traffic returning to the city had lightened, our seats were excellent, and the ballet—top notch. I should have felt relieved by *not* finding the painting. Instead, it left me deflated and disappointed, as though I'd failed in some sort of bizarre self-imposed quest. I'd gotten it into my head that I would crack a case that neither the FBI, nor highly skilled art detectives, nor investigative reporters had done in the past twenty-eight years.

How silly of me.

Chapter Six

"…is yooouuuu!" Swaying my hips side-to-side, I used the spatula as a microphone while belting out the popular Mariah Carey holiday song, *All I Want for Christmas*, currently radiating from the iPod. My finger pointed at Patrick's spiky bedhead as he watched in amusement from his perch at the kitchen island. The batter bubbled, and the spatula returned to its intended use— flipping the fluffy flapjacks. "Perfection."

"Besides dinner, do we have any plans today?" He sipped his coffee.

"Nope. It's Christmas Eve. Congress has left the building, and I have N-O-T-H-I-N-G to do. We're going to eat these pancakes, drink our coffee, read the paper, and laze around in our pajamas until noon."

"What happens at noon?"

"I might consider showering," I sang.

"Maybe we can do that together."

"Maybe so." I winked and turned in a circle to the music.

He grinned. "You're in a goofy mood today. It's nice. I haven't seen you this happy since" —his head tilted in thought— "Thanksgiving? You've been so distracted these past few weeks. I've been a little worried that something else might be going on. Seeing you like this, I realize how much your job must have been stressing you out."

My gaze darted away from his, focusing on the griddle in front of me. So, Patrick had noticed my preoccupation, and he assumed it had to do with work. I didn't disabuse him of the notion. When I awoke that morning, it had been with a sense of refreshing lightness. Thursday night I slept horribly, stewing about the missing painting. By Friday afternoon, I'd had enough. Realizing how stupid it was for me to waste so much of my time over ... what? Since there was no painting on Thursday, now I questioned what I'd seen that night two ... no, three weeks ago. Marty had done nothing to indicate he dealt in shady artwork. Even Patrick had said his father felt art should be displayed to be admired. Friday night, as Patrick and I sat on the couch, watching the movie *Love Actually*, I came to the conclusion that I had been wrong.

Just plain wrong.

And it was time to, in the inimitable words of Disney, let it go.

Decision made, that dirty lump of Christmas coal that had been weighing on my conscience disintegrated. With my outlook reformed and mood improved, I was ready to spend Christmas with Patrick's family, something I'd come to dread after the Dunne holiday party.

Removing the pancakes from the griddle, I placed them on the platter next to the bacon and slid it over to Patrick. "Now we're both on vacation. Tomorrow's Christmas, and it's time I got into the spirit and spread some holiday cheer." I circled around the counter, grabbed his cheeks between my hands, and gave him a rousing smackeroo.

His arms wrapped around my waist, and he turned the silly kiss into something more. Deeper. Sexier.

My cell phone jingled, breaking the moment. I glanced down at the display and saw my sister's face. "Merry Christmas, little sister. I'm surprised to be hearing from you so early. It's only what..." The clock above the microwave read 10:02. "... eight o'clock in Denver."

"Karina?" Jillian's voice shook out my name.

"What's wrong?" Gently, I pushed out of Patrick's embrace.

"Dad's on his way to the hospital. Mom's with him in the ambulance. She asked me to call you." My sister Jillian was a middle school English teacher living in Fairfax, and on a good day I could make it to her place in about thirty minutes. She'd flown out to Denver, however, to spend Christmas at my parents' home.

"Is it bad?" I turned away from Patrick and paced over to the sliding glass door.

A sob answered me. "He said his arm felt numb, then he couldn't speak properly, and he collapsed on the kitchen floor. It was awful. I've never seen anything like it."

My heart plummeted, and a chill shivered up my spine. "I'm coming to you. Do you hear me, Jilly? I'll find a flight out as soon as possible. Tell Mom I'm on my way. Is Tyler there with you?" My brother Tyler, his wife, and daughter were supposed to be spending Christmas at my parents' place along with Jillian.

"I tried. He and the girls were catching a six fifteen flight. They're not supposed to land until almost ten. I'm supposed to pick them up, but I have to go to the hospital to be with Mom. Rina, what should I do?" She was in full-on crying mode, blubbering so hard I could hardly understand what she said.

Jillian had always been the family drama queen. Her teenage years included a lot of door slamming. A boyfriend breakup would necessitate numerous boxes of tissues, dramatic scenes of self-loathing, and Mom calling her in sick to school. I remember she once ran away to a neighbor's house. During college, the drama mellowed. However, if my dad had passed out on the floor, her fears were certainly legitimate. Something like that would scare the bejeezus out of me too.

"Okay, okay, take a breath, Jilly. Take a moment. Count backward from thirty to settle yourself." I waited while the noisy sobs subsided. "Tyler's on the plane, his phone is just turned off. He'll turn it on as soon as they land. Simply text him. They'll have to catch a cab or rent a car. I'm sure once he gets your text he'll call."

"Yes, you're right, of course," she wobbled out.

"Now, I need you stay calm. Okay?" I heard her suck in a lungful of air. "That's good." I stared blindly out the sliding door at the building across the street and listened to the sound of Jillian's breaths as they steadied into a regular pace. "Better?"

"Mm-hm."

"Now, let's think. You might be at the hospital for a while. Grab yourself a cup of coffee and a bottle of water for Mom and throw some snacks in that gigantic satchel you call a handbag. Take a magazine or a book. And don't forget to take your phone charger. You're going to have to field the calls and texts from Tyler and I over the next few hours. You are now mission control. We need you to be strong for Mom and Dad right now."

She cleared her throat. "You're right. Those are good ideas."

"I need you chill and centered. We don't want to add a car accident on top of Dad's…" I couldn't voice the scary words. "…situation. Don't leave until you have yourself pulled together. Understand?"

"Yes, I'm better now. I can do this."

That's the Jillian I needed to hear. "Now, do you know where you're going?" I knew talking Jillian through the mundane details of getting to the hospital would refocus her anxiety.

"Don't worry about that. Mom told me the name of the hospital and I've got my phone, I'll GPS it." Her speech sounded calmer, the initial panic receded.

"As soon as I get a flight, I'll text you. Contact me when you have some information about Dad."

"Will do. And, Rina?"

"Yeah?"

"Thanks."

"No problem. Love you and see you soon." I turned to find

Patrick behind me.

"What's wrong?"

"My dad collapsed."

"Oh, God."

"I need to go."

"But ... tomorrow's Christmas." Patrick's face fell into a despondent frown.

"I'm sorry. I know we're supposed to have Christmas with your parents. But, it's my dad..." I chewed my bottom lip.

"Sh, sh, it's going to be alright." His arms curled around me, and I laid my head on his shoulder.

"Can you do me a favor?"

"Anything."

"My computer's in the bag, by the front door. I need you to find a flight out to Denver."

"I can try. It *is* Christmas Eve."

"I know, and it'll cost me a fortune. But ..."

He stared down at me. "I'll find you something."

"Thanks, hon." I rose to my tiptoes, gave him a quick kiss, and spun out of his embrace. "I'm going to pack and zip through the shower."

My suitcase was buried in the back of the closet, and I knocked over a stack of shoe boxes dragging it out.

"What's your computer password?" Patrick called from the living room.

I rattled it off as I haphazardly threw things on the bed. In general, I was protective of my passwords, especially because it was my work machine, and normally would have gone out to log on for Patrick, but not today. I used that passcode for my computer and other logins. I made a mental note to change them. The pair of jeans I tossed made a direct hit inside the open suitcase.

"There's a flight at twelve fifteen on Frontier," Patrick called.

The clock read 10:40. "Out of DCA?"

"Yes."

"Book it."

"It's $852."

I paused mid-toss and cringed. I'd already spent so much on Christmas gifts, and $852 was more than the cost of one of my college loan payments. Pinching the bridge of my nose, I let out a windy sigh. "Book it. My wallet's in my purse. Use the black credit card, please. I'm getting in the shower now. You'll have to come in if you need anything else."

"Is that an invitation?"

I didn't answer, my mind spun off in too many directions to banter with him now.

"Just kidding. I'll let you know if I need anything else."

****

It wasn't until after nine at night, Denver time, when I found a moment to call Patrick. I'd texted when I landed safe at the airport, but between Jillian, my Mom, Tyler, his wife Diana, and the slow-moving, sporadic information dribbled to us through the doctors at the hospital, connecting with Patrick dropped to the bottom of the totem pole. His cell rang three times before he picked up.

"Hello?" he said in a sleepy voice.

"Hi, hon. Did I wake you?"

"I guess I fell asleep watching *A Christmas Story*. They're running it on TNT for twenty-four hours straight. How's your dad?"

"He had a TIA, or a mini-stroke." It sounded so simple as I spoke the words.

What my simple sentence hid was the hours of waiting around at the hospital for them to wheel my dad off from one room to another for half a dozen tests. It hid the hours of pacing the floors as labs processed bloodwork and random doctors asked my parents the same questions over and over. Tyler, Jillian, and I spent our time putting on a good face for Mom, pretending we weren't scared shitless that Dad would have a Mount Vesuvius stroke right in front of us and drop dead, thus ruining all future Christmas Eves. I felt terrible for Tyler's wife. Poor Diana was stuck back at the house entertaining two-year-old Megan, who kept asking when Pop-Pop and Grammy would be home and wondering if Santa would know to deliver her presents to Denver instead of Seattle. Finally, around six thirty, the doctors agreed on the Transient Ischemic Attack diagnosis.

"That doesn't sound good. Is he going to be okay?"

"Yes. They're keeping him overnight, and they want to put him on high blood pressure and cholesterol meds. He's going to have to lay off the junk food and the cigars, but it sounds as though they'll release him tomorrow."

"That must be a relief."

"You have no idea. I thought the past few weeks at work were stressful. Nothing compares to waiting around a hospital for news of a loved one's health."

"I'm sure. You're back at your parents' house now."

"Yes. Dad and the doctors convinced Mom to come back with us. Jilly and I will pick him up from the hospital tomorrow morning and then do the Christmas thing."

"My parents told me to say they're praying for you and your family."

I grimaced feeling bad about the abrupt change in schedule. "How did they take the news?"

"Obviously, they'll miss you tomorrow. We all will. It'll be quiet with just the three of us. But ... they understand. Like mom said, if he had died and you didn't go..."

"Exactly." It was so nice to know Patrick's family understood. "Thank them for their prayers—and, hon..."

"Yes?"

"Today's been so crazy, I'm not sure I even thanked you for all you've done. Booking my ticket, driving me to the airport, taking care of my place while I'm gone. I really appreciate...." I must have been more exhausted than I realized, because my throat swelled, tears sprang up, a little sob snuck out, and I couldn't finish my thought.

"Hey, hey, sweetheart, it's going to be alright. Is there something you're not telling me?"

I swallowed and sniffed. "No. I think it's ... I'm tired and I've spent all day... It's nothing ... I'm just being..." I swiped at the wetness on my cheek.

"I get it. You're always so even-keeled, remaining strong. You've been sitting on your emotions all day long, haven't you?"

"Something like that," I whispered.

"Talk to me."

I took a moment to breathe, then dumped all my worries, doubts, and the day's frustrations on Patrick in a way I'd never done before. He murmured appropriate things, and at one point I think he zoned out watching television, but whether he heard all I said or not, I appreciated having an ear to chew on. Simply voicing all my uncertainties and fears was cathartic. It was past midnight on the East Coast when I realized Patrick had fallen asleep, and I hung up.

Chapter Seven

I walked on tiptoes into the room Jillian and I were sharing. The *Alice in Wonderland* nightlight, a remnant from our childhood, glowed on the table between the twin beds. Jillian was a lump beneath her fluffy white comforter. Exhausted, I slid between my own cold sheets. The old pull chain on the light sounded loud to my ears as the room went black.

"How's Patrick?" Jillian's voice floated across the darkness.

"He's fine."

I heard her shift. "Do you think this is the guy? You know, is this the one you'll marry?"

It's funny she should ask. Patrick and I had recently gotten into a conversation about marriage—the institution—not the two of us getting married. We'd been watching a sitcom where the couple had a fight over something inane. And of course, in half an hour everything was hunky dory. I'd pointed out how ridiculous the entire fight had been, which led to the discussion. I'll admit, that night I'd certainly been thinking about the possibility of marrying Patrick.

"He ... might be." I hedged. "I mean, I care for him. And we share similar interests."

"Can I ask you a question?"

"You can always ask."

"Do you believe in soulmates? Like there's one person out there for you? Like Patrick could be your one and only?"

"Um ... well ... The current divorce and remarriage rate would say that there are multiple people out there for us. Personally, I believe it's more of the right person at the right time." I thought about Mike and our missed chances because our timing always seemed to be off. Could I have married Mike? "Timing is everything. What do *you* think?"

"I believe in soulmates. I believe there's one person out there that will make each of us as happy as we can possibly be in this lifetime."

A big reader of romance novels, our Jillian, and with her temperament, this wasn't exactly earth-shattering news to me.

I took a moment before responding. "And what if your soulmate dies young, from cancer or a tragic accident? Now you're thirty-five, and you'll never remarry because you've already been with your soulmate? No, I think if you have so much love in your heart for one person, you'll find the capability to find love in another if it came to it."

"Maybe."

"Why do you ask? Have you found your soulmate?"

Jillian's silence spoke volumes. My sister had her fair share of boyfriends in high school and college, but ever since she'd started working at her teaching job, we heard very little about her love life. I knew she'd had dates, but I never heard about a guy past the first few. I think she set a very high standard, and there were a lot of jerks out there just looking to get into a woman's pants. At twenty-six, she had plenty of time to find a guy who would respect her the way she deserved.

"Okay, Jilly. Spill, there's some new guy on your radar. Give me the deets."

"We met at a party; he's a friend of a friend."

"Uh-huh, what's his name?"

"It's Tony."

I waited for her to elaborate. "Great, what's the problem?"

"There is no problem. It's just …"

"Yes?"

"When we met, within the first few minutes of talking, the

thought popped into my head that I would marry him. It was the strangest thing, Rina. I've never, ever had that happen before. We were talking and … BAM! There it was—in my head like a loudspeaker—'I'm going to marry this guy.'"

"I see. Is this where your idea about soulmates comes from, or have you always believed in a soulmate?"

"I'm not sure. I guess I've always believed there's a Mr. Right out there for me."

"So, what does your Tony do for a living?"

"He's an EMT. Did that happen with you when you met Patrick? Did you think, 'this is the one'?"

"No … not exactly. I knew I was attracted to him at first sight, but there was no lightning bolt. Our relationship has worked its way into a comfortable groove."

Jillian clicked her tongue.

"Don't get me wrong," I defended, "we still have hot sex, and we do fun things, like go to the theater … and stuff."

"Well, you're always so even-keeled. Maybe, not being as passionate and deep-feeling as I am, it doesn't work the same way for you as it does for me."

I rolled my eyes. *Perhaps you're just more high-strung, or it's the romance novels talking.* I didn't voice my ungracious thoughts to Jillian. "Perhaps," I murmured.

"That's not a bad thing. You know, when I called you, I was freaking out. I thought Dad was going to die."

"I know. You did a great job keeping everyone updated and Mom settled."

"You helped, getting me to focus on the mundane details of getting out of the house. I don't know what I'd do if we'd lost Dad."

"Yeah, I was scared too." A yawn escaped. "I may not believe in soulmates, but I have to tell you, Patrick was my hero this morning. He got my plane ticket sorted out for me while I showered and chucked everything in a suitcase. Maybe that's what makes a Mr. Right. Someone who's there for you to make plane reservations while you're running around like a Tasmanian Devil. Tell me more about your Tony."

"He's got these soulful dark eyes that see right into me. He's a few inches taller than me, maybe five-nine. And he's got this laugh …"

I fell asleep listening to Jillian's murmurings. However, sleep brought only minor relief. My dreams were riddled with visions of running through hallways, searching for my father who was lost somewhere in the labyrinth of a hospital. For some reason, Marty was also there, and he repeatedly sent me down dead-end passages.

Chapter Eight

"It says the ham will take about an hour and a half to heat." I slid the heavy roasting pan into the oven and turned to Mom. "How long does it take for the sweet potato casserole to cook?"

"About forty-five minutes. I'll put it in around three thirty. Go ahead and set the timer on the stove. I'll use this one here." She wiped her hands on a pink apron that read, 'It's good to be the queen,' and wound up an egg timer painted to look like a baby chick.

Little Megan let out a happy squeal from the living room, and my dad's deep laughter floated into the kitchen. Mom and I exchanged a glance, both of us realizing how lucky we were to be together on this holiday. Yesterday, we'd cooled our heels at the hospital until almost three in the afternoon when the doctor finally got around to releasing Dad. Poor Mom, her normally perfect, short-layered hairstyle had stuck out at odd angles because she hadn't thought to brush it. Bags of sleeplessness had hung below her eyes, making her look far older than her sixty years. Today was Monday, the twenty-sixth, and Mom's hair was brushed and shellacked back into coiffed perfection, and the puffy circles beneath her eyes had lessened considerably.

Thanks to the innocence of toddlerhood, Diana had been able to convince her daughter that since we were in Denver, Christmas was a day later than it normally was in Seattle. This morning Megan got up early and snuck past her sleeping parents down to the Christmas tree to determine if Santa had found Grammy and Pop-Pop's house. At 6:03 a.m., we were awoken by a gleeful little girl, her dark curls flying as she ran from room to room announcing, "Santa came! Santa came!" Pop-Pop, in his green plaid flannel robe and slippers, was the first one to join her in front of the tree as the rest of us groggily shuffled downstairs in search of coffee.

Originally, I'd planned to remain in D.C. with Patrick and his family for the holidays. Even though the reasons for my change in plans had been chilling, now that the danger had passed, I couldn't help but be thrilled to be spending this holiday with my own family. Megan brought an excitement to Christmas I hadn't experienced since I was a child myself. We all spoiled her with attention, love, and a pile of presents. Everyone seemed to realize what a blessing it was to celebrate together, safe and healthy.

"Okay, the rolls only take about fifteen minutes," I said, reading the directions on the plastic over wrap.

"Put those in while the—" The doorbell interrupted Mom.

"I'll get it," Jillian hollered.

"—ham cools."

"Then, I think we're done for now. How about a drink?" I reached into the fridge and pulled out a bottle of chardonnay.

"Rina, you have a visitor."

I closed the refrigerator door and gazed past my sister to find Patrick pulling off leather gloves. Snowflakes melted on the lapels of his overcoat. "Patrick?"

"Hi."

"What are you doing here?"

He gave a sheepish look. "I hope I'm not intruding."

"Not at all." My sister moved aside, seizing the wine, as I flowed into Patrick's embrace.

"No, it's fine, I'm … I'm in shock, that's all. I can't believe you flew out here."

"I was worried. After I didn't hear back from you about your Dad being released … I guess I imagined the worst," he whispered.

"Yes, sorry. I didn't see your text until this morning. By the time I responded, you must have already been in transit. Dad's homecoming was a little chaotic." I frowned. "Goodness, you must have spent a fortune on the ticket."

He shook his head. "Not too bad. I flew standby."

"I'm glad you're here." I brushed the snow off his lapel, and, remembering our audience, turned out of his embrace. "Mom, I'd like to introduce you to Patrick Dunne. This is my mother, and you know Jillian, of course."

Dad and Tyler wandered in to meet the stranger in our midst. Introductions streamed around the room, and soon everyone was chattering at once. When Mom realized Patrick planned to stay at a local hotel, she quashed that idea by insisting he take the foldout sofa in the den. Knowing how ungodly uncomfortable it was, I tried to help him out of an unpleasant night's sleep, but Mom wouldn't be deterred. It was at this point Megan went into meltdown mode, and Diana took her upstairs for a nap. Mom directed Tyler to set up the bed and help Patrick get settled.

While the boys organized Patrick's sleeping arrangements, Jilly and I poured drinks and set out a crudité platter. Eventually, all the adults regathered into the family room around the Christmas tree. Patrick entered, looking delish in jeans and a black sweater, and headed toward where I sat on the hearth, but Mom spoiled his plans by inviting him to sit next to her. She then proceeded to play her twenty-questions game. My poor boyfriend held up well under her softball interrogation, and when I caught his eye, he winked.

The timer rang. The ham had to be glazed. Megan came down from her nap and excitedly dove into her pile of toys. Food went in and out of the oven. Jilly added another place setting, and eventually my rowdy family gathered around the dining room table. Patrick sat on my left and squeezed my hand while we bowed our heads and my brother gave the blessing.

"Oh, Lord, bless this food for which we are about to receive. Lord, thank You for the gifts You have bestowed upon us, for we would not have this bounty without Your blessings. And thank You for the joy of having all our family here, including our new friend, Patrick. Most importantly, thank You, Lord, for giving my father more time on this earth, a gift which we all appreciate. Amen."

An emphasized round of "Amens" echoed my brother's sentiments.

Conversation buzzed around the table as we tucked into a delicious meal of ham, green beans, rolls, and sweet potato casserole. Near the end of dinner, Patrick clinked his fork against his water goblet and rose. "Can I have your attention?"

The chatter stopped, and all eyes turned to my boyfriend.

"First, I wanted to thank you for being so kind and welcoming. I know my arrival was unexpected and unplanned, but you've been so open and warm, I feel like we're already family."

"We're pleased you joined us today, my boy." Dad emphasized the sentiment by pointing a forkful of ham at Patrick.

"Yes, it's nice to finally meet you in person," Mom echoed.

"So, first I'd like to say cheers to my lovely hosts, George and Sarah. Thank you for your hospitality."

We all raised our glasses to my parents.

"Second, I wanted to take a moment to give my gift to Karina."

"Oh, hon." I put a hand to my chest with a pout. "I didn't bring your gift with me. I thought we'd do it when I got home."

"I know. Our plans changed, but now that we're here amidst your family, I simply can't wait any longer." He reached into his pocket and drew forth a small red jewelry box. Pushing his chair back from the table, Patrick sank down to one knee. "Karina, my love, will you marry me?" He opened the box to reveal a pear-cut diamond with ruby baguettes on either side set in rose gold filigree. The stone must have been almost two carats.

Jillian gasped.

Gaudy, was the first thing that came to mind. I slapped a hand to my mouth to make sure the ungracious thought didn't slip out. Everyone froze in place, including me. The only thing that moved were my eyes, back and forth from the ring to Patrick's vulnerable face. The proposal could best be described as unexpected. As I'd told Jillian, we'd discussed marriage, but only as an institution. To be honest, I thought if we were still together then, that it might come on Valentine's Day. Even though I poo-poo'd Jillian's romantic notions, I always thought Valentine's Day was a lovely time for an engagement. Patrick and I would have been dating almost six months by then. I'd also pictured something a little more private, or at least surrounded by strangers at a nice restaurant—not my entire family. However, considering Dad's recent near-death experience, it occurred to me that living in the moment might not be such a bad thing. After all, I was thirty. I had my career. We already spent most weekends together. Why not get married?

I opened my mouth to respond.

Megan's clear, high voice broke the silence. "All done, Mommy."

"Hush, baby," whispered Diana.

I bit my lip to keep from laughing, and my answer came out in a garbled undertone. "Yes."

"Yes?" His brows winged up.

I nodded and a giddy smile broke free.

"Oh, thank God." He plucked the ring out of the fold and slid it onto my waiting finger. "This thing's been burning a hole in my pocket for a week."

The table burst into delighted laughter and applause at Patrick's confession.

Mom jumped out of her chair. "Wait, I have champagne in the garage fridge!"

Before I had a chance to view the ring up close, Jillian snatched my hand. "Ooh ... lookie, lookie. That's quite a rock, Patrick. Diana, check it out." She shoved my hand across the table toward my sister-in-law.

Diana glanced over her shoulder while wiping Megan's face and helping her out of the booster seat, multitasking as only a mother can. "It's lovely."

"Here we go." Mom held a bottle of prosecco in each hand. "Jillian, get the champagne glasses out of the china cabinet."

Having been released from my sister's grip, I was finally able to lean over and kiss my fiancé.

"Do you like it?" he asked.

Patrick's eyes were so sincere I couldn't tell him the truth, at least not in front of my family. Maybe when we got home, we could go together to pick out something more suited to my own style. "Why, yes. It's quite something. Did you pick it out all by yourself?"

"No, it's an heirloom—it was my grandmother's, on my dad's side."

Thoughts of a different ring died an immediate death. "An heirloom? Wow, I'm surprised it fits so well."

"I had it sized." He winked. "Borrowed *your* grandmother's ring. I've seen you wear it on that finger."

My brows knit. "When?"

"A few weeks ago. You've been so preoccupied you didn't even notice it was gone, did you?"

"No, I didn't." Of course, when he mentioned my preoccupation, I thought of his father's hidden painting. My relief that it was no longer there doubled. If the painting had still been weighing on my mind, I've no idea how I would have answered Patrick. Since he did it so publicly, I still probably would have said yes. However, my mind would have been a chaos of doubts.

"Rina, let me see." Mom had handed the prosecco to Dad and leaned over my shoulder. "Oh, it's stunning, simply stunning." She pinched Patrick's cheek. "What a wonderful Christmas this has turned out to be."

Chapter Nine

Two days after our Christmas celebration, Patrick and I flew back to D.C. As delightful as the trip turned out to be, it was nice to return to my own quiet home and bed. Don't get me wrong, I loved spending time with my family, but the full house was exhausting. Tyler and Diana had slept in the room across the hall with a queen bed and a toddler bed for Megan that Mom had borrowed from a neighbor. Like clockwork, Megan was up at six every morning. Her high-pitched voice resonated through the walls, waking Jillian and I every morning. To top it off, my fiancé was only a short flight downstairs, but the uncomfortable old mattress, and my mom's pedantic notions about unmarried couples, kept me from daring to join him.

By the time we returned to D.C., Patrick's parents had already flown out to Utah to spend a week skiing at their condo in Park City. Martin and Molly had been thrilled with the engagement, but Molly showed disappointment that she hadn't seen "the proposal." She made us promise to come over for dinner on the Saturday after their return so she could see how the ring looked on my hand.

****

On the second day of January, I awoke to the tink-tink of sleet striking my bedroom window. The day dawned dark and dreary, as only D.C. can in the middle of winter. I was one to prefer a good snowstorm to the cold, wet drudge of rain. The weather reflected my own gloomy feelings at returning to work after a lovely vacation. Patrick and I stayed up well into the wee hours of New Year's Eve celebrating and, even though I'd napped yesterday, I could have used another day to recover before returning to work.

Because Washingtonians seem to be incapable of driving like normal human beings in the rain, two accidents had me arriving late. Even so, I didn't go directly up to the office, instead diverting into the coffee shop on the main floor of the building. When I turned away from the barista with my gingerbread latte, I spotted a head bent over a cell phone that I thought I recognized.

Mike looked up, our gazes connected, and I waved. "Hello, stranger. Happy New Year."

He flipped his phone over and rose. "Happy New Year."

"What are you doing in my neck of the woods?" We hugged.

"Training course nearby." His fake smile didn't reach his eyes; he stared past my shoulder, and he tapped his thumb and forefinger together like some sort of Morse code.

He just lied to me.

The finger tapping had been a tell of his I'd learned after our first poker session. I never explained to him how I always knew when he was bluffing, simply allowing him to chalk it up to beginner's luck. The movement seemed to be an unconscious action. It surprised me the FBI hadn't trained it out of him. I assumed he was on some sort of mission—maybe a stakeout— after all, why else would he lie about his presence in a coffee shop? It crossed my mind he might be meeting a married woman, although that seemed far-fetched for my old buddy. Either way, I didn't care for it.

"Well ... back to the grind, I'll let you get to it."

"I've got a few minutes. Why don't you join me?" He slid back into his seat.

"Normally, I'd love to. But the traffic was hideous, and I'm running late. Perhaps another time."

"Oh, come on, K.C., can't you spare a few minutes for an old friend?" He looked me in the eye this time and gave that impish grin I remembered from our college days of pulling pranks.

The grin revealed the Mike I knew, and my reserve eased. I checked my phone—twenty minutes late but, then again, half my department was still out of the office and Congress was not yet back in session.

"Besides, you owe me for ditching the Capitol Grille."

"No." I shook my head. "I bought you a swell street vendor hotdog to make up for that. But, I suppose a few more minutes won't hurt."

"Tell me about your holiday. Did you spend it with that Patrick guy you're dating?"

"Mm, we got engaged, as a matter of fact." I sipped my coffee and watched Mike out of my periphery. I could have sworn I saw his face drop, but when I pulled my cup away, he'd recovered with a smile.

"Congrats! That's fantastic," he blustered, and his eyes darted to my left hand. "So, is *that* the rock?" He gave a low whistle.

I explained my sister's panicked Christmas Eve call, my dad's health scare, and how Patrick had flown out to Denver to propose. "And what about you? Don't your parents live in Delaware? How are they doing? Did your mom retire yet? I swear, every time I saw them, she was counting the days to retirement."

He nodded. "Yes, Mom and Dad are good. Mom retired from her bookkeeping job a few years ago, started spending her time volunteering at the church, and she took up golf. Dad's still working. He's talking about upgrading to a larger boat this season."

"Oh, I didn't realize he was a boater. What kind does he have now?"

"A little bass boat. He wants to upgrade to a Boston Whaler."

"Uh-huh, that sounds nice." I sipped my coffee. Fishing boats were out of my league.

"So, have you set a date for the wedding?"

I shook my head. "Not yet."

"What? You're not running around with a bunch of bridal magazines, picking out your colors, and going wedding gaga like all the other girls?"

"Girls?" I frowned. "Honey, I'm a thirty-year-old woman. Besides, I don't know any girls doing that. Do you?"

"My sister, for one." He snorted. "She was a total pain in the ass. For ten months, the only thing she could talk about was the damn wedding. Wedding this, wedding that…"

"Kim? Your big sister got married? When?"

"Two and a half years ago." He rolled his eyes. "She drove Dad and me nuts. 'Mom, which color should the table cloths be, navy or midnight blue?'" he said in a high-pitched voice. "I swear they were both the same color. When I pointed that out to her, she explained, in derogatory and boring detail, why my opinion was wrong."

I laughed. Kim had a nasal voice and Mike perfectly hit her hoity-toity delivery. "I can imagine."

"So, I guess this means that Martin Dunne will be your father-in-law."

"That's usually how it works."

"I hear he's quite the art collector."

"You could say that. He's got a number of pieces in his collection."

"Have you seen them all?"

"Not yet."

He tilted his head.

"Patrick told me there was an upstairs den with more stuff to see. I think there's even a dinosaur bone."

"A dinosaur bone!" His eyes widened.

"That was my exact reaction."

"What kind of art does he collect?"

"Everything, as far as I can tell. He's got a Degas pencil

drawing, an Erté mirror, a Tang Dynasty vase. He doesn't seem to specialize." I leaned in and added sotto-voce, "I have a feeling his art dealer just calls up when he's got something he can't unload because he knows Marty will buy it."

Mike guffawed. "He must have some sort of system."

"Not that I know of." I shrugged.

"Does Patrick also collect art?" He put a hand beneath the table.

Is that a finger tap I saw? "I'm sorry, what did you say?"

"Is Patrick a collector?"

"Nope, he said he hasn't been bitten by the bug. Why do you ask?"

"I guess I was picturing you in that Watergate penthouse hanging your new collection of Picassos and Dalis."

"First, I told you Patrick is not living off Daddy's money. Second," —I stuck my tongue out— "those are modern artists. I'm not a fan."

"Any of Dunne's pieces particularly interest you?"

"Hm…" I stared down at the misspelled name on my cup— *Caterina.* "None in particular." My gaze returned to Mike's direct one. "Why?"

"No reason. The last time we met, I remember we talked about art heists. Did Dunne's collection get you interested?"

The conversation was turning … awkward. It felt like being gently probed with a feather quill. Once again, I returned to the comfort of sipping from my cup to break eye contact. "I suppose it did. I figured I should educate myself about the art world for Patrick's sake." I chuckled. "Although, I don't think he cares. However, I believe it was *you* who brought up the Gardner Museum theft." *There, I said it. Gardner Museum. Ball's in your court, Mike.*

"Yes, you mentioned a couple of thefts; let's see, there was one … in The Netherlands." He didn't pick up the gauntlet, but the gentle poke-poke remained.

I had no idea where this discussion was leading. "Mm. My knowledge only extends as far as the Time Magazine article highlighting the top five art thefts in history. I believe the Netherlands job was in there."

"And the one in Switzerland?" Poke-poke.

Is this a test? I raised a brow. "Do you mean Stockholm, Sweden?"

"Of course, Sweden."

"Yes, it was there. The only other heist I can remember from the article was the Mona Lisa job. The theft is part of what's given her that aura of mystery and intrigue today."

"Have you" —a reminder popped up on my phone as he spoke— "ever heard of—"

"Oh *hell*, I forgot about the conference call. It's in fifteen minutes and I haven't even read the report." I gathered my stuff. "Sorry, I've got to run, Mike. Text me. We'll catch up another time." The door whooshed closed in the face of Mike's adieu.

I scurried to the elevators, juggling my coffee, purse, and computer bag while texting three other people a reminder about the phone call, something I usually did at least an hour beforehand. My head was clearly not in the game today. Luckily, I hit 'send' as the elevator doors closed because service disappeared as soon as the lift rose.

I leaned my shoulder against the wall. Mike's questions seemed … odd. Had it been such a long time that we no longer had the easy friendship of yore? That seemed unlikely. When we met at the National Gallery of Art, it was just like the good old days.

Did my engagement bother him? I couldn't imagine why.

Maybe my initial assumption that he'd been on a stakeout made him cagey. Perhaps he'd been using me as part of his cover. *Yes, that must be it.*

Or is Marty on the FBI's radar? The last question would worry me to death and was not a planet I wished to explore. As far as I knew, the perchance stolen painting was no longer in Marty's possession. *I have nothing to tell.*

Nothing to hide.

Right?

Chapter Ten

The Chevy rolled to a stop and the heater finally kicked in, blasting lukewarm air as opposed to the frigid thirty-degree January cold it'd been circulating on my short drive home from work. I loved the convenience of my commute, but I needed to do something about the heater in my rattletrap of a car. I blew on my arctic cold fingers, then gathered my belongings, making sure to lock the car behind me. Patrick was coming for dinner, and I didn't want another lecture.

The tiny metal mail slot was filled with bills, junk mail, and a late Christmas card. The rip in the corner and black tire tracks let me know the holiday card had taken quite a trip to reach me. The return address was indistinguishable, but the handwriting was easily identifiable as my Aunt Barbara's. Once inside my apartment, I shuffled through the missives. The credit card bill lay at the bottom. Ugh. I was not looking forward to seeing the damage because it would include my very expensive Colorado flight. Not one to procrastinate, I ripped off the bandage.

Huh, not as bad as I thought.

My eyes searched the transactions. This year I'd gotten smart and made a number of holiday purchases in November, maybe that's why the damage wasn't too severe.

I flipped the page over and scanned through to the end of the billing cycle. I returned to the front. *Where is the airline ticket purchase?* I ran my finger down the list. It wasn't on there. The only purchase I found on the twenty-fourth was the taxi to the hospital.

Shit. Patrick must have used the wrong credit card. I had three in my wallet: the black VISA, from the bill in front of me; a bright yellow VISA, which I rarely used because it didn't provide any points or benefits; and a silver Mastercard, issued by my company, and I only used it for company business. Now to figure out which card Patrick charged. If he chose the yellow VISA, it would be fine. It just chapped my ass that none of those dollars would go toward Marriott or airline points. On the other hand, if he used the Mastercard, I'd have to sort it out with work on Monday.

I pulled out my computer to check on the account for the yellow VISA. The statement showed no purchases in the past month. I ran a hand down my face, realizing he'd used the company card. I'd have to talk to the finance department and get it straightened out.

The rattle of a key alerted me to Patrick's arrival.

"Honey, I'm home," he called from the entryway.

I smiled at the cliché. "In the kitchen."

"Are you barefoot and pregnant?" He laid his coat on the stool and came over to kiss the back of my neck.

"Ha. Not yet. How was your day?"

"Fine. Same, same. You?"

"Same, same. Hon, I have a question. Do you remember which credit card you used to pay for my airline ticket? Was it the black or silver card?"

His ears reddened. "Bla-ack?"

"Seriously. You don't remember, do you?"

"Why does it matter?"

"Because I think you used the silver one, and that's my work card."

"I assure you, I did *not* use your silver card."

"It must have been, because I don't see the charges on the yellow card, and it's not here on the black VISA bill. So, you must have put it on the silver one."

He frowned.

"Listen, it's not a big deal. I'll simply sort it out with the finance department on Monday and write them a check for the ticket."

"You don't need to go to your office."

"Of course I do. That's a private charge. I could get fired for misusing a company card if I don't own up to the charge. Look, it's fine. Everyone in the office has done it—whipped out the wrong card. As long as we reimburse the charge, it's all good."

"No, I mean you don't need to reimburse your office, because I didn't put it on the silver card."

I frowned, shaking the bill. "Well, it's not here." I slid it across the island as I put my hands on my hips. It kind of surprised me how stubborn Patrick was being about owning up to such a simple mistake. I mean, if you mess up, just fess up. "Patrick—"

He rubbed the back of his neck. "Karina, I put it on mine."

My hands dropped, and my rising frustration turned to confusion. "What? Why would you do that? I told you to get the credit card out of my purse. Couldn't you find it?"

"I did it because I had an engagement ring in my pocket, and I figured you didn't need a huge bill come January. I did it because I can. And … because … I love you, of course," he added as an afterthought.

"Whoa." I blew out a breath. "First, thank you, thank you." I came around and kissed his cheek. "That's super sweet, and you absolutely win the boyfriend of the month award. Second, I need to write you a check for the cost."

"What if I said it was a Christmas present?"

"Not gonna fly." I shook my head as I dug through my purse, searching for the checkbook buried somewhere at the bottom. "We exchanged presents. You gave me those beautiful new Kate Spade boots, which I know are very expensive. And you covered our New Year's Eve event. I need to pay you for the airline ticket."

"Well … soon enough we'll be joining our accounts. What does it matter if I share the load now?"

I stopped my searching to stare at Patrick. "Okay, let's sit down for a minute, because we've never talked about this. And now's as good time as any."

Patrick followed me and splayed across the couch while I sat on a tucked leg to face him.

"Here's the deal, there are some bills that will never be your responsibility. My student loans will continue to be paid out of my own paycheck until they are retired."

"We could retire them earlier and reduce the amount of interest if we paid them off after the wedding."

I shook my head. "As much as I appreciate your willingness to help in this realm, it's one area where I'm not so willing to compromise. The loans are *mine*. They helped *me* personally get an education which I will value the rest of my life. It doesn't feel right having you take on any sort of responsibility for that debt."

"I thought when we got married, we'd share everything. What's mine is yours and vice versa. It's all a part of our new life together. We'll be moving in *together*, buying houses and cars *together*. Besides, your education is part of what makes you … well, you. It's part of what made me fall in love with you."

"Aww, gold medal boyfriend of the month." I leaned forward to give him a lingering kiss. His lips, soft and pliant beneath mine, tempted me to forget the discussion all together, but rationality prevailed, and I pulled back. "While I appreciate once we are married we'll be making large purchases together, but not my college debt. It doesn't feel right saddling you with it."

Patrick reached out, pulling my hands in his. "What if I told you my father already talked about paying off all our loans as a wedding gift?"

My jaw dropped as I gasped. "Well ... I ... I ... it ... I still have over fifty grand to pay off. There's no way..."

"Karina" —his thumb played with the diamond ring— "you've seen my parents' home ... he can afford it, and if he insists on doing it..." Patrick shrugged. "There's really not much we can do about it. Dad wants us to start our lives debt free. He paid off the loan on my car last year. I didn't ask him to do it, he just ... *did*. He's been asking about my mortgage lately and I suspect he's planning to take care of that as well."

"Wow. That's very..." *Insane? Outrageous? Bat-shit crazy?* "...generous." I chewed my lip.

"He's a generous guy."

A rather unpleasant thought came to mind and I worked to keep my voice and face neutral as I asked, "Will I be expected to sign a prenup?"

Patrick dropped my hand. "No."

"Are you sure your father doesn't expect me to sign one?" My brows rose as I spoke.

His gaze shifted to his lap. "Possibly. But that's for us to determine. Not him."

My fingers caressed the stubble on his cheek. "Patrick, has he already discussed it with you?"

He regarded me. "Do you want to sign a prenup?"

"I hadn't given it any thought. I'm not after your dad's money." I tapped a finger on my chin and frowned. "Divorce law isn't my specialty, but I'm not sure there's any way I could go about getting it through divorcing you. Besides, you don't work for your father, you're not an owner in his business. It's his money, not yours. Right?"

Patrick cleared his throat and shifted. "Well, there was a trust fund that I came into when I turned thirty, and I own some stocks."

"You're a trust fund baby? How much?"

He stared at the unlit fireplace and whispered, "Eight and a half."

"Eight and a half? Eight and a half what? Million?" I asked in a high-pitched voice that defied me by cracking on the last word.

He gave a sharp nod.

"How much in stocks?"

"Mm, maybe a million and a half."

I believe my eyes bugged out to rival Betty Davis. "You *what?*" *My god, over ten million! Mike was right. Patrick could afford to live in a Watergate Penthouse.*

He shrugged.

"How did I not know this?" I frowned.

"I don't advertise. I assumed you knew."

"How the hell would I 'know?' You always made a big deal about how you were independent of your father. You don't work for him. You've got a white-collar marketing job. You live in an ordinary apartment." I ticked off each point. "I assumed you were on the same wavelength as me."

"Sure, I am. Nothing's changed. We never talked about it because … we didn't." He crossed his arms. "Frankly, Karina, I'm rather surprised you're making such a big deal about it. It's just money. I don't get what the big problem is." He looked away. "I'm not purposefully hiding things from you."

His tone had me internally cringing at my behavior. He'd probably never brought it up before because for him it was a way of life. I'd acted in a foolish, accusing manner, like this was a big bad secret. It's not as though he told me he was cheating.

I drew in a breath. "Look, I'm sorry. I didn't mean to be so … so accusing. The new information threw me off guard, that's all. There's nothing wrong with having wealth." I put my hand on his crossed forearm. "Forgive my overreaction."

He allowed his stance to drop and retook my hand. "I probably should have explained more of this earlier, but I've been chased by women for my money. My last 'girlfriend'" —he used finger quotes— "knew I was wealthy and was constantly, I mean, *constantly,* asking me to buy her stuff. Since I could afford it, I didn't think too much about it until I overheard a phone conversation where she was assuring her friend that I would pay for a limousine to take them to a Katy Perry concert that I wasn't even attending. It was then I realized she'd been using me as her own ATM. Worse, the 'friend,' wasn't her girlfriend as she'd led me to believe. I found out later she'd been cheating on me, and the limo was for her and the boy-toy she'd been keeping on the side. Even my brother and father had realized Chrystal's real character and tried to subtly drop hints. I suppose what they say about love being blind is true. I felt like such an ass. After Chrystal..." He shrugged. "Let's just say I'm much more careful."

"Oh, Patrick. That sucks. How did she know about your money? Did you grow up together or something?"

He cleared his throat. "About five years ago, I ended up on one of those most eligible bachelor lists. She'd seen the article and stalked the places it listed where I hung out until we 'met'."

I mashed my lips together, but I couldn't hold back the snicker. "Oh my God, you're kidding. What magazine? I've got to find it." I jumped up. "Where's my phone? Cripes, this purse is like a black hole. I've got to get one with more pockets."

"Did you leave it in your car again?" Patrick pulled his own phone out.

"No, I remember chucking it in here when I got the mail. There it is. Where was the article?"

He sighed. "In the *Washington Hot Spot* magazine."

Sure enough, after a few minutes of searching, the five-year-old article of the top 100 most eligible bachelors in Washington, D.C. came up. "What number are you?"

"Fifty-six."

My finger scrolled the list. "Oh my, I can see why she stalked you. You always look handsome in a suit, but I don't think I've ever seen you in a tux." I gave a catcall. "I'll have to take you to my next rubber-chicken-dinner-fundraiser and make you wear it. I'm surprised you only had one stalker."

He blushed. "Seriously, you never Googled me before now?"

I thought about all the searching I'd done on Marty. "You? No-o."

"That was an iffy no."

"Okay, I Googled your father at one point. But not you. Have you ever Googled me?"

The flush spread down his neck. "Of course."

I made a moue. "And what did you find?"

"A beautiful, smart lady working for a medical association who writes some boring ass policy papers."

"Hey!" I laughed. "I'm proud of those boring ass papers."

He pulled me into his embrace and kissed the top of my head. "I know, I'm proud my fiancée wrote them too."

"However, with this new revelation, I've decided from now on, you're paying for dinner when we go out."

"Done."

"And you can pay for my concert tickets, and I'd like a new Kate Spade handbag to match the shoes, and I could use a new car."

"Done."

"Patrick!" I pushed away from his chest. "You will do no such thing. I'm kidding!"

He tucked my head against his chest. "I know you are. You're very frugal."

I snuggled up, listening to his heartbeat as my head rose and fell with his breathing. "If your dad wants to pay off my loans … I suppose he can. The thought of it doesn't thrill me, so don't bring it up with him. Okay? It makes me uncomfortable."

"Well, we wouldn't want you to be uncomfortable." He

switched our positions, forcing me backward until I lay supine. His lips came down upon mine and trailed across my jawbone. I soon forgot all about money, loans, and credit card payments.

Chapter Eleven

The hideous buzz of the alarm woke me from a lovely dream that included ocean breezes and margaritas on the beach. I cracked my eye open as Patrick rolled over and reached past me to shut it off.

"Isn't it Saturday? Why the hell did the alarm go off? I don't remember setting it."

"I did." He stretched his arms above his head. "I told you about that conference at National Harbor convention center that I'm attending."

"Right. Your sexy shenanigans last night turned my mind to jelly. I'm surprised I remember my own name." I peeked at the clock. It read 6:01. "I didn't realize it started so early."

"Well, I paid to attend the breakfast meeting this morning."

"More power to you." I rolled over and snuggled back into my pillow.

Patrick spooned around me and nuzzled my neck. "Listen, before you fall back asleep, I forgot to tell you last night that my parents got snowed in and couldn't fly home yesterday."

"So, no dinner tonight?" I mumbled.

"No dinner. Since we're not dining with them, there's an evening reception I'd like to attend to do some glad-handing. Do you mind?"

"Go for it."

"You can come, if you want. Be my plus one."

"Is it all a bunch of marketing yahoos talking shop?"

"Probably."

"I'm good. You go have fun."

"What are your plans today?"

"Clean the bathroom. Mop the kitchen. Do some laundry," I murmured into the pillow. "And, if you don't get moving and leave me in peace, I'm going to recruit you to clean the oven."

"I'm going, I'm going." He squeezed my hip and rolled out of bed.

A few hours later, the phone rang as I dumped the last load into the washer. "Hello."

"Karina? It's Molly."

"Hi, Molly. Patrick told me you got stuck in Utah. Are you okay?"

"Yes, we're hoping to get out on a flight tomorrow morning. The snow has stopped and it's supposed to clear up this afternoon, so it's looking good."

"What can I do for you?"

"Well, since we're missing dinner, I'm calling to see if you're available on Wednesday night?"

"Sure, let me check my schedule." With a few swipes, my calendar appeared. "That night looks good. I'll double check with Patrick and get back to you."

"Oh, I already called him. He texted and said it was good for him but told me to speak with you."

"Wonderful. I'm looking forward to it."

"See you then, dear."

"Have a safe flight home."

The phone rang again as I disconnected with Molly. "Hello."

"Hey, big sister, whatcha up to this afternoon?"

"Not much, finishing up some laundry."

"You're not having hot monkey sex with your new fiancé? God, that's weird to say."

"I know what you mean." I glanced at the ring perched above my finger like pink bird waiting to take flight, and pulled a face, wondering if I'd ever get used to it. "No, he's got a conference this weekend. I've got a DVR full of NCIS I thought I'd binge watch. What about you?"

"I've got to find a pair of black slacks and some new winter outfits I can wear to work. Do you want to meet me for lunch and do some shopping at Pentagon City mall?"

"Sure. When and where?"

"Let's say one thirty at Chevy's."

"Done. See you then."

Two hours later, a skinny twenty-something waiter with black glasses and gauges in both ears guided me to my sister's table. The scent and sounds of sizzling fajitas hung heavy in the air.

Jillian slid out of the booth—fashionably casual in her skinny jeans and boots—to give me a hug. "Hey. That's a pretty necklace, I don't think I've seen it before."

"Chico's." I slid into the seat across from her and ordered a Diet Coke.

She crunched up her face. "That's an old lady's store. Mom shops there."

"Women of a certain age, dear, and I know what you mean, but they have some fun chunky pieces of jewelry, and I've also bought a couple of jackets too. I think there's one in the mall if you want to go."

"Macy's first, then we'll see."

"Sure. So, how was the rest of your trip with Mom and Dad?"

"Fine. Tyler and his family left the day after you did, and it was rather quiet. We played cards, went to a movie, and chilled out."

"That's good. Honestly, I was worried it was a little overwhelming for Dad, considering the hospital visit and everything."

"Yeah, we're a noisy bunch. But, you know, they both loved having everyone there. I think your engagement was the highlight for Mom, and it kind of took everyone's mind off Dad's TIA."

She crunched down on a chip and eyed me.

"Yes, it was quite a surprise." My gaze cruised the bar as I debated telling Jillian about his monetary revelations last night. My scan halted abruptly when I caught the eye of a fiftyish man wearing a navy button down shirt and brown sport coat staring at our table. He seemed to be scrutinizing me in particular. His eyes narrowed before he broke contact, and an uncomfortable shiver ran down my spine. The waiter's arrival with our drinks pulled my attention back to the menu.

"Speaking of engagements … tell me about your new fellow. Have you seen Tony since you got back?" I dipped a chip into the salsa and my Alex and Ani bracelets jingled.

She played with her straw.

"You are turning pink as a peony. What's going on, did *you* have wild jungle sex in the back of his ambulance or something?"

"No!" she squeaked.

I snickered. "You're getting even redder. What's going on?"

"Nothing. He surprised me by meeting me at the airport to drive me home."

"Aw. That is sweet. And … did he take you back to your apartment and have his wicked way with you?"

"Rina! Stop it. We did not have S-E-X," she whispered as she spelled it.

I leaned forward. "Why are we whispering?"

She tossed her long, straight blonde hair over her shoulder; it was the one thing I envied my sister. My own shoulder-length chestnut hair had natural wave, which was fine in the dry winters, but once the spring rains arrived and Virginia's humid summer rolled in, my fashionable waves turned into a frizzy pouf on par with that of a Chow-Chow. Thank the lord for Frizz Ease.

"We're not," she said in a normal tone. "We're taking it slow. He said he wants to court me." A secretive smile played around her mouth.

"Court you, huh? Did he use those words?"

"He did, as a matter of fact."

I pursed my lips. "I bet that made your romantic little heart go pitty-pat."

The smile disappeared, and her bright eyes dimmed.

Immediately, I regretted my snarkiness. "Oh, Jilly, I don't know why I'm being a bitch. I'm happy you're dating such a sweet guy. If he's the romantic you make him out to be, maybe Tony is 'The One' for you."

The secretive smile returned. "Maybe." She dipped another chip but before it reached her mouth, her eyes widened and she smacked the table. "I keep forgetting to tell you, did you hear about the sixteen-year-old who wrapped his parents' SUV around a pole two days after Christmas? His younger brother is in my class."

"No, I didn't. How awful." My sister went on to divulge the gory details. While she chattered, the hairs on the back of my neck stood on end, and I subtly glanced at the bar. Brown sport coat was still there, but he seemed intent on his own meal. I gave my head a little shake to dismiss my silly worries.

After lunch, Jillian and I walked across the street to the mall and spent the afternoon and into the evening shopping. Our excursion yielded the black slacks she needed, along with a new dress, two skirts, and a handful of tops. I found a new blouse and jeans, but otherwise remained focused on clothes for my sister.

I was admiring a pair of boots in a shoe store window when Jillian interrupted my contemplation. "It's ten past seven. Do you have time to go to Chico's with me? I'll deign to look at the jewelry."

"Very well, princess. It's in the opposite direction." I made an abrupt about-turn. "Let's…" I forgot the rest of my thought, for directly in my path, about fifteen feet away, stood the man from the restaurant. A black raincoat draped over his arm as he leaned against the balcony rail with his phone up. I could almost swear he aimed at Jillian and me, like he was taking our picture. He lowered the phone, turned his back and strode away at a fast clip.

"Did you see that?" I asked.

"See what?" Jillian manically tapped on her phone with a grin on her face. "Just a sec. I'm responding to Tony's text. He got off early and wants to meet for dinner. I think we'll have to do Chico's another time." She glanced up. "You okay? You've got a funny look on your face."

"I'm fine. Go play with your Romeo. I'm going to stop in at the Black and White store across the way. I see a dress in the window that may need to come live in my closet."

"Ooh, yeah, that would look awesome on you. Thanks for meeting me for lunch and stuff." We hugged. "I'll see you at the Ed Sheeran concert, if not before."

"Sounds good. Drive safe; don't go all moony thinking about Tony and have an accident."

"Yes, *Mom*."

I sniffed and passed the bags I'd been carrying for her. "Get outta here."

She trotted away, weighted down like a pack mule. Even though Jillian had been a pain in my ass growing up, I was glad we'd left all that sibling rivalry garbage behind us. It was nice spending the afternoon with my sister. The moment she got on the escalator, I whipped around and scanned the shopping mall for my disturbing brown-coated shadow. Nothing. I looked over the glass partition and investigated the lower level. Mothers with strollers, a Hispanic family of five, a gaggle of giggling teens, men and women of all shapes and sizes wandered the halls. None of them were wearing a telltale brown blazer and dark hair with graying temples.

The entire episode gave me the creeps, and suddenly shopping no longer held my interest. As soon as I hit the lowlighted parking garage, I speed walked to the car with the keys splayed between my knuckles—a self-defense tactic I'd once read about in a women's magazine. High pitched laughter echoed eerily, bouncing off the concrete posts, and invisible footsteps seemed to dog me. The door I'd exited slammed shut and my heartbeat raced. A woman with short spiky blue hair turned left and walked in the opposite direction. I practically launched myself into the car, throwing my packages willy-nilly onto the passenger seat. Key in place, shoulder harness locked, car in gear, I peeled out of the parking space. Luckily, no one had been driving down the aisle.

It occurred to me what I'd witnessed was an FBI surveillance tail. The meeting with Mike invaded my thoughts. *Is the FBI surveilling Marty and by extension me?* I fished through my purse, and my fingers finally connected with their quarry. I pulled out my cell only to toss it back into the black hole of my handbag when I realized it had gone dead because I'd forgotten to charge it last night. One more thing to blame on Patrick's sexy shenanigans.

I checked my rearview mirror for a tail. A black sedan, three cars back, followed my lane change; I pushed the accelerator down hard, running a light that turned red as I passed beneath it. The traffic behind me stopped at the light. From there on, I drove like an idiot on the way home—putting my left directional signal on and turning right, driving exceedingly slow up and down a few neighborhood blocks and running a yellow light. I received a few rude gestures for my less than stellar driving, but felt reassured that no one followed me. By the time I pulled into the parking lot, my breathing had settled to normal, and I began to think rationally about the encounter. Rational thoughts brought mild relief.

Juggling the shopping bags and my purse, I fumbled with the keys. Before I could turn the lock, the door whipped open and my heart once again sped into a gallop to rival the Kentucky

Derby winner.

"Patrick! Jesus, you scared the crap out of me."

"Where the hell have you been?" he snapped.

I reared back at his thunderous expression. "Shopping with my sister. Why?"

"Your phone's turned off!"

"What's wrong? Is it my dad?" My voice wobbled with apprehension and pent-up fear.

Patrick's frowning mien softened only slightly as he pulled me into the apartment. "No, damn it, it's not your dad."

"What's the problem? I thought you had a reception tonight? What are you doing here?" I did little to hide the irritation in my own voice.

"Here, give me those." He snatched the bags out of my hands, and I marched behind him into the living room.

Every light in the apartment blazed. I dropped the handbag on the kitchen island. "Patrick, *what* is going on?"

He placed my shopping paraphernalia on the couch and rubbed a hand through his hair. "I've been calling and texting for hours."

"I forgot to charge my phone last night. It must have died while I was out. What's the big deal?" I dug said phone out of my bag and plugged it in.

"I didn't know where you were," he grumbled, stuffing his hands into his pockets, his shoulders stiff at attention.

My brows rose, and I drew in a breath. "Do you mean to tell me you skipped your reception and came haring home because I didn't answer my *phone*?"

He shrugged.

"Dude." I walked around the couch and sat down to remove my boots. "What did you think had happened? I was abducted by space aliens?"

Patrick remained in the same position by the island, a mulish look on his face. "I didn't know. You said you planned to stay at the house doing chores. Mom said she spoke to you before noon. I've been trying to reach you since two. It's"— he checked his watch— "quarter to eight now."

"Well, I didn't expect to see you until eleven or twelve." I tossed the first boot on the far side of the coffee table. "When you left, you said you'd be home late and not to wait up. I wasn't aware I had to account to you for my comings and goings when you were away at a conference."

"You should have let me know you'd be going out. What if there had been an emergency?" His mouth settled into a straight line.

It had been a long time since I'd been held accountable to another in this manner, not since I'd left home for college, as a matter of fact. The engagement ring glittered as I shifted, its weight unexpectedly heavy on my hand. I was affianced now; it hadn't occurred to me that my agenda would be important to another, but here we were. Clearly, Patrick had gotten himself into a froth over nothing. On the other hand, how would I feel if I couldn't get in touch with him and had no idea where he was? Honestly, our society had become exceptionally spoiled by smart phones, social media, texting, messaging, tweeting, etc. At any given time of the day, friends and colleagues were reachable, and if they weren't, all you had to do was track their social media. With half the planet inevitably "checking in" to whatever restaurant/airport/event they were currently attending, all their friends and followers knew where they were. In the days before smart phones, you could be gone for hours and no one worried. Life had changed.

I sighed, and the second boot followed the first. "Okay, you've got a point. I should have let you know I'd be going out for the afternoon. Being in a relationship means caring for the other person's whereabouts. I'm sorry I made you worry. I didn't notice my phone went dead until I was driving home."

Patrick's shoulders finally relaxed. He pulled his hands out of his pockets as he came around, pushed the bags aside, and sat on the club chair. "I'm sorry too. I just feel more comfortable when I know where you are. Maybe I overreacted."

"You did, but you're right, I should have texted to let you know that I was going shopping with Jillian. I guess I'm still feeling my way in this relationship."

"I suppose we both are."

"You're missing your reception. Do you want me to get dressed and go back with you?"

He waved his hand. "Forget it. You're right, they're all a bunch of blowhards."

I returned his smile and, with that, our ship on rough waters righted itself.

Chapter Twelve

"My goodness, look at you! Why, you're practically glowing."

Glowing would be a gross exaggeration of my current end-of-long-day state; however, I didn't bother to correct Molly. She opened her arms and I leaned in for a hug.

"Let me see, let me see."

I proffered the left hand for inspection; she took hold and tugged me into the foyer.

"Oh my goodness, it looks fabulous on you." Her fingers splayed across her chest. "Don't you just love it? And it means so much more since it's an heirloom."

"No doubt," I said as Ivan, Molly's shadow, leaned against me, almost knocking me down. I spread my feet further apart to adjust to his weight and stroked his back. "I suppose you heard Patrick's running late."

"Yes, yes. Marty is too. Men and their meetings. But what are you going to do?"

Host us on the weekend? I couldn't help the uncharitable thought. Traffic had been a bear getting out of Alexandria, and I would have preferred it if this dinner had not been held on a "school night."

"Here, let me take your coat and you can put your handbag there on the table. I warned both Patrick and Marty that if they're not home by quarter to eight, we'll eat without them. I'm not allowing dinner to be ruined over some silly meetings. Besides, I'm starving." Molly patted her stomach.

Knowing Patrick and Marty's work life, I suspected the meetings weren't silly. I knew for a fact Patrick, at least, was trying to reel in a million-dollar deal. "I'm sure they'll get here as soon as they can."

Molly's kitten heel shoes and Ivan's nails clicked in unison across the marble floors as I followed them to the family room, where the scent of cooking meat assailed my senses. "Whatever you're making smells delicious."

"Pot roast. Here you go, dear, I poured us a nice chardonnay. It's from Argentina, so it doesn't have that dreaded California oaky-ness. What do you think?"

"Mm, very nice, quite refreshing." I took a deep swallow, then lowered myself into the poufy chair across from Molly. Ivan lay down in front of the fire.

"Feel free to kick off your shoes. It's just family tonight so we can be casual." Molly toed off her own pumps and tucked her feet up. "Ah, that feels better. I've been running all over town today. It was old Mother Hubbard's cupboard here at the house, and I'm still running laundry from our trip."

"Speaking of your trip, how was Utah?"

"Wonderful. Marty and I both got in some skiing. Do you ski?"

"Only marginally. I'm no black diamond skier. I stick with blues and greens."

"We'll have you come out to Utah sometime. I'm a blue and green myself. Sometimes I send Marty on the slopes and stick with the young families on the tubing hill. Have you done that?"

I shook my head.

"Oh, you'd love it." She leaned forward and whispered as though imparting a secret, "Takes no experience whatsoever, you just go bouncing down on a big red tube. It's as fun as can be. And then, there's some wonderful shopping to do. Oh, I can't wait to do all the fun girl things with you. I mean, don't get me wrong, I love my boys, but sometimes … I miss not having a daughter to do girly things with." She held up her wine. "But now

I have you!"

I smiled at her enthusiasm and clinked my glass to hers. "To girly things."

"To my future daughter-in-law!"

We both drank deeply.

"So, tell me… have you and Patrick set a date?"

"Not yet. I was thinking about having a fall wedding. Maybe in October, it's such a beautiful time around here with the leaves changing, all those reds and oranges."

"Oh, I think that would be lovely, especially with your reddish-brown hair. You'd make a beautiful fall bride. And Jonathan will be home by then. Do you know where you want to hold the reception?"

"Not really. We don't know how many people yet. Maybe one of the old estates in the area. Gunston Hall?"

"I've been to a wedding there. They do a nice job at Gunston. There's also the Carlyle House on Fairfax Street in Old Town if you want one of those old Manor homes. We're also members of the Belle Haven Country Club; if you're interested in holding it there, I can arrange it."

"I've never been."

"It's pretty, especially in the fall. We'll arrange to have lunch sometime, so you can see it. That reminds me." She snapped her fingers and jumped up. "I've got something for you. I saw it at the airport and couldn't help buying it. I think I left it on my bedside table. I'll be right back." As she navigated the coffee table, the phone rang. "I'll get it." She picked up the cordless handset off its charger and exited the room. Ivan rose, staring after her. "Hello? Oh, Bonnie, it's you. Hold on just a sec." Molly stuck her head around the entryway. "Sorry, Karina, I've been waiting to hear back from this woman all day. It's about our Junior League fundraiser. She's on the committee with me. I'll only be a few minutes."

"Take your time."

Her voice faded. Ivan watched her exit, then looked at me.

"She'll be back in a minute, buddy."

He must not have liked that answer because a moment later he loped off after her.

I rose and strolled around the room, fingering the bric-a-brac, admiring the Erté mirror in its glass case, smiling at a picture of Patrick and Jonathan as toddlers. Eventually, when Molly didn't return, I wandered down to Marty's study. The door was open, and I had a vague notion of looking through more of his antique law books. I found the white gloves in the desk drawer where he retrieved them last time and pulled out a volume midway through the stack. Like before, I took it to the desk and turned on the desk lamp to see better.

After a few minutes of perusing the archaic laws, I got up and stuck my head out the door. "Molly?"

No answer.

She must still be upstairs.

I returned to the desk and, as before when I'd been in the office, my fingers searched the underside. *The Hunting Party* disappeared and my heart dropped. Instead of the empty space that I'd expected ... the black and white checkerboard floor had returned. Only this time, a thick gilt frame majestically surrounded the painting. I strode across the room to view it up close. Indeed, it was the same music lesson scene I'd observed on all the websites; the orange coloring of the chair dominated the canvas. The paint had a crackled appearance; the minute fissures spoke to its age. Although, some of the research I'd done on forgeries demonstrated avenues for baking those fissures into a newer painting. At the top left of the painting, there seemed to be a small scratch or tear, almost as though fixed with a patch in back. I couldn't tell you how long I stared at the painting before coming to my senses. Retreating behind the desk, I closed the secret hiding place.

"Mom? Karina? Where is everyone?"

Patrick found me leaning in a stupor against the powder room door. "Karina, are you okay? You're white as a sheet."

"What? Uh, I'm sorry, hon, I'm not feeling well."

"You look like you're about to vomit." He scrutinized me. "I heard there's a stomach bug going around. Do you think you've caught it?"

"Maybe so. I think I need to go home."

"Want me to drive you?"

"No. I don't want you to catch it." The hand I held to my mouth kept Patrick at bay. "Please give your mom my regrets. She went upstairs to fetch something. I'm so sorry but I really have to leave." I retrieved my coat and purse and as I opened the door, Molly and Ivan trotted down the stairs.

"Here it is. I'm sorry to keep you waiting. That Bonnie … talk, talk, talk. Oh, Patrick you're here. Wonderful. Karina? What's the matter? Are you leaving?"

"Mom, Karina's not feeling well. We think it's a stomach bug. She's headed home."

"Oh, you poor dear. Is there anything I can do?"

Shaking my head, I trucked down the steps, calling over my shoulder, "Sorry, raincheck."

I must have driven home on autopilot, because I have no memory of the roads, or traffic, for that matter. After texting Patrick to let him know I arrived home safely, my feet directed me to the bedroom, where I flopped down onto the bed and stared unseeingly at the ceiling. The hall light provided a swath of illumination through the doorway into the room.

What the hell is Marty doing with a $50 million stolen painting? Is it real? Why would you hide a copy? It isn't illegal to have a copy of a painting, but the real one… Where did he get it? Why does he have it? What should I do about it?

The last question was the true kicker. What the hell was I supposed to do about it? Tell my friend in the FBI my future father-in-law was hiding a stolen painting in his study? My God, the ramifications. Poor Molly. And what about Molly? What would they do to her? Could she be arrested as well? The thought of Molly's face staring at me with utter disappointment after her exuberance about our upcoming nuptials … Nuptials! What about Patrick? Could he ever forgive me for ratting out his father? I cringed, thinking of the utter betrayal at turning his father into the feds. Could he ever forgive me? Could I ever forgive myself? As much as I'd like to believe we could get through something like that, it would ruin us.

The questions rolled around and around like a marble circling the drain.

"Oh, my stupid, stupid, stupid curiosity." I pulled a pillow over my face. "I couldn't leave it alone, could I?" The last time I looked, the painting had been gone, and the reason for its absence was as clear as day now that a golden frame surrounded it.

The pillow flew to the floor. "Why did I have to look again?" I yelled at the ceiling.

The glass of wine churned, souring in my stomach, and I ran to the bathroom to hover over the toilet and pray for relief. After a few minutes, I realized I wasn't going to be sick. Unfortunate. I didn't have a stomach bug. What I did have was a Catch-22 and no good answers. The mirror reflected my miserable green eyes, pale face, and sagging lips. Legal ethics and loyalties pulled me in opposite directions; I knew the night would not bring the relief I so desperately sought.

Chapter Thirteen

Thursday morning, I left a message for my boss, calling in sick. What little sleep I got was filled with nightmares and coasted right along the edge of sleep and wakefulness. My bloodshot eyes were gritty with fatigue and a low-grade headache throbbed at my temples. The bed looked as though it'd met with a rabid porcupine or a night of turbulent monkey sex. Frankly, I would have preferred either of those options to the true reason it was trashed.

Around eight thirty, I dragged myself out of bed, wrapped in the comforter, and trudged to the kitchen to fire up the coffeemaker. The morning talk shows kept me company while I begrudgingly swallowed strawberry yogurt with a too strong cup of java. By nine thirty, I questioned my reasons for laying out of the office. At least if I'd gone in, there would have been distractions; as it was, the television provided only white noise. No matter how hard I tried to disengage my brain, the squirrel scurried from one nut to another in there.

At ten, Patrick's sing-song ringtone broke the monotony, and my hand hovered over the phone in debate before answering.

"Hello."

"Hi, sweetie. You sound terrible. How's the stomach bug?"

"Didn't get much sleep last night," I grated out in a scratchy voice.

"I'm glad you got home okay. Is there anything I can bring you after work?"

There was no way I could face Patrick. "No. You'd better stay away. I don't want you to catch this, it seems pretty virulent. Why don't we see how I'm feeling tomorrow, or Saturday, before we connect?"

"I don't know. I feel as though I should take care of you. Isn't that my job now?"

"Not at all, your job is to stay well. Besides, I've got saltines and chicken soup. There's really nothing for you to do. I'll be fine. You don't want to catch this one."

"If you're sure."

"I'm sure. The worst is over." *I wish.* "I'll likely head into work tomorrow."

"Okay. Mom wanted to reschedule for Saturday. She wants to plan an engagement party for us."

Engagement party? Cripes! "I …" My mind scrambled for an excuse. "I think I've got a fundraiser. Why don't I check my schedule and get back to you?"

"That's fine. She's just so pumped about the wedding."

I rolled my eyes and replied with sarcasm, "Ya think?"

Patrick sighed. "Karina, I can hear you rolling your eyes. Give her a break. I'm the first one walking down the aisle. She's so excited to be getting a daughter-in-law."

"I know, I know. Sorry, the lack of sleep is making me cranky. It's just that your mom is ten steps ahead on this wedding planning thing, and I'm still processing the engagement."

"That's Mom for you. I should let you go. Get some rest and we'll talk tonight. Everything will look better after you get more sleep."

Like that's going to happen. "Okay, bye."

"Love you."

"You too."

After another half hour of *not* watching the blaring TV, I cracked open my laptop and began searching laws and regulations for returning stolen property to museums. Unfortunately, my initial search revealed little useful information. All the links were about museums that had art or antiquities that had been looted from other countries, like the Greeks' Elgin Marbles, or private Jewish artwork stolen by Nazis.

I typed in the Gardner Museum heist, and in the lower corner of the portion of the Gardner Museum website dedicated to the theft, contact information for the current head of security was provided. It also provided declarations that anyone returning the artwork could be assured of anonymity. Somehow, I doubted that statement. I found it unlikely the museum would keep the name of the returner from the DOJ or FBI. Both agencies remained hot to nail a guilty party.

I spent the next few hours researching Marty, trying to find any sort of shady deals, criminal complaints, or bad press. His name came up surrounding legitimate auctions for artwork, but nothing that would lead me to believe that he dealt in illegal circles. He'd been married for almost forty years. Two years ago, he and Molly co-sponsored a fundraiser with the nonprofit, Africa Children's Aid. It raised close to a million dollars and went toward feeding and providing medical care to refugees. Two of his buildings donated a certain amount of office space to nonprofit entities working domestically and abroad. Hardly the background of a master criminal. His fingers were undoubtedly in several political pies, but as far as I could tell, he kept them as clean as a surgeon's instruments.

Soft rays of mid-afternoon light shone through the sliding glass door when I tossed aside the laptop in frustration. Knuckling my eyes, I plodded to the bathroom and turned on the shower. The plentitude of information I'd just skimmed ran through my head. There was one article, from late October, in the *Philadelphia Weekly*. Buried in the editorial section was a story about a concrete company, Sims Brothers Concrete, which the writer alleged was run by a Philadelphia mafia family. The editorial stated Sims Brothers had strong-armed a smaller, legitimate company into folding, going so far as to burn down their main office building. The anonymous author used the platform to chastise law enforcement from performing their due diligence investigating the fire. The police reported the cause for the fire was arson; apparently, it started with a Molotov cocktail and used gasoline as an accelerant. The only reason the article struck a chord was because Martin's company had recently scored a large government contract, and Sims Brothers Concrete was listed as one of over a hundred subcontractors on the job.

I squeezed the excess water out of my hair and stepped onto the fluffy white mat. *Nah, it's probably nothing,* I decided.

After putting on a clean pair of yoga pants and my favorite Redskins sweatshirt, I microwaved some chicken noodle soup and spent the rest of the afternoon binge-watching my DVR'd NCIS shows. Thank heavens for Gibbs, McGee, Abby, and all the dead military personnel apparently dropping like flies around the D.C. area. Note to Marines and Navy folks—do not put in for a transfer to D.C.—according to NCIS, you are putting your life in mortal peril. At least three times I yelled at the TV, "You know Norfolk is three hours from D.C., and that's *without* 95 traffic!" In the end, it didn't matter how long it took Hollywood to reach Norfolk, because the show did its job taking my mind off the Vermeer dilemma for a few hours.

Chapter Fourteen

Desperate for decent night's sleep, I took a sleeping pill, which knocked me out, but had the unfortunate effect of leaving me with morning grogginess, necessitating a visit to the coffee shop.

I blamed that imprudent pill for the caffeine yen and my own inattention. If I had been on my game, I would have foreseen and avoided the trap I walked into. At minimum, I would have recognized Mike's profile in the window and continued to the elevators. But I didn't see Mike until it was too late. When I turned from the barista—cupping my sugared and caffeinated joe like a crack addict in need of a hit—he'd risen from his seat by the window and flagged me down.

Shit! The thought screamed in my head, and I feared I'd spoken the word aloud. I must not have done so because no one stared oddly at me. For a brief second, I considered ignoring my old buddy and waltzing right past him. Ingrained etiquette overrode my rude intentions.

"Mike." I nodded. "On another stakeout?"

He grimaced, glancing at the man sitting with him at the table. Then he gave a terrible impression of a laugh, so fake it made my teeth clench. "That's a good one."

The guy at the table wore a dark suit, light blue shirt, and nondescript tie. Everything about him screamed 'Fed.' In no mood to pussyfoot around, I asked bluntly, "Who's your friend?"

"K.C., I'd like to introduce you to a coworker of mine, Bruce Patterson. This is a college friend, Karina Cardinal."

Bruce rose. "Hello, Karina." The handshake was firm and

warm compared to my flaccid, cold fingers.

"Bruce. How's it going?" I said flippantly.

"Won't you join us?" His voice was soft but held a tone that told me 'no' was not an option.

I pursed my lips and contemplated the two. "Sure, what the hell? Let's chat." I slid into the extra seat crammed around the minuscule table. "So, what do you do for the FBI, Bruce?"

"He works in the art crimes division," Mike answered for him.

Of course, he does. I'm sure my eyes flared at Mike's revelation, but I'd learned well during mock trials how to school my expression into a look I called "interested neutrality."

I guessed Bruce was in his mid-fifties, his sandy hair liberally sprinkled with gray and receding beyond his forehead, where a pair of reading glasses rested. The wrinkles around his hazel eyes and mouth spoke of hours in the unshaded sun. He seemed to be waiting for me to break the silence, but I had no such intention.

Bruce cleared his throat. "I understand from Mike that you're recently engaged. Congratulations."

"Thanks."

The conversation continued to lag as I sipped my lifesaving drug and waited for the caffeine to work its magic.

"Your future father-in-law, Martin Dunne, is quite the art collector?" Bruce tried again.

I didn't bat an eyelash. "Yes."

"What kinds of art pieces does he have?"

I glanced between the two men. The look of "interested neutrality" returned. "All kinds—paintings, antiquities, sculptures, and statues. He has an eclectic palate."

"Have you ever met any of his art associates?"

"Interested Neutrality" dropped into "Frowning Suspicion."

"How long?"

"I beg your pardon?" Bruce asked.

But I was looking at Mike. "How long have you been staking out the coffee shop to 'accidentally' run into me?"

Mike didn't blush; his jaw flexed and the telltale finger tapped.

"This is only the second time." Bruce again answered on the duo's behalf.

My cup thumped against the table as I glared at my so-called friend. "Seriously, Mike?"

Mike had the decency to look embarrassed.

"Before you begin blaming him, you should know I asked Mike to set this up. And since you're as sharp as he warned, I won't insult your intelligence, I'll get right down to it." Bruce drew his glasses down.

Here it comes. My heart pounded, and I gripped the coffee to keep my hands from shaking. Could I lie to the FBI? Was I going to be the instrument that labeled my future father-in-law a criminal?

His phone had been sitting on the table, and now he flipped it over and held it forth, revealing a grainy candid shot of a man wearing a Russian Cossack hat and long, dark overcoat. "Have you ever seen this man?"

It took a minute for me to realize the photo was not the Vermeer as I'd expected. *What is going on here?* The photo struck a chord. I squinted and leaned closer to the phone. "I'm … not sure."

Bruce swiped right.

The next photo wasn't as grainy, and without the fluffy hat, the white hair stood out like a beacon. I sucked in a breath. "Yes, I've seen that man."

"Where?"

"You tell me."

Bruce licked his lips. "I'm sure I couldn't say."

"Who is he?"

"He goes by many names, Lorenzo Knight, Nick Haldeman,

Javier Durand…"

"Christoph O'Brien?" I offered.

"Ah."

"What I meant—who is he in the art world?"

"Well, that's a good question. As Nick Haldeman, he worked with Interpol to recover a stolen Renoir painting worth $2.4 million. All the other aliases we believe he uses to fence artwork of questionable origin."

Mike remained mute during Bruce's interrogation, watching like a spectator on the sidelines of a Wimbledon match.

"And you're wondering what he was doing at Marty Dunne's Christmas bash," I said.

Both the men exchanged a look, and I realized I'd made a mistake. They hadn't confirmed that he'd been to Marty's house. I shook my head at how foolishly I'd fallen for the trick. The damn caffeine hadn't kicked in yet.

"Where did you clock him? The airport?" I asked.

"He arrived Thursday, December first."

"When did he leave?"

"We don't know," Bruce admitted.

"So, he's still in the area?"

Another look passed. Bruce cleared his throat. "We believe he used a different alias, a new one, to leave the country. We've lost track of him."

"What about all that facial recognition software?"

"He's a master of disguise, and he's got connections." Mike finally entered the conversation.

"What do you want to know?" I ignored my friend and spoke directly to the elder agent.

Mike shifted uncomfortably, but Bruce, all business now, swiped the phone again. "Have you seen this painting in Mr. Dunne's home?"

And here it is. My fingers tightened on the coffee cup, and I forced my eyes to look down, but once again my gaze did not see the expected painting. Instead, a colorful pastel piece depicted a row of men singing. They wore Spanish pantaloons and feathered caps. My entire body sagged in relief, and I answered with full honesty, "No, I have *never* seen that painting."

Bruce removed his Cheaters and the uncanny tawny eyes scrutinized me. "You're sure? Look again."

I humored him. "Nope. Why do you ask?"

"It's a Degas."

I waited for the punchline.

Mike leaned forward. "It was stolen from the Cantini Museum in Marseille."

If he was expecting some sort of shocked reaction, he was sorely disappointed, for "Interested Neutrality" returned. "Recently?"

"2010," Mike said.

"Hm." I sat back, crossing my arms. "And you think Christoph had something to do with the theft?"

"No, but there's been talk that he might be seeking a buyer." Mike fidgeted with a napkin.

"What's it worth?"

"Valued at $1.1 million."

"Sorry, I can't help you. Never seen it." With that, I decided to draw this little discussion to a close. Gathering my purse and laptop bag, I rose. "The next time you want to talk, Mike, just call ... or text. There's really no need for this cloak and dagger business."

"Wait." Bruce rose with me. "Take my card. If you see Christoph again, please contact me. He's a person of interest in an ongoing investigation."

I stuffed the piece of cardstock into my purse and shoved the glass door out of my way. A thought occurred to me and I caught the door on the backswing. "By the way, whoever you put on duty to tail me last Saturday sucks at it. He should go back to the FBI academy to retake Surveillance 101."

"I didn't put a tail on you." Mike managed to sound affronted.

"Whatever." I rolled my eyes as I stalked to the elevator bank. Lucky for me, one opened, divesting its passengers. Once the doors slid shut, I fell back against the wall, my head spinning.

"Shit," I whispered, "shitty, shit, shit, *shit*." *What the hell is Marty into? Does he have more stolen paintings from Christoph/Nick/ Lorenzo? Is Marty a fence for stolen goods? Is he up to his neck in this?*

Though I didn't directly lie to an FBI agent, I withheld information on an unsolved case. Technically, I could be charged with obstruction of justice. The only thing currently working in my favor was the fact no one knew I'd seen the stolen painting. I'd never spoken about it with Patrick or my family. Marty didn't know I'd seen it. Only my conscience knew. And that damn painting weighed on my conscience, heavy as a school bus.

The doors opened, and I stomped down the mint green hallway to my office. My purse and computer bag dropped unceremoniously onto the desk. *Something is missing.* "Damn it. I forgot my coffee!"

"There's a fresh pot in the kitchen," Latesha called from her office next door.

"Thanks," I grumbled as I sorted out my computer, plugging it in to boot up.

"Rebecca said you were sick yesterday. I hope you're feeling better. Because if not, you can turn your butt around and go right back home." Latesha stood in my doorway, wiggling her finger. Her braided extensions swayed in mesmerizing unison as she shook her head. "We don't need any of that around here."

I collapsed on the desk chair. "Ugh. No, I feel fine."

She lowered herself onto my single guest chair, and her amber eyes examined me. "You don't look fine. What's going on with you?"

Desperate to share my secret, I had to bite my lips. Latesha oversaw grassroots advocacy mobilization for the profession, and we'd been office neighbors for the past five years. We were friendly office coworkers, but not close friends. For an instant, I thought about confiding in her. She wasn't in the midst of my world, but rather an onlooker, at a distance, that neither Patrick nor my family could claim.

"Something wrong in paradise with your new fiancé?"

"No." I pressed fingers against my eyes. It wouldn't be fair to drag Latesha into my Lifetime movie drama. Besides, I feared she'd tell me to go to the authorities, and I simply wasn't in a position to do that. "I'm sorry, I'm cranky. I just need to mainline some coffee."

She stood. "If you say so. But, if you need to talk … my door is always open."

How I wished I could take her up on the offer. My phone rang, and Latesha exited, closing the door behind her.

"Karina Cardinal."

"Karina, it's Molly. How are you feeling, dear?"

"Hi, Molly. I'm sorry I left so abruptly the other night."

"Oh, goodness. Don't worry about that. Are you doing better?"

"Yes, much," I lied.

"Good, good. Patrick told me you're busy tomorrow night, so I was wondering if you were available for lunch instead?"

"Lunch? This Saturday?" My mind scrambled for an excuse.

"Yes."

"Well … I'm free … but I believe Patrick has an indoor soccer game on Saturday afternoon."

"Great. Then it's a date."

"But Patrick—"

"No worries. Marty isn't available either, which is perfect for what I have in mind. It'll be us girls. We can talk about the engagement party. The men aren't interested in that planning stuff anyway."

Right now, I'm not interested in it either. "Uh, sure, I guess. Where do you want to meet?"

"I thought we'd eat at the club. It'll give you a chance to get a tour. Why don't you come to the house at noon, and I'll drive us over?"

"Sure," I said with resignation.

"Great. See you then."

The line went dead, and I thunked my head against the desk. A whistle at my elbow announced a new text. It was from Mike.

> *Sorry about ambushing you this morning. I didn't have you tailed.*
> *Whatever.*
> *Can we meet? I think we should talk.*
> *Go away, Mike. I'm busy.*
> *Please.*
> *I'll think about it.*

I turned off my phone and resumed head banging until an unpleasant thought intruded.

If Mike is telling the truth, who is creepy mall guy, and why was he following me?

Chapter Fifteen

The windshield wipers cleared away the fat flakes of snow drifting from the ashen skies. I prayed the clouds would unload and turn into a blizzard. Patrick's ringtone sang out from my purse and I pressed the Bluetooth at my ear.

"What's up?"

"Hi, I was going to come over tonight to check on you, but it looks like I'll be working late. We've got a presentation first thing Monday morning and our concept art isn't coming together." Patrick sounded harried.

"No problem." *Thank God.* "You should stay at your place in the city tonight."

"Are you sure?"

"Definitely. I just witnessed five snowflakes. Any moment, Washington will be declared a federal emergency."

He chuckled. "I'll keep that in mind. We'll talk tomorrow."

"I'm supposed to have lunch with your mom tomorrow."

"Great. You can regale me with her plans afterward."

"Will do."

****

"Mother Nature, you suck," I groused at the postcard perfect scene laid before me. Bright morning sunlight bounced off the dusting of snow that would melt well before lunchtime, leaving me no excuse to ditch Molly.

At noon on the dot, I rolled into the Dunne's driveway, holding the steering wheel in a death grip. The only good thing I could say about this lunch—it wouldn't be held at the house. At least I wouldn't be tempted to look at what I'd come to refer to as "that damn painting," the current bane of my existence.

I rubbed a hand against my jaw—sore from grinding all night long. At bedtime, my fears turned to anger, and I roundly cursed Marty for bringing that damn painting into my life. Then I cursed Christoph for bringing it to Marty, Mike for lying about putting a tail on me, that Bruce character for convincing Mike to stake out the coffee shop, and my own stinkin' curiosity. After talking to the dark ceiling for an hour, I'd come around to cursing Molly and this stupid lunch, and Patrick for proposing in the first place. Finally, I cursed myself for being late to the wine tour, because then I never would have met Patrick, and even though I'd still be unengaged, at least I wouldn't be cursing the walls like a madwoman.

I waited in the car for a full five minutes, hoping Molly would see me out the window and make my day by trotting out.

No such luck.

With a grunt, I unfolded from the car, dragged myself up the front steps, and rang the doorbell. No one answered. I pressed the button again and knocked. As my knuckles rapped against the heavy wooden door, it swung inward.

That's odd.

I pushed it further and stuck my head through the opening. "Hello? Molly?" No alarms beeped or lights flashed, so I stepped further into the foyer, glancing left and right. "Yoo-hoo, Molly, it's Karina. I'm here for our lunch date."

Nothing.

"Marty?"

The master bedroom was at the far end of the second story hallway, and I climbed halfway up the stairs to get a little closer in case she was changing. "Molly? Hel-lo!"

My calls were met with silence—the silence of an empty house. Not even the dog trotted out to greet me. A shiver ran down my spine, and my hair stood on end.

Where is everyone?

Thanks to a recent NCIS, my imagination conjured up a home invasion, complete with bloodstains and hacked off limbs. I remained frozen in place, unable to move up or down. My cellphone broke the silence, and a tiny scream erupted from my mouth.

"Hello."

"Karina, good. Are you at the house yet?"

"I've just arrived."

"Sorry, I should have called earlier. I've got to cancel. I'm at the vet with Ivan." Molly's voice pitched in agitation.

"What's wrong? Is he going to be okay?"

"They're taking x-rays now. When I brought him inside this morning, he threw up and then cried pitifully. I think he might have eaten something he shouldn't have. Maybe something poisonous."

Home invasion carnage disappeared, replaced with the much likelier reality of Molly scrambling around to load gentle-giant Ivan into the car while collecting keys, phone, and a handbag. "Oh, no. Is there anything I can do?"

"I don't think so. We'll just have to wait and see what the vet has to say."

"Is Marty with you?"

"No, he had meetings at the office today. I've got to go. The vet just came out. We'll talk soon."

She hung up before I could tell her about the open front door. It didn't matter; even though I didn't have the key to lock the deadbolt, the doorknob had a lock, and I twisted it to the right. It would have to do. I was about to pull it closed behind me when my footsteps paused at the threshold. Common sense fought a battle with interfering nosiness.

"Hell," I muttered, closing the door.

Moments later, that damn painting stared back at me and

dragged me into its world. The singer's figure was so delicate and fine, and I could almost hear her birdlike soprano voice fill the room while the teacher tapped time with his foot in tune with the harpsichordist. Vermeer created a hypnotic scene; it was no wonder audiences remained delighted by his works even 350 years later.

One thought kept banging away in my head: *This should be in a museum.*

In 1903, Isabella Stewart Gardner opened her lavish, Venetian-style palace doors for the "education and enjoyment of the public forever." I was not one to subscribe to ideals like fate or destiny, but I began to wonder if I was here for a purpose. Did I stumble into this stolen art because it was my job to return it to the walls of Isabella's home? Why should Marty alone be able to enjoy such a masterpiece? Who was he to keep this hidden from the world?

I dragged one of the wing chairs in front of the fireplace and climbed up. The house alarm and security cameras were obviously off. However, Patrick's description of the pressure plates led me to believe they remained on continuously, which had me running my hand around the frame in search of a wire. I didn't find one, but that could mean nothing. The wiring and pressure plate mechanism could all be behind the canvas. Crossing my arms, I stared at the painting. One question kept coming to mind. *Why would you wire a hidden painting? Wouldn't hiding it be enough security?*

Taking two fingers, I pushed the frame to the side, shifting it cockeyed on the wall. No sirens went off. *How do pressure plates work?* I mentally kicked myself for not investigating pressure plates during my manic research on Marty and the Gardner heist. *How long would it take the cops to arrive if I did set off an alarm? If they came, how would Marty explain the painting?* The latter question led me back to the former. *Why would you wire a hidden painting?*

"Enough!"

I grabbed the frame on either side, drew in a breath, and lifted.

The dark green wall showed nothing but a sturdy hanger—no shrieking alarms sounded, no steel doors slammed shut over the windows. I laid the painting by the fireplace, returned the chair to its home, making sure the feet fit back into the rug divots, then closed the secret compartment.

As I walked past Marty's desk, my hip brushed against a manila envelope, knocking it to the floor. The contents spilled across the Persian rug, and I bent to retrieve them when something caught my eye. It was a close-up eight-by-ten glossy of me, at the Pentagon City mall ... five days ago. My sister's green sweater could barely be seen in the right corner as I stared straight into the camera. The pinched look I gave the photographer was not particularly attractive, but clearly defined my irritation with the man in the brown coat.

"What the hell?" I sat down hard on the floor and shuffled through the other photos. "What are you doing, Marty?"

There was an attractive profile of me, taken at the restaurant, and another sifting through a rack of dresses at Macy's. *Is Marty running a background check on me before I become a family member?* Patrick hadn't mentioned the prenup again, but that didn't mean his father wasn't pressuring him to have me sign one. However, sending an investigator to follow me around seemed a bit beyond the pale.

Sorting further into the stack confused me even more. I found a grainy photo of Patrick entering his office building, and another of him at the corner coffee shop about a block from his apartment. There were three pictures of Molly: two in the same red suit on a sidewalk somewhere in D.C.—the third, even more disturbing. She wore sweatpants and a down coat, and was walking Ivan less than fifty yards from the house. I could see the Dunne's black iron fence in the background.

"What on earth *is* all this?"

The entire package duly creeped me out and pissed me off. I could have sat further pondering the ramifications of the photos, and I even considered waiting for Marty to get home to confront him, but I had more pressing business to take care of. That damn painting called to me from its perch against the fireplace. I paid little attention to order as I stuffed the glossies back into the packet and replaced it on the desk.

Returning to the task at hand, I reconsidered my next move. Originally, I planned to walk it out the front door. However, if Marty was having me watched, or the FBI was surveilling Marty's house, going the front-door-route was perhaps not the best idea. The French doors in Marty's office opened out onto the back patio. It was a short walk to the driveway that led to the three-car garage.

I left by the front door, locking it behind me, and backed the car down the curving drive around to the side of the house. My trunk housed an old pink blanket that Patrick and I had once used for a picnic; I spread this out and trotted around to Marty's office. A camera right outside the door pointed directly at the entryway, and I was relieved the system was turned off.

Again, I stared at the painting, only this time my heart pounded and sweat broke out along my upper lip. There would be no coming back from this road—what that road entailed was still unclear. As soon as Marty found the painting gone, the proverbial shit would hit the fan. So far, I hadn't done anything I couldn't walk back. It would be so easy to stick that damn painting back on the wall and forget about it.

Who am I kidding? I gave myself a mental head slap, knowing I'd *never* be able to forget about it.

"*Hell!*" I scooped up the painting and made my move before I chickened out.

A few minutes later, *The Concert* lay—gently wrapped and secured by my gym bag and briefcase on either side to keep it from sliding around—inside the trunk as I drove out of the Dunne's neighborhood.

Once I returned to my apartment complex, I left the painting in my trunk and took the stairs down to the basement. Each homeowner was provided a storage unit in the basement. I didn't have much in my unit besides my bike, old college books, a few odd pieces of furniture, and about two dozen packing boxes I'd kept after the move. The four-by-six-foot chicken-wire cages, piled with other tenants' dusty random stuff and lit by a few dim bulbs, didn't help my state of mind as I weaved my way through the maze to my own unit. Immediately, I found the picture box I'd been looking for and returned to the car.

The parking lot was surprisingly busy. I mumbled greetings to two different neighbors as they walked past me into the lobby. My gaze took in the panorama and found a couple walking their dog, another car arriving, and a pair of kids playing tag on the front sidewalk. The complex was simply too busy; I shoved the box in the back seat and drove down the GW Parkway to a place I expected to be empty in the middle of winter. Fifteen minutes later, I pulled into Fort Hunt park and found a secluded area where I could transfer the painting into the box and formulate my next move.

Chapter Sixteen
MARTIN

The heavy Mercedes keyring made a loud *clunk* as Marty tossed them into the wooden bowl by the garage door. The green light on the keypad remained steady, and Marty called out, "Molly? Are you home?"

No answer.

He removed his gray parka, hanging it on one of the wall hooks in the mudroom, and headed toward the kitchen.

"Molly?"

When he didn't receive an answer the second time, he pulled the phone out of his pocket and texted her.

Are you still at the vet?

Yes. They are performing a procedure on Ivan.

Will call when I know more.

Martin ground his teeth, knowing that Molly, in her agitated state, forgot to turn on the security system … again. He didn't bother to point out her mistake. First, she was clearly upset about Ivan. Second, his loving, but occasionally forgetful, wife had left the house without turning on the alarm many times, which is why the pressure plates and outside security cameras remained on at all times. A few taps on his phone pulled up a convenient monitoring security app, which showed no plate or glass break alarms had been triggered.

Marty grabbed an apple from the fridge, poured himself a glass of water, and headed down to his office. The Grandfather clock struck two, its pendulous bongs resonated through the house. Marty placed the bottle on the desk blotter and stared at the manila envelope. Its presence filled him with unease, and he picked it up to sort through the photos one more time. Two people held dear to him, and the third, a lovely girl engaged to his son, were pictured in them. His fingers stopped at the one he found the most deeply disturbing—a photo of his wife walking Ivan in front of the house.

"Damn it." He tossed the packet down in frustration and fell into the leather chair. "I never should have accepted it in the first place!"

****

Six months ago, it all seemed so perfect. The company won a government contract to build a new office building for the Veterans Affairs Department in Bethesda, Maryland, near Walter Reed Medical Center. When his partner Jeff Jenkins suggested subcontracting out to Sims Brothers Concrete, a business in Philadelphia, Marty didn't think twice. This wasn't their first government contract, he and Jenkins had been around the block before, and he saw no reason not to trust his partner's judgement. But then Marty's secretary had forwarded him an article from a local Philadelphia newspaper about a fire, ruled to be arson, and pointed the finger at a local mafia family. Sims Brothers Concrete business was listed as one of the companies connected to this family.

When Marty broached the subject with Jenkins and told him to cancel the contract, it was the first time he met with resistance from his partner. Initially, Jenkins told Marty he was making a big deal over nothing. Then Marty found another article, an editorial this time, pointing at a corrupt police department financed on the side by the same family, and so he returned to Jeff and put his foot down. Either the concrete company went, or Marty would remove Jeff from the contract all together. The two had a terrible argument which finally ended with his partner agreeing to dump the contractor.

A few weeks went by and Jeff came up with one excuse after another why he hadn't cancelled the contract, always promising to do so. Then Jeff's wife was diagnosed with colon cancer. When Marty again confronted his partner over the concrete company, Jeff finally broke down and tearfully explained. Years ago, when his daughter was an infant, his marriage was still young and on rocky ground from lack of sleep, and the beginnings of his first company was wavering, he'd gotten into trouble gambling at a backdoor poker game. He was in the hole for close to a hundred grand and only found out the game was run by the Russian mafia after he'd been threatened with physical harm and his family's life was threatened. Twenty-four hours later, an anonymous benefactor paid off his debt with one caveat: he would owe the patron a favor. He didn't know when or what the favor would be, but it was made clear that when the chip was called in, there were no questions asked, and refusal was not an option. Desperate, Jeff agreed to the conditions and was given a 1000 lira coin to remember his promise.

Years passed. Dunne and Jenkins combined their two middling companies to become the multi-million-dollar firm they were today. In the back of his mind, Jenkins kept waiting for the marker to be called in. Thirty-eight years passed. His children grew up. He divorced and remarried. He forgot about the coin. Until, that is, the day after Dunne and Jenkins won the VA contract, when in response to a request for proposal, a hand-delivered one landed on Jeff's desk. When he pulled the contents of the envelope out, taped to the top page was a 1000 lira coin—a coin that was no longer in circulation—and a handwritten note that said, "Time to pay up."

Marty had been both shocked and angered by Jeff's story and chewed him out for his stupidity. They finally came to an agreement; the concrete company would keep the contract, but Marty would keep an eye on their work. If anything seemed fishy or was subpar, he would deal with them. Jeff was no longer a decision-maker on the VA contract. Jeff agreed, and since his wife was dealing with cancer treatments, the pair decided it would best for him to take a leave of absence. Marty reached out to the managing partner at Sims Brothers Concrete to let them know Jeff was out of the picture, and he was in.

Two weeks later, a tall man with a narrow, acne-scarred face came to his office and introduced himself as Vincent, Mr. Monaldo's assistant.

"Sit down." Marty indicated the guest chair opposite his desk and resumed his own seat. Marty knew exactly who Monaldo was. "Before we proceed, Mr. Vincent—"

"Just Vincent, or you can call me Vince."

"Very well. Vincent, let me be clear. I am not my partner. I do not know, nor do I owe Mr. Monaldo anything. As you may have heard, Jeff is currently on leave due to his wife's illness—"

"Yes, I spoke to Mr. Jenkins a few days ago and was saddened to hear about his wife's turn of health. Mr. Monaldo sent a large fruit basket."

"Erm, yes, well, you need to let Mr. Monaldo know that there won't be any funny business on this contract. I expect first-class work out of his concrete company. Anything less, and I will fire you for cause as listed under section 203, subsection B in your contract."

The weaselly man bowed his head. "I can assure you nothing less than exceptional product and workers out of Sims Concrete. Mr. Monaldo will see to it. Mr. Monaldo hopes this will be the first of many contracts the two firms could work on together."

Inwardly, Marty cringed at the thought, however, he kept on his tough face and crossed his arms. "We'll have to wait and see."

"Mr. Monaldo would also like to give you a gift for agreeing to honor his contract."

"That is quite unnecessary."

"Nonetheless—"

"Nonetheless," Marty cut in, "in case Mr. Monaldo is unaware, it would be illegal for me to accept any gifts from a subcontractor. This is a business arrangement. Nothing more."

Again, Vincent bowed his head in that subservient manner. "If you insist."

"I do. Now, is there anything else you would like to discuss regarding the contract?"

"I don't believe so." Vincent stood and extended a business card. "Mr. Monaldo sends his regards. Here is my direct line in case you have any problems or concerns."

He heard nothing more from Vincent, Monaldo, or the managing partner of Sims Brothers Concrete. The original strip mall where the new structure was to be built had been leveled and the land cleared in readiness for the new construction.

Then on the day of the Christmas party, Christoph O'Brien, bearing a set of antiquities credentials, showed up at his door with a package he insisted be opened in private. Marty assumed this was the man delivering the Georgia O'Keefe flower painting he'd bought ten days ago from Sotheby's auction house, a Christmas present for Molly. It wasn't supposed to be delivered for another week, so Marty was pleasantly surprised when O'Brien showed up early. He poured the two of them a glass of brandy to celebrate. When he pulled the painting out of the crate, it took him a few moments to comprehend what he held in his hands.

This was no O'Keefe.

Vermeer did not sign all his paintings; however, by 1990, Martin had begun his own collection and the Gardner Museum theft was front page news. *The Concert*, considered the most precious of all the paintings stolen, had been splashed across the newspapers. One could never forget the orange chair and distinctive checkered floor—used in a few of his paintings. Like so many, he'd followed the story, going so far as to subscribe to

The Boston Globe at one point.

"What is this? It can't be." He turned it this way and that. "It must be a copy. Right? If it's not a copy, then…"

O'Brien shrugged and smiled. "So much like the original. No? Do you like it?"

"The workmanship is magnificent. Whoever did this knows what he is doing." Marty pulled a magnifying glass out of the desk drawer. "The fine strokes provide such depth, and the craquelure, it's amazing … the artist must be a master of the baking technique."

He flipped the painting over. The canvas had browned to the color of a tea stain, and the fibers certainly looked as if it had aged 300 years. In the upper left-hand quadrant was a small round patch, much whiter and newer. Did the copyist use a canvas from the period? The stretchers, too, looked brittle with age.

"Done by one of the best."

Even as a copy, Martin wanted it. He wanted it so badly he could taste it. "What does he want for it?"

"I beg your pardon?"

"Who is the artist? I want to meet him."

"Impossible, sir. The artist … passed on, some time ago."

"The seller then, what is his price?"

"Price, sir?"

"Give me a number."

"I thought you understood … but where are my manners? Of course." He made a show of pulling a paper from one pocket and a pair of reading glasses from another. "I am to tell you, 'This is a gift, from a family man.'"

Marty sucked wind. "There must be a mistake. I made it clear to Vincent that there were to be no gifts."

"I don't know any Vincent." He returned the paper and glasses to their respective pockets. "My directive was to deliver the painting."

"Where did it come from?"

O'Brien shook his head. "Think of me as a courier. I deliver valuable items from point A to point B. I do not ask questions, and many times things are done anonymously."

"How did you find me?"

"I was provided the address."

"I'm afraid you'll have to take it back," Marty said with some regret.

O'Brien cupped the brandy, held it up to the light, and swirled the amber liquid around the bulbous crystal. "I can't simply take it with me. I would have to contact the shipper to … identify an appropriate means of returning the item. You see this requires the utmost of delicacy. One can't simply … take it to the post office." He sipped from his glass.

"I can't accept it. You must return it." Marty leaned the painting against the crate and, as much as it hurt him to do so, he let it go.

O'Brien held up his palm. "Patience, dear sir. I didn't say I wouldn't take it back, I simply said it would take time. Have you somewhere you can keep it until I work out the details of the return?" O'Brien coughed. "Perhaps somewhere…"

"Out of sight?"

"As you say."

One of the reasons Martin had decided to purchase the house was the secret hiding place in the wall behind the fireplace. The original owners used it to hide the television out of sight. It originally worked via remote, however, he'd had it hardwired to a button under his desk.

The relatively small painting had no problem fitting in the space. He'd almost been caught with the painting uncovered by his son's fiancée when she entered the room unexpectedly. Luckily, he'd been able to close the cavity before she noticed anything, and using her good nature, he pawned O'Brien off on her so he could handle a different business concern. O'Brien left the name of his hotel, and they agreed to speak the following day. After the party wound down, Marty returned to his office and spent close to an hour admiring the artwork while sipping the rest of his brandy.

However, when Marty called the hotel the following day, there was no record of O'Brien, nor at the thirty other area hotels he tried. The man was a ghost, and Martin realized he'd been duped into taking the painting.

His initial instincts were to contact Vincent and insist on having Monaldo take the painting back. The first few days, upon returning home from work, Marty stared at the magnificent artwork, telling himself he'd call Vincent tomorrow. Tomorrow would arrive, and the day would get away from him, and by ten at night, he would tell himself he'd call tomorrow.

Meanwhile, the longer he studied the copy, the more convinced he became—it wasn't a copy at all.

Marty had been collecting art for almost thirty years, and along the way he'd met artists, experts, and lab technicians. On day four, Marty took a paint sample and a thread from the canvas to a lab tech that owed him a favor.

The response—the canvas for a certainty dated back to the 1600s. Initial analysis of the paint chips revealed they, too, dated back at least two hundred years. However, the lab tech told Marty he would need to pass them along to another department for further analysis to get more conclusive results.

Marty's burgeoning concerns that the painting was indeed the original had him refusing further tests and retrieving the threads and chips from the tech. The next day, he brought home a handheld moisture imager from work. He couldn't see signs of another painting beneath *The Concert*, although this meant nothing, as the handheld device was made to find moisture behind concrete walls. The oils appeared fully dried according to the little machine, and Marty knew it could take fifty to one hundred years for oil paints to dry completely. Still, the device was made for construction purposes and not high-quality artwork.

He reached out to Vincent and left a message requesting to know the provenance of the painting. Vincent did not return his call. In the meantime, with apprehension growing that the painting was not what O'Brien had led him to believe, he did something completely frivolous. He framed it. He took the measurements to a local frame shop, chose a thick gilt frame, worthy of such a masterpiece, and ordered the framing materials. Once the materials came in, he removed the painting from its hiding place and took it to his own basement workshop to make the frame for it. It took him three evenings to complete the process before he replaced it behind the wall in the study.

Again, he phoned Vincent and received no response. The Christmas holidays arrived and things converged at once. Patrick and Karina's original plans were derailed by her father's stroke. Patrick flew out to Denver and became engaged, upsetting Molly terribly because she'd missed it. Then he and Molly flew to Salt Lake for their ski vacation, and they were forced to remain for two extra days due to a snowstorm. Marty didn't forget about the painting, but he put the return of it on hold until after the New Year.

Spending time away from the painting put one thing into perspective—no matter, copy or original—Marty wanted to keep it. He knew it was wrong, but the painting was nothing short of magnificent—even if he was the only one to appreciate it. Then something changed. Three days straight, he noticed the same strange car in his neighborhood and again in front of his office. Paranoia led him to wonder if he was under law enforcement surveillance. He thought about turning it in to the feds or contacting the museum. But they would ask questions—

questions Marty wasn't willing or stupid enough to answer. It seemed easier to get it returned to Monaldo—if that meant hand delivering it to the mobster in person, then so be it.

His third phone call to Vincent had been pointed—arrange for the painting to be picked up, or he'd leave it on the FBI's doorstep.

Twenty-four hours later, outside his office, a sandy-haired man in a brown overcoat approached him.

"Martin Dunne?"

"Yes. Can I help you?"

He held out a large nine-by-twelve envelope, and Marty automatically took it.

"Mr. Monaldo suggests you keep the gift and your mouth shut."

Marty blamed himself for not taking care of the situation with O'Brien immediately. He now realized the courier chose that particular night to deliver the painting. After all, with the party going on, he'd been assured Martin wouldn't make a scene. Now Marty had a painting he didn't want in his possession. At least, he wanted *not* to want it.

He couldn't return it to the mob, and the threat made it clear that if he went to the FBI, the mafia would take away everything he held dear. He shuffled through the photos for the dozenth time. The only person who hadn't been in the photos had been Jonathan, no doubt because he was overseas in Afghanistan. The idea that his youngest was currently safer in a war zone than at home gave him little comfort.

The painting had become more trouble than it was worth. He'd run different scenarios in his head for mailing the art directly to the Gardner Museum. However, every scenario, short of driving up there himself and dropping it at the back door, could be traced back to him. Even dropping it at the museum would expose him to countless security cameras. He couldn't see a way through that didn't involve spending time in jail or putting his family at risk. He concluded the safest plan of action would be to leave it behind the wall.

Chapter Seventeen

MARTIN

Throwing his feet up on the desk, Marty pressed the button to reveal the painting. Immediately, his boots slammed back to the ground, and he gaped at the empty space.

"No, no, no!" As anyone is wont to do when something isn't in its proper place, Marty searched the hearth. There was no sign of it. He scratched his head. "Did I leave it in the workshop?" He rushed to the basement, but his hunt through the long, narrow space did not reveal the artwork, and he returned to the study to check the security cameras on the computer.

He forwarded through the morning activities of Ivan going out and in, and then Molly pulling the car around front and heaving the dog into the back of her SUV before rushing off to the vet. An hour later, the camera revealed another car pulling around front, and a few minutes later, Karina strolled up the front steps. Martin paused and rewound the tape twice; she knocked, then pushed against the door, and watched it swing inward. He gritted his teeth, realizing Molly not only forgot to set the alarm, she didn't actually close and lock the damn door. Karina disappeared for eight minutes before the front camera captured her stepping out on the porch, but just as she was about to close the door, she paused, then returned inside the house. It took seventeen minutes before Karina popped back up on the security cameras, leaving through the front door. Her car disappeared, but reappeared a moment later on the camera by the garage. She popped the trunk and walked out of sight, reappearing on the backyard camera, then looked directly into the lens surveilling the

French doors to his office before entering.

"What are you doing, little girl?" he ground out.

Twelve minutes later, she exited the office, painting in hand, placed it into the trunk, and drove off. Marty watched the footage multiple times. Over and over and over. Disbelief turned into dread, which turned into anger.

"Thieving bitch!" The water glass slammed into the hearth, shattering upon impact.

"Mom? Dad?" His son's voice pitched with panic and Marty heard footsteps pounding against the hardwoods. "Are you okay?" Patrick skated through the study door as *The Hunting Party* slid back into place. "Dad? What's going on? I thought I heard breaking glass."

"I'll tell you what's going on. Your girlfriend is a thief!"

"*Karina*? A thief? What *are* you talking about?"

Martin slammed his laptop shut. "I warned you about signing a prenup." He pointed a finger at Patrick. "She's a gold digger, just like the rest. Just like that Chrystal bitch. Only this one's going to rain down hell on the entire family."

Patrick's face flamed. "Father! That's my fiancée you're talking about!"

"I'm aware."

"She's *not* a damn gold digger! And I don't believe for a moment she would steal from you."

"Believe it."

"What are you missing?"

"A painting."

"Which one? Perhaps you misplaced it. Maybe Mom moved it."

"No one misplaced it."

"What painting?" Patrick slammed his fist on the desk.

It was at this point, Marty came to his senses. He'd allowed his anger to get the better of him, and now he had to find a way to keep Patrick out of this mess.

"Is it on camera? Show me."

Martin cleared his throat and took a beat as he spread his hands across the laptop surface. "I apologize, Patrick. I misspoke. I've just realized—" The desk phone interrupted his lie. Caller ID read 'Unknown' and normally he'd let it go to voicemail, but intuition had him picking it up. "Martin Dunne."

"It's Karina … do you know why I'm calling?"

"Of course."

"Who is that?" Patrick asked.

Marty put his hand over the receiver. "Business call."

Patrick crossed his arms and remained looming above the desk.

Marty swiveled the chair around. "How much do you want for it?"

Karina's indrawn breath could be heard across the line. "You mistake."

"I have money."

"That's not what this is about. I don't want your money."

"Name your price."

"The item doesn't belong to you."

He pinched the bridge of his nose. "What do you want?"

"I want to know why you have it? Did you have anything to do with its … original retrieval?"

"Good God, *no.*"

"Do you know who did?"

"Nope."

"Did you realize what it was when you acquired it?"

"That's a long story. Probably best discussed in person." Marty glanced over his shoulder. His son remained in the same position, staring stormily at him. "Listen, I don't think you realize what you've gotten into here. I think it would be best if we could meet to work out the details. Why don't you come to my office?"

"No. The front steps at the Lincoln Memorial. One hour. Bring your cell phone."

The line went dead.

Slowly, Marty rotated the chair around to face his angry and confused son. "Patrick, let me start by apologizing. I was mistaken about your fiancée and the painting. There's been a mix up."

"I *believe* I deserve an explanation."

"I simply jumped to conclusions. I forgot the painting was going out for a cleaning. Karina entered the house because your mother left the door open when she rushed off to the vet. Karina actually locked up for her. That's all. When I saw her enter the house and the painting was missing because I forgot …" He shrugged.

Patrick squinted at his father. "Thievery is quite an accusation to level."

"As I said, mea culpa."

"Why do I get the feeling you're not being straight with me?"

Marty rose. "I don't know what you mean."

"What painting?"

"Pardon?"

"What painting is out for cleaning?"

"Why…" Martin's mind searched the paintings upstairs in the den. "The Macey Williams, of course."

Patrick pulled out his phone. "I think I'll call Karina."

"There's really no reason…" Marty needn't have worried; the call went straight to voicemail. "I'm rather embarrassed by my behavior. Your fiancée is above reproach…"

But his son was no longer listening. He tapped away on his phone and mumbled to himself, "Why isn't she coming up? Did she forget to charge her phone again?"

"Something wrong?"

Patrick looked up. "Uh, no … I don't know. If everything is

okay, then I've got to head out. I've got to find ... I mean, there's something I forgot to do."

"Of course. We'll just keep this conversation to ourselves, if you don't mind."

"Sure thing, Dad." Patrick put the phone to his ear as he exited.

The front door slammed, and Marty breathed a little easier. The video mocked him as he watched it one last time before removing the Beretta M9 from the locked desk drawer.

Chapter Eighteen

I hung up the cheap burner phone I'd purchased at the gas station and slipped it into my pocket. The miniscule gift shop on my left beckoned me with its warmth. I'd given Marty an hour and had time to kill. A hefty pair of tourists browsed the bookshelf. I took off my gloves and stood in the corner behind them, above one of the brass vents blowing hot air. The day had grown colder, with a brisk winter wind, and my fingers were like icicles.

I wasn't sure if the FBI was surveilling Marty's phones, and it occurred to me my old friend or his buddy may have tapped mine. The uncertainty of everyone's intentions was part of the reason I'd turned off my phone and removed the battery. How much the FBI knew or if they were simply on a fishing expedition remained unclear. However, a few things had become obvious in the past few hours. First, by possessing the painting, I'd broken the law. If I didn't give it over to the FBI or the Gardner Museum soon, my intentions could become misconstrued, and I could find myself an accessory to an infamous crime. Thoughts of my face splashed across front page news, on a perp walk, had me cringing. Additionally, someone *had* been spying on me. It wasn't my imagination. The photos in Marty's office needed an explanation. Which left me with one last realization; if the surveillance was done at Marty's behest, then Mike had told me the truth.

Mike.

It occurred to me I might need a safeguard. As much as Marty had banked his rage during our phone conversation, there'd been an edge to his voice. A little protection never hurts. In either case, it was time Mike and I talked.

The elderly clerk eyed me. The tourists had moved on, and my vent hovering had drawn her attention. I removed a random tome on Lincoln and flipped through the pages. A group of rowdy teens entered, diverting her stare. I slid the book back in place and glided out the door.

Abraham Lincoln gazed down at me, his face stern and unyielding, as though admonishing me for my sins. I was eight the first time my parents brought me to visit the Memorial. At that time, I'd thought Lincoln's face inviting and asked if I could sit on his lap for a photo. My parents immediately put the kibosh on that idea. Today, as he frowned down, I was inclined to climb up onto the hard marble lap and ask for his measured advice. I'd visited the memorial dozens of times since I was a child, and its architectural magnificence never dimmed. I contemplated the statue of the man who clung to his beliefs—the abomination of slavery—though his country nearly tore itself apart over them. If this poor Kentucky-born, self-educated President could see his way through a civil war to abolish slavery, surely, I could do something so simple as seeing a painting returned to its home safely … without getting arrested … or breaking up my engagement. Couldn't I?

I descended the front steps; to my left, in stark contrast to Lincoln's white marble Doric columns, rose the black granite panels of the Vietnam Memorial. On my right, seven-foot stainless steel statues of soldiers in full combat gear walked through strips of granite and juniper bushes. I'd always enjoyed visiting the Korean War Memorial by night because the lighting bounced off the steel, giving it an eerie glow. The surrounding trees, shed of their leaves, contributed a harshness and austerity to the entire monument site—a reflection of my current state of mind. I much preferred the area during the spring and summer when the trees bloomed lush and full.

Half an hour before Martin was due to show, I replaced the battery in my cell and texted Mike.

> *I think it's time we talked. Meet me at the steps*
> *of the Lincoln Memorial in 45 mins.*
> *I'll be there.*

Multiple texts and phone messages from Patrick awaited me but, before I could listen to them, the phone rang and my sister's smiling face appeared.

"Hey, Jilly. What's up?"

"He called."

"Uh-huh."

"He seemed pretty antsy to know where you were."

"What did you tell him?"

"What you told me. I didn't, nor *do I,* know where you are."

"Thanks. Did he seem … angry?"

"No, he sounded … jumpy, and a little irritated. Are you going to tell me what's going on?"

"Someday. Just not right now."

"Are you in some sort of trouble?"

"Nothing that need concern you, Jilly."

"Rina, I'm not a baby anymore. If there's something I can do to help … I've got a shovel."

"Why would I need a shovel?"

"For burying the body," she said sotto voce.

Even though my stomach was tied in knots, I mustered a laugh.

"Hey, I'm just saying, I'm there for you."

"Thanks, Jilly. There's no body, but you might be able to help later. I'll let you know." I didn't want to drag Jillian into any of this mess, but it was good to know my sister had my back … and a shovel.

Chapter Nineteen

I scanned the steps with the opera glasses I'd found in my glove box, stopping on my quarry.

"Right on time," I mumbled.

Martin, in the same black overcoat I'd seen him wear to *The Nutcracker,* stood at the base of the Lincoln Memorial steps. His right hand was tucked in his pocket while the other held his cell phone. Sunglasses hid his eyes even though leaden clouds had turned the day gloomy and bleak.

I pressed the send button on the burner phone and waited.

"Yes? I'm here," Martin answered.

"Take a walk down the pathway to your right on the Korean Memorial side—not the one right next to the reflecting pool, the one lined by trees. About fifty yards down, you'll see a green bench that doesn't match the rest. Have a seat."

He jammed his phone into his pocket and strode down the steps to the reflecting pool, veering right. While he walked, I searched the area to see if he'd brought any friends. I didn't see anything or anyone out of the ordinary. He sat, and my plan B arrived early.

Mike, with his shoulders hunched, turned away from where I watched him. A moment later, a text message whistled on my phone.

I'm here. Where are you?

Running a bit late. Meet me on the steps in front of the reflecting pool.

Marty reclined, an arm thrown across the back of the bench seat, his feet spread apart—the picture of nonchalance. I approached from behind, coming around on his left side, and plopped down next to him.

"Hello, Martin."

"Karina. Did you bring it?"

"No."

"Where is it?"

"Somewhere safe. That's not what we're here to talk about."

"You're correct. I'm not here to talk. I'm here to retrieve what you took. Now very carefully we're going to get up and take a walk." His right hand had remained in his pocket; now he gestured with a gun—pointing at me.

"Martin, Martin, Martin," I tutted. I didn't believe he was a bad guy, but he did surprise me by bringing a gun. Had we not been sitting in a very public place, I might have been afraid. "Are you threatening me with a firearm? Is that weapon registered? Do you possess a D.C. concealed carry permit?"

"Get up," he said between clenched teeth.

"Or what? You going to shoot me? Right here? I don't think so. And let me tell you why. First, I'm your son's fiancée, how are you going to explain that to Patrick? You're also in Washington, D.C., and there's practically a camera on every corner, not to mention D.C. police. But that's not the real reason you're not going to shoot me right here."

"You seem awfully sure of yourself. What you don't seem to realize is that you've made me a desperate man."

"Well, if you shoot me, Martin, the FBI will swarm you like bees to honey. See that jogger coming our way in the purple spandex, black coat, earmuffs? FBI. She's jogged past you once already. There's a guy on the reflecting pool steps; here, take my glasses. Navy blue and white parka. I don't know if there are more. They've been watching you for a while. Ever since the night Christoph O'Brien, a known fence and international fugitive, showed up on your doorstep."

For the first time since he sat down, Martin fully took in his surroundings, scrutinizing a mother pushing a stroller, and a homeless man a few benches away. The stones crunched beneath her feet as the jogger passed us. I didn't know if he'd buy my bluff about the jogger, but knowing Mike was close gave my voice conviction.

"Is that why we're here? This is a set up?"

"No, Martin. I want to help you."

He snorted.

"It's true. I have no interest in seeing you behind bars—ruining your life, Molly's life, your children's lives over this."

"So, what is it you want?"

"I want it returned. I want you to come out of this smelling like a rose rather than yesterday's garbage. I believed you when you said you had nothing to do with the original theft and that you don't know who did. I need you to tell me the story, Martin."

He removed his hand from the gun in his pocket and rubbed it against the denim on his knees. "What do you want to know?"

"How it came into your possession. Wait," I held up a finger, "first, do you have your wallet?"

"Yes."

"Give me the lowest denomination you've got."

"What for?"

I sighed and held out my hand. "Just do it, please."

He frowned at me as he dug into the interior pocket of his coat, drew out his wallet, and pulled forth a twenty-dollar bill.

With a thumb and forefinger, I retrieved the cash and stuck it into my own pocket. "Consider me your lawyer. Anything we discuss is now covered by attorney-client privilege. Understand?"

He nodded.

"As I said, I want to help you. Now, tell me your story."

Chapter Twenty
MARTIN

The grass-green eyes that stared back at him seemed sincere, and knowing her relationship with his son, Marty believed she wanted to help. And maybe she could see her way through the problem in a way he couldn't. However, he also realized there was no way in hell he would put his family in the mafia's crosshairs. No good would come from implicating Monaldo.

If I did, what can the FBI offer? Witness protection? Give up my work? My home? My life? And what about my children? Implicating Monaldo also implicates me. Would the feds give me full immunity? Can I risk it?

No.

Martin scrutinized the lovely auburn-haired girl sitting next to him. Did she have any idea what he said here and now could change her life forever?

She wanted a story? He'd give her one.

"What do you know about the dark net?"

She drew in a breath. "I know it's where you can find assassins, gun runners, drugs, and human trafficking."

"You can also find art on the black market."

"I see. And do you regularly visit the black market dark net?"

"I had never done so" —he shifted— "until an email was sent to me right around Thanksgiving."

"Okay, so you're saying someone reached out to you? Who?"

"I have no idea. One day, I opened an email with the subject line, 'Art for Sale.' Now, you see, I get these kinds of emails all the time. I'm on several auction site lists and when certain artists, or types of artwork, come on the market an email automatically gets sent out to me. So, I didn't think twice about opening this email."

"Makes sense." She nodded.

"What I found was something different. It was a thumbnail picture of the painting and a lot number next to it. When I clicked on the image to enlarge it, the email disappeared."

"What do you mean … disappeared?"

"Gone. Like I hit the self-destruct button. My internet browser automatically opened up to a tutorial on how to download and use TOR."

"TOR?"

"The Onion Router."

"You mean the dark net."

He shook his head. "TOR is not the dark net. It's simply a browser that allows you to access the internet anonymously. Like Chrome, or Explorer."

"And you downloaded TOR?"

"I didn't have to. I already had it on my computer—"

"Wait, back up. Why would you have TOR on your computer?"

"TOR isn't only used for illegal underground. Every day people are using it to protect their privacy against unscrupulous marketers, identity thieves, or protect communications on the regular internet. Certain countries censor legitimate internet sites, such as news and social media sites. *I* use it to protect my company's communications and for personal electronic security."

"I had no idea."

"Many don't. You should look into it." He removed his sunglasses. "You realize TOR wasn't created by unscrupulous hackers."

"Who created it?"

"The Navy. It was originally used for protecting online US intelligence communications."

"I guess it's true, you learn something new every day." She scrutinized his face, as if weighing the truth of the story. "Continue. You got on TOR and then what happened?"

"Nothing. Like I said, the email completely disappeared. Gone from my inbox, the server, everything. I decided to access my email through the TOR browser, and I found something new. Same subject line, only this time instead of a picture there was a numbered website address and encryption key. I followed the link—"

"What *the hell* is going on here?" Patrick snapped.

"Patrick!" Karina jumped up.

"Son." Marty stood.

"Dad."

"Did you tell him we were meeting?" Karina asked.

"No. I didn't tell him anything."

"Tell me what?" Patrick crossed his arms.

"Son, what are you doing here?"

"I've been searching for Karina. What are *you* doing here? Last time I saw you, you were raging about how she was a thieving gold digger."

"A gold digger, eh?" Karina's mouth twisted.

"Now, now, I explained it was all a misunderstanding."

"So, what are you two scheming? You look pretty cozied up."

"Does he know?" She stared pointedly at Marty.

"Do I know what?" Patrick asked.

"No," Marty said at the same time.

"What don't I know?" Patrick glared at his father.

"Wait a minute. Time out." Karina made a T with her hands. "If Marty didn't tell you … how did you find me?"

"Did you follow me?" Marty asked in an accusing voice.

"No! I didn't follow you."

"How did you find us?" she asked with slow deliberation.

Patrick tugged his ear. His eyes darted around and wouldn't

meet Karina's or his father's.

"Patrick ... how did you find us?"

He cleared his throat. "Through the tracking app on your phone."

Karina mashed her lips together. "There's a tracking app ... on ... my phone?"

"You were always losing it ... and it helps me to know where you are and that ... you're ... safe."

Her eyes turned to slits as Patrick bumbled through his explanation.

"In other words, *you* "—her perfectly manicured finger poked at him— "put a *tracker* on *me*."

Patrick cleared his throat again.

"I cannot believe you put a goddamned tracker on me," she hissed. "Like ... like a stalker."

"It wasn't like that."

"No. I'm sure it wasn't *like* that. As a matter of fact, I'm positive you put it on to make sure I wasn't cheating on you. Like your past girlfriends. Is that what it was *like?*" Her fists clenched and unclenched at her sides.

"No ... maybe. If you're innocent, why should it matter?" he said in a defiant voice.

"Oh, son," Marty sighed.

"It's called trust, Patrick. Something I value highly, and which I now wonder if you understand at all."

"Yeah, well, here I find you with my father..."

"In a public location," Karina said between clenched teeth. "What? You think we're exhibitionists, into some sort of sick, sordid public fornication? Or did you think we'd sneak off behind the bushes over there?" Her face bloomed red and Marty was suddenly glad he wasn't in his son's shoes. She waved her finger under Patrick's nose. "Don't, for one minute, think you're going to accuse your father and me of something so ridiculous as having an affair."

"I wasn't. But I'm not an idiot. I know something is going on, and I think I have a right to be told the truth."

Karina crossed her arms and a coat of self-possession draped itself across her shoulders. "As your father's attorney, I am not at liberty to discuss our interactions with you," she said in a flat voice devoid of emotion.

"His *attorney!* Why would my dad need *you* as his attorney?"

Martin remained silent. Karina's jaw clenched.

"Dad, what the hell is going on here?"

"Son, why don't you go back to your apartment? Once Karina and I finish our business, I'll come by, and we'll talk."

"Oh, shit." Karina looked past both men toward the Lincoln Monument. "Too late."

"What's too late?" Patrick followed her gaze.

"Martin, you and Patrick need to leave. *Now.*"

Marty had seen what Karina saw. Their little contretemps had drawn the attention of the FBI agent she'd pointed out on the reflecting pool steps, and he was now walking toward their coterie.

"Go. We're not ready for this. Martin, you're concealing unpermitted. So, unless you want to explain that to a judge…" she spoke quickly in undertones.

"Got it."

"We'll make other arrangements to meet. Stay by your phone." Karina didn't wait for an answer. She pushed between the two men and strode toward the FBI agent.

"Other arrangements? What is she talking about? Concealing what?"

"Keep your voice down," Marty admonished. "C'mon. It's time we left." He took his son's arm and started pulling him in the opposite direction of his fiancée.

Patrick jerked free. "I'm not going anywhere until I get some goddamn answers."

"This isn't about you. It's about me. And right now, you're putting your fiancée and me in danger."

Patrick's head bobbed between his father and Karina's retreating back.

"Take it from your old man, you'd be wise to let her cool off."

Reluctantly, Patrick turned and walked in step with his father.

Chapter Twenty-one

"Wasn't that your fiancé?"

"Yes. He and his father had a bit of a misunderstanding. I suggested they take a walk and work it out. Wouldn't want to get in between a father and son." I tucked my hand into the crook of Mike's arm. "Brr, I'm cold. Let's walk a bit to warm up."

Neither of us spoke as we strolled in front of the reflecting pool and wandered the path on the opposite side of where I'd met Martin. My head whirled with emotions about Patrick's perfidy and questions over his father's revelations. The original plan had been to talk Mike into offering Martin a deal: immunity in exchange for the painting and any information he could provide. However, Martin hadn't finished his story, but what I had heard, and my limited knowledge about the dark net, made it highly unlikely Martin had any idea who the seller was. I had a feeling when he finished his story, the only person he'd be able to identify would be Christoph O'Brien.

No. We weren't ready to make a deal—which abruptly changed the purpose of my meeting with Mike.

He finally broke the silence. "I'm not having you tailed."

I'd forgotten that accusation. "Oh … okay."

"I'm serious. It's not me."

"I believe you."

"I'm concerned that you believe you *are* being followed."

"As am I." One more thing I hadn't had time to address with Martin. Although considering Patrick's revelations … could he be the one having me followed? No, that didn't make sense, why would there be photos of his mother and himself?

"Do you have any idea who might have you followed?"

"Maybe." I adjusted my sunglasses. "Mike … you're a cyber guy. Right?"

"Yes."

"Can you take a peek at my phone and see if you find some sort of tracking app?"

"You think your phone is being tracked?"

I swiped the code and held out my phone. "Could you just look?"

It didn't take him long. "You're right. It's called Youth Tracker 3000."

"Youth Tracker 3000? Where?"

"One of the latest in parental tracking apps. Looks like it's been running in the background."

"What kind of information does it provide to the other person?"

"I'm not sure. We can look online. Here." He handed the phone back to me and pulled out his own, entering the app's name into the web browser. His brows turned down. "You're not going to like it."

I sighed. "Tell me."

"Well, it provides a GPS location—"

"I figured."

"But that's the least of it. It monitors who you call, what you text, what apps you're running."

"Emails?"

"Not the content, but who you're emailing, when, and subject lines, yes. This one even tracks the speed of your vehicle."

The cold no longer bothered me. My ears and face blazed, and I believe if it hadn't been attached, my head would have popped off. I was past angry. Patrick's intrusion into my privacy went far beyond any concern for my safety, or his own whacked out worries about cheating. This phone was my work lifeline. He invaded the privacy of those in my office, possibly Hill staffers. Hell, there were even representatives and senators who, on occasion, directly texted me. His intrusion went beyond anything I'd ever experienced and left me wondering if I really knew who I was engaged to. Moreover, his distrust hurt me to the core.

"This is serious. Whoever's doing this isn't only tracking you, they're invading your cyberspace."

"How would someone go about putting this on my phone? Would they need my physical phone, or is it something that can be done remotely?"

"The phone … and your passcode."

I was sure Patrick had seen me swipe my thumb through the passcode enough times to memorize it. Something else came to mind—I'd given him the passcode for my computer to purchase the plane ticket, and I'd yet to change it.

"They probably have enough to steal your identification. I can take it back to the office and trace the phone it's connected to." He held out his hand, but I didn't pass him the phone.

"Can you remove the app?"

"Yes. But if I do it now, we won't be able to run the trace back to the origin."

"Okay. Please shut it down. Remove it."

"I don't think you understand how serious this is. It's stalking at minimum and possible identity theft. We need to dig further and find out who's doing this to you." He got in front of me and took hold of my upper arms. "K.C., I don't like this. I'm … concerned. This isn't good. As a matter of fact, I recommend you stay with your sister or your boyfriend until we figure this out. I don't like the thought of some creep having this much access to you."

"There's no need. I know who activated the app."

Those dark eyes assessed me and, even though my thoughts and stomach floundered with turmoil over the hot mess I was in, my heart did a little double beat, something I hadn't felt since college.

"You're sure?"

Confusion and embarrassment had me looking away from his intense scrutiny. "I'm sure. Can you please … just remove it?" I picked at an invisible piece of lint on my arm.

"K.C. … tell me…" He placed a hand on my shoulder.

A lump formed in my throat at Mike's gentle words, and, to my dismay, the prick of tears rose as anger and humiliation over Patrick's betrayal warred in my chest.

"Karina?" He ducked his head to meet my gaze, his face drawn with concern. "Who's doing this?"

I crossed my arms and cleared my throat, but it still came out as a choked whisper, "Patrick."

"Oh." Multiple expressions flitted across his features as he reassessed the scene he'd witnessed across the way. "That's kind of—"

"Fucked up?" I gave a mirthless laugh and brushed away a tear.

"Yeah … sorry. I'll remove it now," he said quietly. "This should take care of it. While I'm in here, I'm going to activate the email notification. Any time a new app is added to your phone, you'll get an email notification. That way … you'll know."

"Thanks."

"Of course."

"And, Mike…"

"Um, hm." His fingers flew across the tiny smartphone keyboard.

"I'm sorry I accused you of having me followed."

He paused. "I'm sorry we ambushed you at the coffee shop. That wasn't very nice. And … I realize it isn't the ideal time to tell you this, but Bruce would like to meet with you again."

"Am I under investigation?"

"You? No."

I debated asking the next question, unsure I wanted to hear the answer. "Is Marty?"

"I couldn't say."

In other words, yes. I guess my bluff wasn't such a bluff. Maybe the jogger really was FBI. "Why don't you have Bruce give me a call next week, and we'll arrange a time?"

Mike held out the phone. "You're all set."

An awkwardness hung between us. I hated it. I so desperately wanted to be transported back to our easygoing college days when there were no secrets and I could fling myself into his arms for the hug my spirit craved.

"I'd better go. There's someone I need to have a … talk with."

"If you need a sounding board or … someone to watch bad romantic comedies with…"

That brought a genuine grin to my face. Mike and I had a deal back in college. He'd go to see the romantic comedies if I promised to watch the superhero movies with him. We both put on a show about how big a favor we were doing for the other. The truth was, I enjoyed the action of the superhero movies, and, even though his machismo would never admit it, he laughed at the rom-coms too.

"I appreciate that." I felt his eyes on me as I strode away.

Chapter Twenty-two

COOL MOM, read the license plate of the white minivan parked in front of me. I stared at it, unsure of my next move. *Should I track down Martin and have him finish the story? Or should I deal with Patrick? Are they still together?* I pressed fingers against my eyes and, making my decision, dialed the number.

"Where are you?" I asked when Marty answered.

"At my office."

"Are you still with Patrick?"

"No, he went home."

"We need to finish our discussion."

"Come to my office."

No way was I about to give Martin the high ground by meeting at his office. The evening sky waned, and it wouldn't be long until the shroud of darkness covered the city. My brain raced to find a public location. "No. Union Station food court, in front of the Chipotle. Twenty minutes."

"Really, Karina. There's no need for this cloak and dagger business."

"I beg to differ. You brought a gun to our last meeting, and your son's put a tracker app on my phone."

"I had nothing to do with that."

"And the gun?"

"I'm sorry about that."

"I suggest you leave it at the office. Twenty minutes."

Chapter Twenty-three
MARTIN

Leaving the gun locked in a file cabinet at his office, Marty arrived at the appointed place only five minutes late. Patrick's interruption had given him more time to finish devising the story he'd started to tell Karina.

His phone rang. "I'm here," he answered.

"Turn around to your eight o'clock. I've got a table for us."

Pedestrian traffic was light. She'd chosen a small, round table without ears close by. He sat across from her, and she pushed a coffee cup toward him, along with a pile of sugar packets and a little creamer.

"I didn't know how you liked it."

He ripped open a pair of sugar packets and dumped them in. "Thanks."

She appeared pulled, with a strained look in her eyes.

"Karina, about Patrick … you need to understand—"

"How's the dog?" she interrupted.

"The dog? Ivan? Molly's home. They're keeping him overnight. Twisted stomach. It can happen."

"I hope he'll be okay."

"I'm sure he'll be fine," Marty said dismissively. "Listen, about Patrick—"

"I'm not here to talk about your son. I'll deal with him later."

"It's just that…"

"I know what it's just. He thinks it's okay to betray my trust, invade my privacy and accuse me of having an affair. The tracking app…" Karina's lips pinched together.

Marty opened his mouth, but she cut him off again.

"You haven't much room to talk. *You* believed I was a gold digger. I believe you wanted me to sign a prenup."

He shook his head.

"Don't deny it. Patrick told me. And lest we forget, you thought it was okay to threaten me with a gun. Frankly, I'm rethinking joining this family. Molly and the dog seem to be the only people who trust me. And right now, they're the only ones I can trust."

"I'm—"

"You know what, Marty, I don't want to hear it. Why don't you finish telling me the story? It's why we're here. Right now, I'm not a prospective daughter-in-law. I'm your lawyer. So ... you said you went to the numbered site..."

Marty sighed. "Very well. I went to the site. It was clearly an underground auction. The painting was listed and there were already other bidders."

"How did you know it was the real one?"

"I didn't. There were about two dozen photos showing close-ups of the painting."

"How many people were bidding?"

"I've no idea. The entire thing was anonymous. All you saw was the price go up when someone made a bid. The auction closed thirty minutes after I signed on."

"What did you think? Did you bid right away?"

"I didn't know what to think. I figured it was a fake. However ... I decided to bid."

"Why?"

He shrugged. "For the hell of it."

She opened her mouth, seemed to rethink her question, and shut it. "And you won?"

"Yes."

"How did you pay?"

"Bitcoin."

"How did you purchase the bitcoin?"

"I didn't, or at least not then. A friend told me about it and recommended I purchase some bitcoin in 2010, a year after its release."

"So, you already … what … had a bitcoin bank account?"

"Something like that. It's called a cyberwallet."

"How much did you purchase in 2010?"

"Fifteen thousand."

She sat back and whistled. "You must be sitting on a tidy sum of bitcoin."

"Yes." He didn't elaborate.

"So, what did you pay for the painting?"

"About one-two."

"One-two? You mean one point two … as in million?" She leaned closer. "I don't believe it. It's estimated at over fifty million. Why would someone let it go for such a low sum?"

"That's the black market. Infamous" —he glanced around— "artwork isn't as easy to move as you'd think. Sellers are lucky to get three to five percent of a painting's worth. Remember there was absolutely no way to authenticate it."

"And Christoph?"

"The messenger … and he authenticated the bitcoin exchange."

"Do you believe he's the seller? The one who ran the auction?"

"No."

"You said that awfully fast. How can you know?"

He took another sip and relaxed back against the chair. "As you said, he's a fence. I assumed he was the courier. Nothing more."

"Could you identify him in a line up?"

"Could you?"

"Yes, of course. But he didn't deliver the painting to me."

"If the FBI found him," Marty said with a shrug, "I would be able to identify him."

"What were your plans for the painting?"

"At first, I believed I'd purchased a fake. A brilliant one, but a forgery nonetheless."

"Why did you think it was a fake?"

He raised a skeptical brow. "Because someone could make a cool one point two mil doing it."

"When did you realize it might be the real thing?"

"When I framed it ... I don't know, call it intuition."

"How did you know? Are you an expert?"

"An amateur only. It was more a gut feeling. But I had some paint chips analyzed and it dates to the period."

"You had paint chips analyzed?"

"Called in a favor. The guy had no idea what he was looking at."

"Why didn't you contact the FBI or the museum?"

"I was trying to figure out a way to do so ... anonymously." That one was closest to the truth of the cock-and-bull story he just fed this young woman.

"Do you have any of the emails? The transaction?"

"Yes, and the encryption key. But, after the auction ended, the site disappeared or the encryption key was changed. If I give you the location, you'll find a black page."

"What about the bitcoin? Can we track the transaction?"

Marty shook his head. "That's the reason so many criminals use it, that and an encrypted site ... makes it difficult for anyone to track. Government can't track the bitcoin transaction the way they do an FDIC insured bank transaction. Some might say it's better than a Swiss account."

Karina sat back and contemplated the dregs of her cup. "It's not much to bargain with. Still ... there is O'Brien."

"I don't want to go to jail. I just want the painting returned, quietly and with as little fuss as possible."

She had the temerity to laugh at him. "Are you kidding me? Beyond the Mona Lisa, it's one of the most famous paintings stolen in history. It's been missing for twenty-eight years. There is no way this goes quietly. Whether or not your name stays out of the press, that's a different story." She got to her feet. "I'll be in touch in twenty-four hours."

"What are you going to do?"

"Try and figure a way out … for all of us." She wove through the tables and disappeared around the corner.

Marty swallowed the last of his coffee and wondered if his story would hold up against FBI interrogation. He figured it would, because all of it was true. Just, it wasn't the Vermeer; it'd been a Mary Cassatt, and he'd lost the bid.

Chapter Twenty-four

The yellowish-orange streetlamp outside the window and the glow from the computer screen were the only lights in my darkened office. In an effort to be part of the Green movement, the top brass installed a fancy new lighting system. After eight during the week, and on the weekends, the hall lights were left in power-saving mode, which meant motion sensors turned on sets of fluorescent lights ahead of where a person walked. They shut off a few minutes after you left the sensor's range. I was one of the staff members who regularly worked late, or popped by on the weekends, and my office was in the far corner of the building. The system had been a bit disconcerting to get used to. Today, I liked it because hall lights would give me ample warning if another staffer came trotting down the hall.

I'd come here following the meeting with Martin to bone up on the laws and cases regarding returning stolen artwork. My mind conjured one scenario after another of how to return the painting to the FBI. Unfortunately, the end of each scenario left Martin and I in a small interrogation room at FBI headquarters answering questions, while they obtained a search warrant and proceeded to ransack his house and possibly my condo. I'd seriously considered playing the friend card with Mike. However, it would put him in an awful position, and I wasn't sure on which side of the line he'd fall. Worse, if he did do something … say … in the gray areas of ethics, I couldn't forgive myself. I feared he'd eventually hate me for crossing that line. Or worse, himself.

No, I couldn't do that to him. I wasn't willing to ruin a relationship over Martin or that damn painting. I gave the brown box residing against the wall a dirty look.

My cell rang.

Patrick's smiling face lit up the display, and I swiped the X for ignore … again … and stuffed my feelings back down into the file cabinet of my heart where I planned to keep them until I was ready to deal with that part of my life. Unfortunately, the emotions were starting to ooze and drip out the sides of that rusty old cabinet, leading to things like the minor fit I'd had in my car on the way over to the office. Maybe minor was an understatement. I suppose calling my fiancé every dirty word I could think of, at the top of my lungs, as I raced down the GW Parkway qualified as an … outburst.

Okay, I'll admit, I totally lost my shit.

A man in a Lexus, who'd pulled up next to me at a red light, stared with wide eyes while I carried on. Lucky for me, as I realized my Vesuvius-style eruption was being observed, the light turned green, and I'd hit the gas.

I clicked on an FBI link about the stolen artwork and halfway down the page, it hit me. I was looking in the wrong place. I was so close to Mike, I'd completely forgotten—the FBI wasn't the owner of the painting, the museum was. *Why go through the FBI at all?*

I navigated my way back to the Gardner Museum site and found what I was looking for—a page unto itself about the heist. Sitting at the bottom … a phone number to reach the head of security. The clock on my phone read 6:33 p.m. According to their website, the Gardner Museum closed at five. On the off chance someone in the security office would pick up, I dialed the number using my burner phone.

It went to voicemail, and I hung up.

The main information line began with a general recording about museum hours, then moved on to extensions for the box office, gift shop, events coordinator, etc. First, I tried the events coordinator. It went straight to voicemail. After that, I tried the gift shop and got a recording telling me the gift shop was now closed. I didn't hold out much hope to get a live person at the box office, but the third time was indeed charmed.

"Gardner Museum box office."

"Good evening."

"How can I help you?"

"I'm a … freelance journalist working on a story about stolen artwork …"

There was a sigh at the other end. "Don't tell me, you're writing about the 1990 heist."

"It's … part of the story, and I believe I've stumbled across something that I should speak with your head of security about."

"Hold on, let me get that number for you."

"No, wait. I've already called the number on the website, it went to voicemail. Can you tell me, is that an office line or cell number?"

"It's an office number."

"And will Mr. Bradigan be in tomorrow checking his voicemail?"

"I doubt it, he's in D.C. at a security conference this week."

I drew in a breath. *He's right here. In D.C.* "It just so happens I'm in D.C. I'm writing the article for *The Washington Post.*" *Geez, when did I become such a liar?* "Would it be possible to get his cell number?"

"No, ma'am, it wouldn't."

"What if I gave *you* my cell number to pass along to him?"

There was a pause.

"Look, I'm on a deadline, and I think I've got a lead for him. If it's what I think it is, it could make my story front page news, and your museum very happy." I held my breath, at least one of those statements was true.

"I suppose. What's your number?"

I reeled off the burner phone number.

"And what's your name?"

"It's Karina. Thanks so much!" I hung up before she could ask more questions. For good measure, I called Mr. Bradigan's landline again and left a short message.

I spun the chair around and stared out the window at the gas station across the street. My stomach grumbled, reminding me I hadn't eaten since breakfast, and the coffee I drank with Martin did nothing to fill the hole.

The kitchen refrigerator revealed a questionable yogurt, a dozen salad dressings, some grapes on their way to the raisin zone, and a variety of condiments. I pulled the freezer drawer open to see if there was something more appetizing ... or at least more filling. Normally, I kept a couple of Lean Cuisine meals on hand for lunch, but I'd eaten the last one and hadn't replaced my stock. What I did find was a ten-inch supreme pizza marked with Brian Mendoza's name on it. As it circled around the microwave, I silently thanked him and made a mental note to replace the finance officer's lunch on Monday.

The microwave binged at the same time my burner phone rang. Caller ID revealed the same Boston area code as the Gardner Museum.

"Hello."

"This is Sam Bradigan with the Gardner Museum. Is this Carrie?"

"Hello, Mr. Bradigan, thank you for returning my call." I didn't bother to correct my name. "I don't know what the woman I spoke with told you ..."

"She said you were a reporter doing a story."

"Um, journalist ... freelance, doing a piece on art heists. As I was ... researching the Gardner Museum heist, I ... came upon a lead that I thought you might want to follow up on."

"Uh-huh, what's the lead?" His clipped voice gave nothing

away.

"Well, it's rather involved … since you're here in D.C.—"

"How do you know I'm in D.C.?"

"The woman at the museum told me."

The line went quiet for a few moments.

"I see."

The way he said those two words led me to believe the woman at the box office was in for an ass chewing when Mr. Bradigan returned home.

"Anyway, I'm in D.C. as well, and I was hoping you might be willing to meet me for twenty minutes, so I could present you with my research."

"What paper did you say you worked for?"

"*The Post.*"

"I suppose I've got some time tomorrow before my flight. When and where would you like to meet?"

"Um." My mind scrambled. I hadn't planned a meeting place. "Are you flying out of Reagan National?"

"Yes."

"What time's your flight?"

"Nine fifteen."

"I'll meet you on the metro platform at, say, seven thirty? We can find a place to get breakfast inside the terminal."

"Fine. Seven thirty. How will I know you?"

"I'll be wearing a long red coat, no hat, red gloves."

"Tomorrow, then."

"Tomorrow." I hung up and pulled the pizza out of the microwave; steam spiraled upward from fat-laden, cheesy goodness. Its sustenance would help me get through the next twelve hours. I finished the entire thing before calling Martin.

Chapter Twenty-five

The buzz of the alarm launched me out of bed as if zapped by a cattle prod. An ear-ringing head rush followed, and I flopped, face first, back onto the unfamiliar pillow. The neurons filtered back into my brain, and I slapped at the clock. I'd checked into the Sheraton, two blocks from the office, close to midnight. Patrick's phone calls continued every hour, and I figured there was a good possibility he'd be camped at my condo. In order to keep that file cabinet closed, I turned off my phone and avoided my home.

The clock number flipped to 5:47 a.m., and I groaned rubbing my tired eyes. Sleep didn't come easily last night. Twice I woke from dreams that I'd lost that damn painting. It currently resided in my office, boxed up, between the desk and the wall. I should have brought the damn thing with me to the hotel, but I didn't want to be seen carrying it around.

A few minutes later, the in-room coffee pot percolated a dark Colombian roast while I showered. About two weeks into my time on the Hill, I ended up working on some legislation that had me staying with a colleague overnight to pound out acceptable language. I was the only fool who hadn't known to keep what they called a "go" bag under my desk—change of clothes, makeup, toothbrush, hair products—and spent the following day looking like a wrinkled mess and smelling like a fast food hamburger, while my coworker showered and changed appearing fresh as a spring daisy. Lesson learned. My current office "go" bag sat on the bathroom countertop and included Visine for the bloodshot eyes.

An hour later, I paced the platform in an area that provided a visual of the comings and goings of train passengers. The 7:15 Metro arrived. A dark-haired man of average height with broad shoulders and a black overcoat zeroed in as soon as he debarked.

"Mr. Bradigan?"

He removed his sunglasses; blue eyes speared me. "That's me."

I held out my gloved hand. "It's good to meet you."

He ignored my outstretched hand. "Young lady, do you mind telling me what this is all about?"

I stepped back at his accusing tone.

"I called the managing editor at *The Post*, and they've never heard of you, or an article being written about art heists. Furthermore, your phone number comes up in my caller ID as Luis Rodriguez."

I cleared my throat. "You're right, Mr. Bradigan. First, my name isn't Carrie. It's Karina. Your receptionist misheard the name and I didn't bother to correct her, and ... I'm not a reporter, I'm a lawyer." I handed him a plain white business card that I'd printed up at the office. On it was my name, credentials, and burn phone number. Nothing else.

He glanced at the card, flipping it over and back again. "And what does a Washington lawyer have to do with the Gardner art heist?"

"Art isn't exactly my field, I'm doing some freelance work."

His brows crunched together. "Go on."

"Can we speak in hypotheticals for a moment?"

"Be my guest." He crossed his arms.

"Let's say I have a client who came across a painting they initially believed to be a fake. They purchased the painting at no little cost. However, after possessing the painting for some time, they concluded that perhaps it was the real thing."

"How long?"

"I beg your pardon?"

"How long, hypothetically, did he possess the painting?"

"Over a month."

"Did any paperwork come with the painting?"

"No."

"Where did he purchase it from?"

"Hypothetically?"

"Hypothetically."

"From an auction ..."

"What kind of auction?"

I stared back into those unblinking eyes.

"In other words, it was an illegal auction."

Coughing, I glanced away.

"Okay, why does he think it's the real thing?"

The next train arrived and belched out a dozen fast moving passengers. Mr. Bradigan and I watched the last pair, a rotund couple—dragging matching green suitcases and speaking at the top of their lungs—disappear from the platform.

"By the way, where is *your* luggage?"

"My flight's not until nine tonight."

"Ah, I see. I'm not the only one who didn't correct a misunderstanding."

"I like breakfast. You had a nice voice on the phone." He shrugged. "Why does your client believe he's got a real painting?"

"He had paint chips analyzed. They date to the period."

That got a mild eye-widening reaction. "Which painting are we talking about?"

"Hold on. We're not there yet."

"What do you want? The ten-million-dollar reward?"

"I'm not so foolish as to believe you'd hand it over for one painting. The reward is for leading to the recovery of *all* the artwork. Second, my client isn't looking for money."

"What does he want?"

"He'd like to give you the painting to be assessed by your people. If it is indeed a fake, he'd like it returned. If it's not … the museum keeps it."

"That seems a little too easy. How do I know other missing pieces of artwork weren't sold on this black-market auction site?"

"There was only one painting. This one."

"How do I know that to be true?"

"He's assured me, and I'm assuring you."

He stared at me. "I assume there's more…"

"First," I said as I reached into my coat and pulled out a manila envelope. "My client had nothing to do with the original heist; he has an alibi which puts him in Park City, Utah, at the time, and no ties, of any sort, to the people you believe did the heist."

Bradigan nodded and pulled the two-page document out of the packet.

"If the painting turns out to be real, he's willing to provide the dark website address he purchased it on, and the manner in which he was contacted, along with the encryption code." I didn't bother to tell him the site was now defunct or that the encryption key didn't work.

"In return …"

"In exchange for the painting, you keep our meetings confidential. Anonymity. Provide me an assurance the FBI, or Justice Department, or the press isn't going to crawl up his ass, or mine, with a microscope. You don't tell the FBI where it came from, because even though the statute of limitations has run out on the theft itself, we both know they can still pursue action against my client for possessing stolen museum works under US Code 668."

"I see you've done your homework." He scanned the second page of the document.

"Those little letters after my name aren't just for show, Mr.

Bradigan."

"Call me Sam."

"Do we have a deal?"

"I'll have to run this document by our counsel."

"No."

His lips pursed, and his brows rose. "No?"

"There's a time limit on this deal. You are the head of security, and, as such, I'm sure you've been given the authority to go pretty far to get those paintings returned. As a matter of fact, I wouldn't doubt you've been given authority to provide a stipulated amount of money for any good leads. Let's not dick around, you've got" —I glanced at the screen listing the incoming train times— "six minutes to decide."

"That's not a lot of time. This is a big ask."

"Bullshit. My client had nothing to do with the theft. He's trying to do what is right here."

"Why the anonymity?"

"Let's just say, this is a well-respected person of the community who has no interest in having the press or the FBI crawling all over the business or family. It could do unforeseen damage."

"In other words, there are other parts of his business life he wouldn't like scrutinized."

A heavyset black woman, talking on her phone, walked onto the platform. She glanced at Bradigan and I, then trotted to the end out of earshot. "Not that I know of."

"Then why the cloak and dagger? Your client's done nothing wrong. According to you, he's the hero."

"He held onto the painting for over a month, that's long enough for the FBI to question motivations. No, we're not willing to take the risk."

"And, what if I say no? Then what?"

"Hypothetically?" I pulled my coat collar tighter to keep out the cold breeze.

He sighed and his eyes drooped. "Hypothetically."

"I don't know." I pursed my lips in thought, then leaned closer and whispered, "Maybe it would accidentally fall into a fire."

Bradigan blanched and choked out, "He wouldn't."

"You asked for a hypothetical." I shrugged. "Accidents happen."

He dug a hand into an inside pocket, pulled out a pen, slapped the document against a nearby post, and scribbled his signature along the bottom line. Then he brandished it in front of me. "When do we meet to make the exchange?"

Our conversation came to a halt again as the next train whooshed into the station, dispatching another group of people. Like before, the area cleared quickly as they hurriedly wheeled their luggage behind them. A nondescript passenger—dressed in a long calf-length trench coat with the hood pulled up, black gloves, and dark glasses—stood with one foot in and one foot out of the train halfway down the platform. I slid my sunglasses to the top of my head and retrieved the documents from Bradigan's outstretched hand. The floor lights along the platform blinked, and a bell dinged, indicating the train doors would be closing. The hooded passenger shoved a box onto the platform, leaning it against one of the posts, and stepped back onto the train as the doors closed.

"I'm sorry, Mr. Bradigan, but we won't be meeting again."

His nostrils flared. "What?" he yelled over the retreating train.

"And the exchange happens now." I lifted my chin. "Behind you."

The security director pivoted and spotted the package. I heard him cursing under his breath, probably from the pathetic covering I'd used for his precious painting. He scooped it off the ground and held it to his chest.

"By the way. It's the Vermeer."

I heard his indrawn breath from across the tiles.

"I have your number," I told him. "If it's a fake, I'll arrange for its return."

"If it's real? When do I get the dark net information?"

"You have my number."

I spun on my heel and strode away. Once out of eyeshot, something spurred me onward. Running along the moving sidewalk, I called out to a slow-moving septuagenarian, "On your left." I pounded up the garage stairs, two at a time, to the third floor where I'd parked the car. My heart continued to hammer as I paid and rolled out of the garage.

My fingers fumbled to dial the cell.

Martin picked up on the second ring. "Karina?"

"It's done."

"Let's hope this works."

I pressed end and tossed the burn phone into a cup holder. I was deadly relieved to have turned over that damn painting. However, the document the security director signed wasn't guaranteed to stand up in a court of law. It wasn't even guaranteed to keep him from talking to the FBI. However, it was the best play I could think of on short notice. If he did leak my name to the FBI, sure as a frog's ass is watertight, I'd have Mike and his buddy, Bruce, knocking on my door … and Martin's, for that matter. There were absolutely no guarantees—once the painting went back on display at the museum—that they wouldn't put two-and-two together and be knocking on my door anyway.

Chapter Twenty-six

To my relief, Patrick was not camped outside my door when I arrived. I tossed my keys in the bowl, dropped my bag, and went directly to the fridge to grab a flavored water and gulp down a few swigs. The strawberry infused liquid felt good sluicing down my throat.

"Where were you last night?"

"Eeeugh!" I spun around and instinctively chucked the half-full bottle across the island at the intruder. Water flew everywhere.

He swatted the projectile away, and it landed with a thunk on my hardwoods.

"Jesus, Patrick. You scared the hell out of me. Have you been here all night?"

"I went back to my place a few times to see if you went there … you didn't."

"No, I didn't."

His clothes were wrinkled, hair mussed, and he shared my bloodshot eyes. "We need to talk."

"You're right, we do need to talk. I'm just not ready to have this conversation with you now."

He rubbed a hand down his face. "Yes, now. I don't think we should let this simmer."

"Oh, really? I'm not so sure that's a good idea, *Patrick*," I said his name rather nastily. "Right now, I'm mad as fire at you. I haven't had enough time to think about what I want to say." I snatched a kitchen towel off the oven door and wiped up the watery mess so it wouldn't damage the hardwoods.

He followed me. "Well, I know what I want to say. Why don't you let me say my piece, and then when you're ready to talk, you can … call me."

"Really, Patrick. I'm tired and cranky, and I think we should just wait for a better time." I dropped the wet towel and bottle into the sink. Again, he followed behind me like a puppy.

"Please, I think I have the right to explain, and we need to talk so we can, you know, move on. I don't appreciate the silent treatment I'm getting from you. We need to deal with this in a mature manner."

Seriously? A mature manner? "Fine." I rolled my eyes, pushed past him, and parked my butt on a stool, putting the island between us. "No, no. You stay there and talk." My imperious finger pointed across the counter.

"Okay." He held up his hands. "First, I want you to know that I had your safety in mind."

My brows rose.

"And it's not as bad as you think. Yes, I'll admit, it gave me peace of mind knowing where you were and that you were safe. But, I'd also like to point out that I used it to help you find your phone a few times."

I rested my chin in my hand. "Do go on."

"And if you'd been in an accident or something, like when you went home at Christmas time, I would have known and could have helped."

Christmas? Key-rist, when the hell did he put this on my phone?

"Well, I … uh … realize it's unorthodox, but I just didn't want to get burned, like I did in the past. You know, with Chrystal. That really messed with my head, and I just didn't want to be blindsided like that again. I'm sorry it upset you."

I didn't answer. He picked at a hangnail.

"Besides, parents do it to their kids all the time. It's no big deal."

If my hand hadn't been holding up my chin, it would have fallen to the floor. Silence reigned. Patrick shifted his weight from foot-to-foot.

"Rina, say something."

"It's … no … big … deal?"

"Uh, well…"

"When did you put the app on my phone?"

He crossed his arms, chewed the hangnail, and shrugged.

"It's not rocket science … when did you put it on?"

He mumbled under his breath.

"What? I didn't hear that."

"Thanksgiving."

Thanksgiving! I tapped my nails against the granite. They sounded loud in the silence. Events ran through my head. Patrick finding my phone when I'd left it in the car. Patrick showing up at my parents' house rather than the hospital, because he knew I'd be there. One incident stood out: the day I went shopping with my sister and came home to find Patrick in a froth because my phone had run out of battery, even though he was supposed to be at the marketing conference. Clearly, it had shut down his tracking app.

"You know, the most disturbing thing you said to me in this little speech is the fact that you're 'sorry I'm upset.' Not 'sorry for betraying my trust.' Not 'sorry for putting a stalker-like tracking app on my phone.'"

"How did I betray your trust?"

"Are you fucking kidding me?" That dark, leaky file cabinet drawer burst open, with all its volatile emotions. "Without my permission, you put an app on my phone so invasive as to see who and when I was texting; when I sent emails, their subjects, and to whom; incoming and outgoing phone calls." I ticked them off one-by-one.

His face reddened as I spoke. "Uh, how did you know about

that?"

"I had my FBI pal, you remember the one at the Lincoln Memorial—"

"Yeah." His hands slammed down on the counter. "Speaking of the Lincoln Memorial, we need to talk about that little incident as well."

"No, *we* don't. You violated my privacy, and that of those I work with. I get texts from senators and congressmen, and their staffers. None of those texts are for your eyes. Not only could I bring a suit against you, but anyone who's emailed, texted, or called me in the past month and a half could, too."

"File suit! Come on, Rina, you're blowing this all out of proportion."

"Am I, Patrick? *Am I?* You have betrayed my trust at the highest levels, and from what I can tell by this conversation, you're not even remorseful of your actions. You've spent more time trying to *justify* them, rather than apologize *for* them. I'm not sure you even believe what you've done is wrong."

"I said I'm sorry."

"No, *you said,* 'I'm sorry you're upset.' *NOT,* 'I'm sorry I did this thing.' *Not,* 'I'm sorry I betrayed you.' *Not,* 'I'm sorry I invaded your privacy.' *Not,* 'I'm sorry for stalking you'!"

"I didn't stalk you," he said through clenched teeth. "I'm your fiancé, *not* a stranger stalking you."

"That's *exactly* what you did! It's made worse by the fact that *you are my fiancé!* I don't care what justification you have. You put an app on my phone behind my back! You followed me out to Colorado. You followed me to a meeting with your father."

"No. I went out to Colorado to *propose.* Yes, I followed you yesterday and found you in some sort of shady, clandestine meeting with my father. A meeting neither one of you has seen fit to explain to me."

"You know why that is? Because it isn't your damn business

to know! Attorney-client privilege means exactly that. I can't talk about it. I'm not allowed to do so. But you know what? Even if your father gave me permission to do so, I wouldn't. You know why? Because you're a weaselly little turd and I can't trust you!" My voice had risen to a high-pitched screech, and I slapped my hand against the hard stone for emphasis. It stung like the devil, but I refused to acknowledge it while Patrick and I stared at each other. The clock ticked away the minutes, and my angry pants slowed.

"There's no cause for name calling," he murmured, breaking eye contact.

"No, there isn't." I rubbed my temples. "Patrick, I think you should go."

"I think so, too. I caught you at a bad time. You're tired and out of sorts. We can talk about this when you're feeling better."

He walked past me to get his stuff.

"Leave your key."

"What?"

My gaze didn't waver from its hard stare directly at the oven. "You heard me. I want my key back."

"Rina, you're upset. You don't mean that."

Spinning around on the stool, I speared him with my gaze. "Yes. I do. As a matter of fact," I said in a calm voice as I slid from my perch, retrieved my own keys, and removed his from the ring. "Here."

"No, keep it. You'll come to your senses."

"Patrick, that's the problem in a nutshell." I placed the key on the counter and unseeingly removed the engagement ring, placing it atop the key.

His face drained of color.

"You think I'll come around to your way of thinking. I won't. This wasn't okay, and the fact that you can't see how this has absolutely devastated our bond—our relationship—tells me we'll never get past it. I can't trust that you'll never try something like this again, and I can't live like that. I can't live with someone who doesn't trust me enough to be loyal to him. Someone so hung up on a hurt from the past that he can't trust what he's got right now." I gulped back the lump in my throat and drew in a breath. "This isn't going to work, Patrick."

"Rina," he whispered my name across the air, "I'm sorry. Truly, for everything. The phone app, following you, the thing with my dad. Don't do this."

"*I* haven't done this."

"Okay, I'll admit it. Is that what you want? *I made a mistake.* Okay? I shouldn't have done it. I was wrong to do it. Does that make you happy now?"

"Oh, Patrick. Just the way you're saying it. You're trying to placate me. This isn't about making me happy by tossing off an admittance of guilt. It's about truly realizing the utter wrongness of the action. It's about getting past what Chrystal did to you. It's about releasing that control you crave, so you can have a trusting adult relationship."

"But ... we love each other."

I focused on my boots and shook my head.

"Maybe ... maybe I can see someone, a shrink or something, get some counseling, you know," he bargained. "Isn't that the answer to everything? A shrink? What do you think? Maybe we can go together."

"Patrick, I can't start a marriage that's already on the rocks. One already shaky due to mistrust. This is supposed to be the carefree honeymoon phase. The time when all we want to do is make love, eat cake for breakfast, make googly eyes, and send sexy texts, and ... and ... fun stuff. This isn't just a blip in our relationship. It's trust ... it's a deal breaker."

His jaw muscles flexed as he removed the key and gently placed it on the counter, but he didn't retrieve his own or the engagement ring. "We'll talk in a day or two. I think we both need some time to cool off."

I didn't bother to argue the point, and the door closed gently behind him. The ring taunted me as memories of better times played through my head. Like the time I was supposed to meet him for lunch and had to cancel because I was stuck at work, and he brought it to me instead. His possessive hand on my back the night of his parents' party, and that smoldering gaze that could get me hot and bothered from across the room. Purchasing my plane ticket and paying for the fare to Colorado. I twisted the ring between my fingers; the stone caught in the light and made prisms against the wall.

Was the tracking app so bad?

Mike's voice rang in my head—texts, phone calls, location, emails. The diamond clinked against the counter as it dropped; a tear followed.

Chapter Twenty-seven

Time passed. The crying came and went in little bursts. The day waned. I lay on my bed and watched the sun's shadows shift across the ceiling. My mind wouldn't turn off as it bounced from Patrick to his father. I still had one more issue to address with Martin—the photos. So focused on getting the painting returned, I'd let the packet of glossies slide. I knew I'd have to confront him … just not today. My drained emotions and I couldn't muster up the energy to go one more round with the Dunne boys.

For dinner, I drank more than half a bottle of wine. It put me to sleep at nine, and I woke at six the following morning to a rhinoceros sitting on my head. Actually, it turned out to be a pillow. But, even after I threw it off, it still felt like a large animal was crushing my little brain cells.

"Ugh." I rolled out of bed and hit the shower.

****

Before entering, I checked the coffee shop for anyone I might know. Luckily, I recognized no one but the barista. For once, the problematic men in my life had left me alone this morning. Java in one hand and computer bag in the other, I walked with a heavy tread toward my office and was almost run over by Latesha as she rushed out of her own.

"Sorry, didn't see you there. Whoa! Nothing personal, but you look like hell."

I had to give Latesha credit, she didn't sugarcoat the truth.

"What's up? Rough night? A little too much of the bubbly? An all-night hanky-panky session with your lo-ver?"

I couldn't seem to help the tears that blurred my eyes.

"Hey, hey, what's this?" She looked past my shoulder and pulled me into her office, shutting the door behind us. "Here now, sit down and tell Tesha what's going on. And don't try to brush me off. You haven't been right since we got back from the holiday break. Is it your dad? Did he have another stroke? Oh lord, he didn't die this weekend, did he?"

I shook my head and took the tissue she held out to me.

"Then what is it? I can tell you need to talk. Something's wrapped up your emotions, and it's taking you off your game."

"What do you mean? Don't tell me ... what did I screw up?"

She sighed. "I found some typos in that brief you sent last week. Silly things, nothing big. I fixed them before forwarding it up the chain."

"Christ." I rubbed my eyes. "Thanks for covering for me."

"What's going on?"

"I broke up with Patrick ... I think."

"You think?"

"Well, I tried to give the ring back, but he's not really accepted the situation, and the ring is still sitting on my kitchen counter ... torturing me."

She whistled. "What did he do? Wait, don't tell me. You caught him doing the nasty with another woman?"

"No."

"That boy better not have hit you. I will go kick his bony ass right now. No one hits one of my friends and walks away unscathed."

"No."

"I'm serious, Karina. If that boy hit you, I will junk punch him so hard ..."

That brought forth a slight smirk. "Thanks for the offer, but it's nothing like that. He'd never do that."

"Then what, honey? What'd he do that was so bad?"

Of course, I'd spent the night second-guessing my decision.

Really, was the tracking app so bad? Maybe another woman's opinion was needed. "He put a tracking app on my phone. He's been able to see all my texts, know when and to whom I made phone calls, emails ... not to mention the GPS signal that gave him my exact location at any time of day or night."

She sat back, her eyes wide and unbelieving. "No, he didn't."

My head bounced up and down.

"Holy Shi—zzlesticks." She covered her mouth.

Latesha had given up cursing as a New Year's resolution, and I bit my lips to keep from smiling at her word choice. "He tapped your phone?"

"Sort of. He tracked all my communications. It even told him how fast my car was traveling."

"How'd you find out?"

"He tracked me this weekend and showed up where he shouldn't have. When I asked him how he knew where I was ... it all came out."

"Wow."

"Am I blowing this out of proportion?"

"Why'd he do it?" She leaned her elbows on the desk.

"He got burned in a prior relationship. She cheated on him. And, he claims, it was for my own safety."

"Your safety? He said it was for *your* safety? Oh, honey."

"I just couldn't get past ... the broken trust. And the fact that he stood in front of me and spent twenty minutes trying to justify his actions. He tried to get me to agree putting this app on my phone was ... okay. It's not. Right? I'm not overreacting, am I?"

"Is that what he made you believe? That you're blowing this out of proportion? No, ma'am. Don't you dare allow that boy to make you second-guess yourself. What he did was wrong. Absolutely and completely wrong. There is no justification. Did he apologize?"

"He was 'sorry it upset me.'"

"Sorry it upset ... what the heck kind of apology is that? Look at me, don't you let that fool undermine your confidence and keep you up at night. Don't start making justifications for him."

"Thanks, Tesha. You're right, I've been second-guessing myself all night long. It helps to ... get a second opinion."

"Here, take some extra tissues and trot down to the bathroom. The single one. Get yourself cleaned up. We've got a staff meeting at ten. It's time to get your head back in the game."

"You're a doll." I took her hand and squeezed. "Thank you."

"No thanks necessary. We ladies have to look out for each other. Can't allow those men to mess with our heads. You stay strong now."

My day turned out to be so busy, I ate lunch—an apple, granola bar, and a half bag of chips I found at the back of my drawer—at my desk. Luckily, Brian wasn't in the office today, because I didn't have time to replace his borrowed pizza. At ten past seven, I found myself in the city, a few blocks from Martin's office. I decided to put one more matter to rest. On a mission, my boots quickly ate up the pavement. Marty happened to be exiting the lobby elevator as I spun through the revolving door. One glance at my determined face had him escorting me up to his office.

"Can I offer you a drink?"

"No thanks." I removed my coat.

"To what do I owe the pleasure?" He indicated a small seating area and I folded myself onto the loveseat.

"Here's a copy of the document Bradigan signed."

He glanced at the paperwork as he sat in an armchair across from the coffee table. "I certainly hope this works. If it does, I owe you one."

"Me too." My gaze roved the walls, taking in the artwork. One looked like a Degas. "Are they real?"

"That one is by a local artist. The rest are reproductions I had commissioned."

I nodded. "Martin, when I handed the painting over to the security director, I assured him you had no ties to the Boston mafia, or anyone that would have been a part of the original theft. I wasn't lying ... was I?"

"Not that I know of."

My brows lifted.

"What I mean is ... I meet a lot of people in this business. Architects, engineers, electricians, hundreds of subcontractors."

"You're hedging."

"Not at all, it's the best I can do."

It wasn't the assurance I'd been looking for, but I supposed that was the best I would get out of Martin. "Fine. I'm not actually here for the painting. I have a question to ask you."

"And what would that be?" He rose. "Are you sure I can't get you something to drink? I've got a twenty-year-old scotch ..."

"No, thanks."

"You don't mind if I ..."

"Not at all."

I waited until he began pouring the spirits into a crystal highball glass. "I want to know about the photos."

The bottle clinked against the glass. "What photos?" he asked quickly. I'll admit he did a good job covering his consternation.

"The surveillance photos in your home office. Let me see if I can remember—me at the mall. Patrick outside his office and in front of the coffee shop on the corner of his block. Molly walking the dog in front of your house."

He took a swig. "I'm sure I don't know what you're talking about."

"I accidentally knocked them off your desk ... when I retrieved the item. Initially, I thought the FBI was tailing me. But when I found the photos in *your* possession, I realized I'd been wrong, and figured you'd hired a PI to look into me because

Patrick and I were getting married. But what I couldn't figure out was why you'd get pictures of Patrick and your wife. Then it hit me."

He swallowed the rest of the whiskey in one gulp. "What hit you?"

"Are you being blackmailed? Is someone threatening your family?"

"Why would someone be threatening me?"

"Does this have to do with your business?"

He put the glass down with a thunk. "Is there anything else we need to discuss, Karina?"

I rose. "Who's following me, Martin? Besides your son."

"It's nothing that should concern you."

"Don't be ridiculous. It concerns me. I was followed, Martin, and the man who followed me wasn't overly covert about it. Is someone threatening you to sign or not sign a contract? Am I still being followed?"

"Karina…so many questions over nothing."

"Martin." I folded my arms across my chest. "You're lying to me. You know I have FBI connections. I can get you help."

"I don't think it's a good idea to put me in front of the FBI right now. Is it?"

He had a point.

"Besides," he continued, "it's been taken care of."

"That fills me with confidence."

He poured another two fingers into the glass.

"What are you into, Martin? Does it have something to do with the painting?"

"Why would you say that?"

"Because that little voice in my head isn't so little anymore, it's starting to shriek at me. Why don't you tell me the real story?"

"I told you …"

"Bullshit."

Martin's fist clenched around the tumbler, but otherwise he didn't show any other outward concern. He was certainly a cool customer. I doubted he'd come clean with me, and maybe that was for the best. Perhaps knowing Martin's dirty secrets would only drag me further into his mess. Did I really want to represent him in a blackmail case? Not an attractive prospect.

"Fine, if it's handled, then it's handled. Stick to your story, Martin. Don't make me regret covering your ass over that damn painting." I snatched up my coat and purse. "But, heed me, if I get one whiff of a tail, I'm calling the FBI." With that, I swept out of the room.

Chapter Twenty-eight

On Friday, I received a text from Patrick asking to see me. I had to give him credit, he'd left me alone for the entire week. The ring and two keys remained lined up on the counter where they'd been left on Sunday. I did my level best to ignore them when I passed by in the mornings and evenings. That's about all I did, too. Monday's work compounded as our department jumped aboard a new legislative initiative by House Democrats, and my eight- to ten-hour days turned into fourteen-hour days. I counted the additional work as a blessing, because I fell into bed exhausted with nothing on my mind except the following day's schedule. Neither the painting nor Patrick kept me awake, and I finally caught up on sleep. Doing so put a few things into perspective.

First, though I missed Patrick and having his warm body next to mine in bed, I simply couldn't marry him. Not only because of the tracking app incident. Maybe my sister had been right when she cooed into the darkness about knowing when you've met "the one," or of having that flash of insight or intuition. When I looked back at our relationship, I'm not sure I gave it my all. Yes, the sex was good, and I enjoyed doing things with Patrick, but perhaps I'd been simply riding the relationship train because it'd been convenient and nice. Marriage shouldn't be "nice," it should be more, and maybe in his own twisted way, it had been for Patrick. However, relationships can't be one-sided. It wouldn't be fair to either one of us. Also, I'd said yes to the proposal before I was ready—throwing caution to the wind because I came face-to-face with mortality through my dad's medical scare. Finally, Martin's lies were stacking up. Even though Molly was a doll, I didn't feel safe in the Dunne family environment. The dishonesty appeared more and more a family trait and not one I wanted to risk my heart over.

I agreed to meet Patrick at his place around eight. At ten 'til, he texted.

I'm running late. Let yourself in.

That was fine with me, because it gave me time to gather my things. I'd already packed a duffle bag of odds and ends he'd left at my place—toiletries, a sweatshirt, a couple of T-shirts, sneakers, etc. I neatly laid those items on his bed and packed up my own leaving the bag by the door. I regarded the ring one last time—it wasn't so bad, but perhaps the first inkling that we weren't meant to be—and placed it inside the red box. The lock rattled.

"Good, you're here." He hung his coat and keys on the rack. "You look lovely." He gave me a peck on the cheek as though nothing had happened. "Have you eaten yet?"

"Yes, we had Chinese at the office. You?" I followed him to the living room, crossed my arms, and leaned against the wall, watching him sort through the mail.

"I had a big lunch with a client around two. How was your day?"

"Fine."

"I heard about the new bill the Dems are working on. Are you a part of that?"

"Yes, we are."

"Bet that's keeping you busy." He finished with the mail and finally looked up at me.

I'd been unsure what to expect. This nonchalance was not it. "Mm-hm."

"Can I get you a drink?"

"This isn't a social call."

He sighed and pushed a hand through his hair. "Okay … why

don't we sit down."

I folded myself onto the couch and turned to find him staring at the ring box and key I'd left on the coffee table.

His jaw flexed, but otherwise he hid his emotions. Instead of sitting next to me, as I expected, he paced the room. "This week has given me time to think. And, I'll admit, you were right. I put the tracking app on your phone because … because of Chrystal. Chrystal and every other sucking leech in my life. She wasn't the first girl to cheat on me. There was Claire, in college."

"Did you really think I'd cheat on you?"

"No … yes … I don't know! I didn't think you would, but I'm having trouble trusting my own choices."

"And me."

He stuffed his hands in his pockets. "I just know that I felt secure knowing I could check up on you. But, I promise you, I never read your emails."

"What about phone and texts?"

"Well…" His face reddened. "I'll admit I checked the phone logs occasionally, and there were a few texts I read. But, jeez, nothing of importance. I mean, what do I care about some boring-ass US code and how it relates to a legislative amendment?"

I gritted my teeth. The conversation he spoke of was discussed between half a dozen industry professionals and a House staffer, *none* of whom would be pleased to know that my boyfriend had read it. However, I understood it meant nothing to Patrick, so he decided it was unimportant.

"Let's reverse the situation. What if I secretly hired a PI to follow you around, and I got on your phone while you were in the shower to check your emails, texts, and phone records. Your professional contacts, your clients, conversations between you and your boss or staff?"

"I didn't set a PI on you."

I gave him an arch stare.

"Okay, I get it. I'd be pissed. I crossed a line. I'm sorry. That was not cool."

I rubbed my face. "Well, thank you for coming clean."

"Do you think you can forgive me?" He stared at the red box.

"I think, eventually, I will forgive you. But … Patrick, look at me … I can't marry you."

"Because I've broken your trust?"

"That, and because I don't love you enough to do so. It's unfair to you and me. You're not 'the one,' honey. It's best for both of us if this ends now."

"I don't believe that." He shook his head. "I simply don't believe that. We got engaged."

"Maybe we acted too soon. I always thought we should have waited, but with my dad's near death experience the day before … I lived in the moment, jumping with both feet, and hoping it would all work out."

"I think you're wrong. You need time? I'll wait."

I found Patrick's unacceptance of our breakup a mite disturbing. "Get some help. You need to get past Chrystal if you are to have a quality relationship." I rose and donned my coat. "Now, I've gathered my things, and the stuff you left at my place is in your bedroom."

He followed me to the door. "What if I get help? What if I seek counseling? Will that change things? Will you reconsider?"

I could tell Patrick didn't want to let it go. I scooped up my duffle and opened the door. "Goodbye, Patrick. I wish you the best."

"Wait, Karina, there are still questions you haven't answered. Karina …"

Patrick's elderly Indian neighbor across the hall opened her door, trash bag in hand as I exited.

"Hi, Mrs. Lapook." I waved scurrying down the hall toward

the elevators, and thanked my lucky stars. Mrs. Lapook's arrival seemed to ward off what may have become an ugly scene. Patrick did not follow me as I'd begun to fear.

I expected more crying on the way home, instead, there remained a sad sense of relief. Whether or not Patrick accepted the breakup, I did. I got closure. The painting was where it belonged. All was right with the world.

God has a funny sense of humor.

Chapter Twenty-nine

I pulled the duffle out and slammed the trunk to find a dark figure looming by the side of the car. My heart went into jackhammer mode as adrenaline flooded my system.

"K.C."

"Mike? What the hell? You scared me to death. Christ, I'm surprised I didn't drop from a heart attack here on the pavement. It's past nine, what are you doing skulking around my place at this hour?"

"We need to talk."

"Ever heard of a phone? It's that little rectangular thing in your pocket, you can dial it, or use the text messaging app, or even send an email." Another car's headlights swept through the parking lot lighting us up; Mike turned away from the glare.

"Do you think we could go inside for a few minutes?"

"Sure. Here, carry my computer for me." Even though my heart returned to normal speed, on the way up to the apartment, my brain's cogs spun on their axis faster than a racecar at Indianapolis. Mike's brooding silence didn't help.

I plopped the duffle in the front hall and indicated Mike do the same with the computer bag before he followed me into the living room. Hands to hips, still wearing my coat, I turned to him. "What's going on?"

"There's a rumor the Gardner Museum got one of its stolen paintings back."

"Okay …" I'd been waiting for this. I thought it would take the museum longer to do its authentication of the painting. "And…"

"I thought you should know."

"Thanks. I'm sure the museum is thrilled."

He released a snort of disbelief. "Damn it, Karina, you're neck deep in this, aren't you?"

"Why do you say that?"

"Hm … our past conversations and the fact that you showed zero surprise to my announcement."

"Keeping a straight face is part of my legal training. You should know that, agent."

"Don't bullshit me. I *know* you."

I mashed my lips together.

"Does this have something to do with your boyfriend and his father?"

"He's not my boyfriend."

"Fiancé, boyfriend, whatever."

"He's not my fiancé either. We broke up."

"Oh."

"Why are you here, Mike? Are you questioning me in an official capacity? Do you have an FBI buddy waiting downstairs to take me in for questioning? Is this another ambush?" I defiantly jutted my chin out.

"I came as your friend, damn it! I shouldn't even be talking to you. I could lose my job by coming here." He spun and paced away from me.

My hands dropped from their perch and I rubbed my temples. "I'm sorry, Mike. What's the rumor?"

"The painting was anonymously returned to the museum's security director."

"Who's investigating?" I asked.

"I don't know. Bruce hasn't returned my call."

My head bobbed.

"What's going on?" Mike prodded.

"I can't talk about it."

Mike removed his badge, gun, and cell phone, placing them on the dining room table. "K.C., right now, I'm your friend, not Agent Finnegan. Tell me what's going on. I can help you."

"No, it's not like that. It's an attorney-client privilege thing."

"You're representing him?"

"That depends upon whom you speak of. In either case, I can't talk about it."

He rubbed at the scruff on his chin. "I hope you know what you're doing."

That brought a smirk to my face. "So do I."

We assessed each other for a few moments. I desperately wished to tell my friend Mike everything, but I knew Agent Finnegan was another facet of his life, and they were both intimately connected. Also, getting disbarred over that damn painting by revealing my client didn't fit in my plans.

"Mike, I hate to ask you for another favor."

"Name it."

"Don't tell them about the tracking app. It has nothing to do with ... well, anything."

"If it comes out ... I can't lie."

"I get it. Just—don't ... bring it up. Play least in sight."

He frowned. "I'll see what I can do."

"And don't contact me like this again. I'd hate to see you lose your career. It's not worth it. I'm not worth it."

Mike opened his mouth and stepped toward me, his hand out—something flickered in his eyes, as if rethinking. Instead, he stuck that hand in his pocket and removed his wallet. "This is the name of a good lawyer. She's gone up against Justice in the past and won. Don't leave yourself—or your client—exposed." The business card landed silently on the dining room table next to his gun and badge, which he returned to their respective holsters.

I walked him to the door where he turned back to me before opening it. "You're wrong, you know."

"Wrong about what?"

"You *are* worth it." He grabbed my shoulders and his lips descended on mine in a hard kiss. It ended as quickly as it started, and I stumbled at his abrupt release.

The door slammed.

I pressed my fingers against tingling lips. "I'll be damned."

Chapter Thirty

The other shoe dropped on Monday. I'd just finished a two-hour department staff meeting and returned to my office to find our receptionist standing in my doorway. She tapped her foot and held out a sheaf of little yellow message slips.

"These are for you."

"Why didn't you send them to my voicemail?"

"It's full, so they bounced back to me."

"Sorry, Rochelle, I'll clean them out now."

"S'all right. You guys must be working on something big. Reporters from *The Post* and *New York Times*, and a bunch of TV news channels called."

"*The New York Times?* What the—" My cell phone, which I'd left sitting at my desk, read twenty-eight messages and began ringing as I looked at it. I didn't recognize the number and sent it to voicemail.

A bad feeling crawled into my gut as I punched in the code for my office phone and Stephen Hawking's electronic voice pronounced, "You have twenty-three messages."

Twenty-three? In two hours? What's going on? I typed in the CNN website and in another browser opened up the Local 9 News site.

A knock at my door distracted me from the loading sites. "Come in."

Latesha stuck her head in. "Karina, I think you should hear this message some reporter from the *Baltimore Sun* left."

My office phone rang, and I stared at it like it was an adder about to strike.

"You gonna get that?"

"No. Let me hear your message."

Latesha's phone rang as we stepped through her doorway. "Latesha Jones." Her eyes darted to me. "She's right here."

"Who is it?" I whispered.

"It's Joanne."

Oh, great, our Chief Operating Officer. "Hi, Joanne. What can I do for you?"

"Karina, there's an FBI agent here in reception asking to see you."

"What's his name?"

"According to this card he handed me, it's Bruce Patterson."

If it'd been Mike, I would have sent him up. However, I'd been dodging Bruce's calls since last week, and I was pretty sure I *didn't* want to see him until I figured out what the hell was going on.

"Karina?"

"Right, can you please ask him what it's regarding?"

Joanne repeated my question to Bruce. "He says it's about the Gardner Museum."

"Does he have a warrant?"

"Do you have a warrant? I'm judging by your face, that's a no. What would you like me to do, Karina?"

"Send him on his way. There's nothing he can do, and I don't have to speak with him."

"He says it's better if you talk with him now."

"Ha, of course he does. Tell him I'm busy and to call to make an appointment." I handed the phone back to Latesha. "I'll listen to the message later. I've got something I need to do first."

I returned to my desk. The CNN site was loaded, and I found it on the Breaking News crawl: *Stolen Painting Returns Home to the Gardner Museum in Boston.* My gaze scanned the article and identified the reason for my phones blowing up.

Unconfirmed reports state one of the original paintings stolen in the infamous 1990 Isabella Stewart Gardner Museum heist has returned home. Allegedly, through a series of Deep Throat style meetings with the museum's head of security, a lawyer representing an anonymous client arranged to have the painting returned safely to the museum. Both the law firm and the donor remain anonymous, however a report from the Boston Globe is claiming a museum source revealed the Deep Throat lawyer's name is Cardinal and practices either in New York City, or Washington, D.C. The painting's condition has yet to be revealed.

The article went on to rehash the 1990 heist and then bring in an expert's opinion on how the painting could be authenticated at this stage.

My butt sank into the chair. "Son of a b—"

"Karina, can I see you in my office?" Joanne stood inside my doorway with a grim look on her face. I could tell the request wasn't optional.

It felt as though every eye in the office followed us as we traversed the halls to Joanne's office. She closed the door and indicated I sit. Instead of going around her desk, as I'd expected, she sat next to me in the other guest chair.

"Tell me, please, what on earth is going on? Rochelle has taken dozens of calls, the FBI showed up on our doorstep, and you're looking green at the gills."

"I think it's best if I show you." I rose and went around her desk. "Do you mind?" I indicated her computer.

She shook her head and in a moment the CNN site came up.

I rotated the computer screen around for her to see. Her eyes scrolled back and forth as she read the article.

"That's quite a story. And you think everyone is calling because they believe you are the Cardinal referred to in the article?"

I sank down into the chair and sighed, "I *am* the Cardinal from the article."

"How can that be? What do you know about stolen paintings?"

"The anonymous donor is my client."

"Your client! This isn't a law firm, and you're a director of legislative affairs."

"I'm also a lawyer, and a member of the bar in both Virginia and D.C. As such, I'm bound by attorney-client privilege and can't discuss more with you. I'm sorry, Joanne."

She stared at me as though I spoke a foreign language. "Are you moonlighting on the side?"

"Out of necessity."

"Ah, I get it. Someone you know is involved."

"Interested neutrality" settled across my features.

"Are *you* the anonymous donor?"

I didn't blink.

"Well, now, what are we supposed to do about this?"

"I could take a leave of absence until the furor dies down. The press is likely calling every lawyer between here and New York with the last name of Cardinal. It'll pass."

"I don't imagine having the FBI show up on our doorstep has helped your cause to remain anonymous."

"They'll get nothing out of me. It'll die down as soon as the next scandal hits."

She tapped a finger against her chin, contemplating my suggestion. "Your team is going to kill me, but you might be right. Let's say a week… for now. Knowing the news cycle, this will probably have blown over by then."

"Yes, ma'am."

She stood, and I followed suit. "By the way, the rumor mill says you've gotten engaged. Congratulations."

"Actually … we've called it off."

"Oh! Well, then, I'm sorry to hear that. Maybe this week off is for the best."

"Yes, ma'am." The door swung inward at my touch.

"By the way, how do you want us to handle the press?"

"I'd stick with 'no comment.'"

She nodded.

Latesha waited in my office. "Is it true? Did you help get that painting returned?"

I sighed and collapsed into my ergonomic desk chair. "I can't talk about it."

"I'll take that as a yes. Who's this mysterious client?" Her brows wiggled.

My phone vibrated and lit up; I sent the call to voicemail. "I can't talk about it. It's confidential."

"What did Jo say?"

"Officially, I'm taking leave."

"For how long?"

"A week … to start. You know, until it dies down."

Her shoulders deflated as she sank into one of my guest chairs.

"I'm sorry," I told her, "I know it leaves the department short-handed with this new initiative."

"Rochelle said there are some reporters out front."

"Crap." I wheeled over to the window, but since it didn't face the front door, there was nothing to see.

"Need some help?" Latesha offered.

"Would love some. Any ideas?"

"Well … I might have one. Get Wendy in here."

"Wait, Wendy, a.k.a. Wild Wendy? Office party animal?"

"That's the one."

"This better be good," I mumbled, dialing her extension.

"It will be. Wendy's up for anything."

Twenty minutes later, Wendy—a young staffer working in the membership department and a girl with few inhibitions, Latesha's main reason for including her in this harebrained caper—sat in the front seat of my car, wearing a scarf over her head and large sunglasses a lá Audrey Hepburn in *Breakfast at Tiffany's*.

"Okay, make sure you give us a fifteen-minute head start," Latesha instructed.

"Yeah, yeah, no problem. We'll cruise down the GW Parkway for a while, then I'll weave my way through Arlington. I know those streets like the back of my hand. I'll get these guys so lost. Now you two better get back into the stairwell. They'll be able to see in here once I open the garage door."

"Thanks for doing this, Wendy." I tapped her shoulder through the open window.

"Anytime. Just call me Black Widow." She cranked the engine and shifted into drive.

My brows furrowed in confusion.

"You know, from the Avengers. Now get out of here. Go, go."

Latesha punched in the code and we disappeared behind the heavy fire door as "Black Widow" headed toward the exit.

"I hope she doesn't have an accident," I said over the clacking of our heels against the concrete stairs as we headed down one level to the lower garage that let out the backside of the building.

Latesha had three kids and drove a large black SUV to cart them around. The height and darkened windows gave us an advantage. Even so, I hunkered down, sharing the floorboards with some sticky change, a purple sock, a variety of forgotten crayons, a mini Etch-a-Sketch, and a handful of fast food french fries that looked as fresh as the day they'd been delivered. She threw a black blanket over the top, closing me in with the scent of spilled apple juice and ... well, I'm not sure what that other odor was. I'm fairly certain I didn't want to know. I shuddered and put a hand over my nose.

"Stay down until I give the all clear."

The car shifted, and we slowly rolled around the corner and down a short ramp. The noisy clanking of the automatic garage doors could be heard through the blanket.

"So far so good. It looks clear to me."

I felt a thump-thump, indicating we'd crossed the drainage grates and exited the garage. Latesha pulled to a halt at the stoplight at the corner of our building. I peeped out of the blanket and saw her glance from side-to-side as we waited for the green and drove forward.

"Turn right on King Street. Keep an eye on your tail. Take note of anyone who turns with you," I said.

"About six cars followed us."

"Okay, take the next right."

She followed my direction.

"Now, put your right blinker on, but turn left at the next cross street ... that's good. Drive real slow. Is anyone following?"

"No, but the guy behind me is flashing his lights and I think ..." She rolled down her window. "Oh yeah, up yours, pal!" she yelled, displaying the corresponding finger gesture. "What the ... is that? Oh hel-licopters, I can't tell who's back there. I'm going to put an end to this nonsense."

The car came to a halt.

"What are you doing?" I hissed.

My friend stuck her hand out the window again, but this time waved the traffic around. Two SUVs and a sedan passed by before she took her foot off the brake and continued forward.

"No one's following us now."

I couldn't help the chuckle that escaped as I tossed the smothering blanket aside. "Brilliant. I've got to remember that one."

It didn't take long before she pulled into my complex. "Uh-oh, get down."

Immediately, I dropped back down onto the smelly floor. "What?"

"Looks like a pair of reporters found your home."

"Damn. Go to the left and drive around back. There's an emergency exit. Big gray door. We'll have to take the stairs."

"No sweat." She spun the wheel. "Coast looks clear."

A few minutes later, we were climbing the back stairs.

Latesha grabbed the handrail and panted. "What floor did you say you live on?"

"Fifth."

"What floor are we on?"

"Uh ... we just passed third."

"Jesus and Jehoshaphat, I've got to get to the gym. Whoa, give me a moment." She bent over, placing her hands on her knees.

I figured it wouldn't help to tell her that, since we'd gone around back, we had actually entered via the basement, thus adding an additional level to climb. I'll admit my thighs were burning a bit, but I often took the stairs around Capitol Hill, so I might have had a slight advantage.

"Okay." She straightened. "Let's go."

We finally reached my floor, and I cracked the stairwell door. We both peered around it like a Lucy and Ethel skit.

"I don't see anyone," Latesha whispered, "do you?"

"No, but my door is around the corner."

She tsked and shoved the heavy door all the way open. "Then what are we waiting for?" On tip-toe, she moved down the hall in stealth mode. Considering Latesha outweighed me by a solid fifty pounds, her silent pace impressed me.

A door opened on my right, and I couldn't help a sharp squeal as my seventy-year-old neighbor exited with her black cat in tow. "Well, hello, dearie."

I gave a nonchalant wave. Latesha had gone ahead and peered around the corner. "C'mon." She flapped her hand. "The coast is clear."

"Have a nice day, Mrs. Thundermuffin." I gave a weak smile.

"You, too. Come along, Mr. Tibbs." She tugged at the leash and minced toward the elevator. Mr. Tibbs followed regally behind her.

Latesha gaped unabashedly at my neighbor's multicolored caftan style coat, bright white turban, and purple glitter stilettos. Mrs. Thundermuffin ignored her curious stare. Once the elevator doors closed, Latesha glanced back at me, eyes wide.

"Was that a *cat* ... on a leash?"

"Yup."

"And did you call that woman Thundermuffin?"

"I sure did."

Her glance ping-ponged back and forth between the elevator and me. "You got weird people here."

"You have *no* idea." I couldn't imagine Latesha's reaction if she knew about Jasper, my neighbor two doors down, who housed a multitude of terrariums filled with snakes, lizards, and a carnivorous frog. One time he knocked on my door to ask if I'd seen Godzilla, his gigantic monitor lizard, who was on the loose. I hadn't. Thankfully, the next day, when I saw Jasper in the elevator, he informed me Godzilla had been located under the dishwasher.

My coworker collapsed onto the couch where I joined her and stared morosely at the blackened TV screen. It began with a small snort, then a slow chuckle, and turned into gulping laughs. Latesha's laughter, a combination of high pitched giggling and honking hoots, was so funny unto itself, I couldn't help joining her.

"That old lady's—*hee hee*—name is—*hee hee*—Thundermuffin! How—*hoot, haw*—do you talk to her—*hoot, snort*—with a straight face?"

"It's a challenge."

Suddenly, she jerked and her merriment ended abruptly. Then she pulled the phone from her pocket. "It's Wendy. She says her mission was a success and is coming our way. What should I tell her?"

"Here, pass it over. I'll send her around back. She'll be able to use my key fob to get in."

Half an hour later, a banging against my door had the two of us jumping. I checked the peephole to confirm it was Wendy before whipping the door open and pulling her in.

"You" —a skinny black painted nail pointed at my nose— "need to move to the first floor. Christ." She grabbed her side.

"Come in and take a load off. I cracked open the wine."

"Red or white?"

"We couldn't decide, so I opened both." I indicated to the two bottles on the coffee table. "Have a seat, I'll get another glass."

"Bring me some water, too, or Gatorade, or Pedialyte, or something. I'm dehydrated from my climb." She collapsed on the club chair, splayed out like a starfish.

"So, tell us what happened on your end of things." Latesha said.

I passed Wendy a large water and placed a clean goblet on the coffee table. "Yes, we're dying to know how the subterfuge went."

Wendy held up a finger and gulped down half the glass before answering. "So, I crept out and when they saw me, I tore outta there and watched in the rearview mirror to see them scramble to catch up with me, which didn't take long because I went down Washington Street and got caught at some of the lights. I think there were three of them following, and I hooked a U-turn, losing one at the light. So, with two hot on my tail and another trying to catch up from behind, we cruised down the GW Parkway around to Arlington. They stayed with me as I wove around traffic, through a Safeway parking lot, around some city busses. After about twenty minutes, I decided I'd given you enough leeway to make your own getaway. I wasn't far from my dry cleaners, so I stopped to pick up my cleaning. A beat-up Jetta and white panel van pulled into the parking lot behind me. Before I got out of the car, I removed the scarf and sunglasses and" —she let out a low whistle— "they were pissed when they realized they'd been led on a wild goose chase. The third guy caught up when I came out with my dry cleaning. He was from the *Washington Times* and he actually laughed. He asked me for my number." She waggled her brows.

"Tell me you didn't." I handed her a glass of wine.

"Yes, I did. His name is Greg, and he was cute, and had a nice butt."

"Lordy-bee, Wendy, you know he just wants to pump you for information."

"Oh, Tesha, I know that. But, I promise you, Karina, scout's honor." She held up four fingers, making me wonder if she knew what scout's honor meant. "He'll get nothing from me. At least not any information. If you know what I mean." She licked her lips and made a lewd sexual gesture with her tongue. "So, what happened on your end?"

"Tesha was great. She stuffed me into the back of her Mom-mobile."

"Hey, now, I don't drive a Mom-mobile."

"Seeing as I spent half an hour on the floor with a handful of six-month-old french fries, and a kid's purple sock, I beg to differ." I grinned.

"No, no." She shook her head. "A minivan is a Mom-mobile, I drive a high-class SUV."

"Whatever, *old ladies*, just tell me how it went." Wendy waved her glass at us.

"Old lady?" Latesha balked.

"As usual, Tesha handled the high-pressure escape with her usual aplomb." I made a sweeping gesture. "We think one guy followed, but we're not sure."

"With my honed evasion tactics, we were able to throw off the dogs." Latesha grinned.

"Yes, I especially enjoyed it when you came to a complete stop in the middle of Princess Street and waved half a dozen honking cars around your behemoth SUV."

"Hey, it did the trick."

"It did. And I haven't thanked you both for your expert spy plan to get me out of the office and home safe." I raised my wine glass.

"Anytime," Wendy laughed. "I had great fun."

"And a date," Latesha drawled.

"Yeah. Let me know if you need to do it again." Wendy took a gulp. "So, what's next?"

"I suppose I'll start culling through my voicemails and determine a course of action." My cell phone, which I'd left on the kitchen island, vibrated as I spoke. I ignored it, as I'd already done half a dozen times since leaving the office. My home phone started up. Caller ID revealed Martin's number. I stomped over and yanked the cord out of the wall. The room went silent.

"You show that phone who's boss," Wendy snickered and gulped more wine.

But Latesha, who knew me better, watched me with a furrowed brow. "What can I do to help?"

"You've done it." I glanced at the clock on the mantel. "And it's past four thirty. You need to go get your kiddos."

She frowned. "It's okay, there's still time. And I can call to pick them up late, or maybe my ex can get them."

"I don't think so." I shook my head. "I've heard you complain. It's twenty-five bucks for every ten minutes you're late. You and I know your *was*-band is a dick when he's called in to do something when it's not *his* day. Besides, you've got to drop Wendy off at the office first, so you need to get moving. Now, I will be just fine." I reached down and pulled her to her feet. "Are you okay to drive, or do I need to call you an Uber?"

"I'm fine. I only had half a glass."

Wendy slammed the rest of her wine as we gathered up their belongings.

"Good luck." Wendy gave me a floaty wave and headed out.

"Are you sure you'll be okay?" Latesha's eyes searched my face.

"Don't add me to your worry list, Momma. It'll all work out." I pulled her into a hug. "Thanks again for your clever plan. You executed it brilliantly. Now go fetch those beautiful children of yours."

"Call me tomorrow."

"Will do." I spun the deadbolt behind them and thumped my head against the door.

Chapter Thirty-one

I contemplated the opened bottles. It would be so easy to stick my head in the sand and drink them both, but I knew I'd only be putting off the inevitable. After clearing away the wine and dirty glasses, I pulled out a yellow legal pad and fired up the voicemail on my cell phone. There were half a dozen messages from local reporters, some I knew from the Hill and some I didn't; Martin; Patrick; Martin again; two local news stations; Patrick again; my sister; Bruce Patterson; Mom—who blessedly seemed unaware of the situation; and Mike, whose message was the most succinct. "Call me."

Mom's message was anything but succinct. "Hi, darling, it's your mother. Your father and I were wondering if you and Patrick had set a wedding date yet? I saw a beautiful purple dress for the wedding—you know how I love purple—at Nordstrom, but it's long sleeved so wouldn't be good for summer. Also, your father and I thought we should make plans to visit and meet Patrick's parents, and we can start shopping for your dress. I was thinking I could spring for a weekend for us to go up to New York and visit Kleinfeld's, you know that show, *Say Yes to the Dress.* Maybe we could get on the show. Wouldn't that be exciting? If you're not up for that, there are some lovely bridal shops in D.C. We'll coordinate with your sister, she'll want to come. We can go to lunch and make an afternoon of it. Girl time! Call me back. Oh, and your father sends his love."

Like a punch to the gut, that call. As Ricky Ricardo used to say, "Lucy, you got some 'splainin' to do." Mom's excitement was palpable. I hadn't told anyone in my family about our break up.

Once I finished with the cell messages, I dialed into my office account. It was more of the same. A few were business calls I needed to return. One a heavy breather. *Pervert.*

Then came the last one. "Keep your trap shut or there will be consequences. Starting with those you love and ending with you." The male voice held a deep, gravelly note, and the phone number must have been blocked.

I'd made a couple of enemies in my time—it was impossible not to in this line of work—however, this was my first death threat. It added an exhilarating new joy to a banner day. I listened to the message two more times, trying to determine if Martin was stupid enough to threaten me, his lawyer. It didn't sound like his voice at all. Neither did it sound as though he'd been using any sort of voice-altering tech, like they do on the procedural shows.

What idiot hires someone to threaten his own lawyer?

I punched Martin's cell number.

"Hello."

"Martin, what the hell do you think you're doing?"

"Karina? Is that you? I've been trying to reach you for the past hour. Have you seen the news?"

"Of course I've seen the goddamn news. That bastard Bradigan revealed *my* name, and my phone's been ringing off the hook ever since."

"That must be why I couldn't get through earlier."

"Well, your messenger sure got through. Where the hell do you get off having someone threaten me?"

"Threaten you? What are you talking about?"

"Come off it, Martin."

"Karina, I have no idea what you're talking about."

"Oh, so you didn't hire, or have one of your 'yes men' wandering around your office leave a threatening message on my work voicemail?"

"No, I didn't. What did he say?"

"Raspy smoker's voice. He said if I talked, there would be consequences, threatened me and my loved ones. Come on, Martin, you and I both know you're the one with the most to lose here. Who else would be leaving me threatening messages?"

"Karina, trust me, I *did not* threaten you."

His voice held sincerity under-laced with a trace of fear, and I began to realize there might be more behind the message than I initially believed. My original anger dissipated, and I eased back down into the chair. "Okay …. but I get the sense you know who did."

Silence.

"Martin? Are you still there?"

"Karina, just don't go out alone at night … and don't talk to the press or FBI."

"You're starting to freak me out here. Does this have something to do with the photos?"

A deep breath whooshed over the lines. "I can't talk about it without putting everyone in danger."

"Jesus, Martin. What the hell have you gotten into?"

"Nothing … it's … look, I'm handling it. Just stick with the story."

"Stick with the story? You mean the story you told me about the painting. That story?"

"Yes. I mean, no. Just maintain my anonymity and everything will be fine. I've got to go."

He hung up on me.

I stared at the phone, feeling a bit like Alice after she fell through the rabbit hole, only a little more pissed off. Women's intuition blared in my head like a fire engine racing through traffic. I believed Martin didn't have a hand in the message. I also believed he knew who did and that it had something to do with that damn painting. Maybe he knew more about the underground auction site than he let on. Or maybe, the entire auction site story was a load of horseshit and he was connected to the mafia.

Great, that makes me a mob lawyer. I pinched the bridge of my nose.

My next phone call, made with my trusty burn phone, was to the person who brought this media barrage down on my head to begin with.

"Samuel Bradigan."

"I'm assuming by the media storm the painting checked out."

"Ah, Luis Rodriguez a.k.a Karina Cardinal. How good of you to call."

"Is it the real thing?"

"Preliminary reports are looking good."

"How long will it take to come to a conclusion?"

"Well ... perhaps ... another few days."

I clicked my tongue. "You've sure got the press riled up."

"Yes, that was a mistake, allowing the story to leak so soon. It's not what I wanted and once I find out who did it, they will be dealt with swiftly."

I rolled my eyes at his denial. "I'm sure the perpetrator is quaking in his boots. And releasing my name? That wasn't part of our agreement. I believe we said our meeting would remain anonymous. You know, my phone hasn't stopped ringing since the story broke." I'd hoped it would take longer, or the museum would want the information about the auction site badly enough that Bradigan would keep his mouth shut. I'd miscalculated.

"I didn't give them your name."

"Technically, you've broken our agreement. There's no reason for me to encourage my client to provide the auction information."

"Now you wouldn't want to do that."

"Why not?"

"I haven't confirmed anything with the FBI or the press ... yet."

"I've already been threatened once today, Mr. Bradigan. Are you threatening me too?"

There was a pause. "What kind of threats?"

"It's nothing." I rubbed my forehead. "Never mind. Neither you, nor the press, nor the FBI will get me to reveal my client. *Capisce?*"

"What kind of threats? Was is serious?"

"Why? Having a sudden bout of conscience?"

"Not really, because I wasn't the one to give the press your name."

"Right." Sarcasm oozed off my tongue with that single syllable. "Then who did?"

"You might want to look a little closer to home. I'll admit someone from the museum leaked the painting. When I got a call from the FBI, it wasn't I who brought your name into the conversation. Agent Patterson asked if I'd heard of you and gave me enough of a description that I had no problem identifying you as my friendly metro station lawyer."

"And you told him about our meeting?"

"On the contrary. The information you're currently withholding is valuable to me. I'm not willing to jeopardize our deal. If you're looking for the press leak ... it may be coming from the FBI."

"To what purpose?"

"Smoke you out? See if you slip? Force some sort of confession? Get your client to cut a deal? I can think of a dozen reasons. None of which help my cause."

Bradigan had a point. If he didn't leak my name, Patterson may have been angry enough at my dodging tactics to do so.

"By the way, our museum director is still willing to give a percentage of the reward money to your client."

"My client's not interested."

"Repay him for the cost of obtaining the painting? It's the

least we could do."

"No."

"We could make the check out to you. Take a percentage. Perhaps you could use the two hundred and fifty grand."

"Bribery? And a paper trail? Nice try."

Bradigan paused, and I waited for his next offer to sweeten the deal. "You know, Miss Cardinal, I did a little research on you. You and Patrick Dunne showed up in the society papers last month, and rumor has it you're engaged."

"The rumors are wrong."

"His father, Martin, is a known collector in the art community."

"Your point?"

"Either he's the donor, or he knows who it is," he said bluntly.

"That's quite a stretch."

"Is it?"

I refused to rise to the bait.

"If I can figure it out with half an hour on Google … it won't take a decent investigative reporter long to start making connections."

"Again, your point?"

"For your own good, you may want to get yourself a lawyer, or one of those damage control spin doctors to deal with the press. I understand they grow on trees down there in D.C. Once we put it on display, I can't stop Justice or the FBI from asking questions, and if I am subpoenaed, I could be forced to confirm your name. I'm not *your* client. We don't have privilege."

"I have signed documents."

"Witnessed only by you and not notarized, which may or may not hold up in court."

No dummy, our Mr. Bradigan. He pointed out the exact weakness that concerned me from the beginning of this crazy scheme. I'd been in such a hurry to unload that damn painting, I'd cut corners. It was sloppy.

"Look, I'm not trying to screw you. I have a feeling you've been caught in the middle of a family affair, and you're doing your best to cover your future father-in-law's ass. Take my advice, get yourself some help. You can bill your client for it."

"I'll take that under advisement. When will you really know about the painting?"

"Soon. We're having the paint analyzed right now."

"I see. If you make an effort to divert the press from my doorstep, I'll do my best to provide the rest of the information."

"If I don't?"

"Your leads on any future paintings will end with the one in your possession. I don't care what you tell Justice or the FBI."

"I'll see what I can do."

Patrick rang my cell phone as I hung up with Bradigan. I figured from the dozen messages he'd left at my varying phone numbers, I'd better speak with him. "Hello."

"Karina? Finally! I've seen the news. That's you, isn't it? The painting, it's my father! My God, Dad's been hiding a goddamn stolen painting! That's what all the secrets were about, wasn't it? Was it in the house?"

"Keep your voice down! Where are you? Are there people around?"

"No, I'm in my car. I'm right, aren't I?"

"I can neither confirm nor deny any implications you've made."

"Damn it! Karina, it's me—don't jerk me around."

My own temper rested on the singed edge of a wire, and Patrick wasn't helping the situation. I spoke through clenched teeth, "Patrick, I'll admit your father is my client. I can tell you nothing further. Please stop calling me and, for the love of all that is holy, watch what you say in public. What I do know, whoever had the painting could be in big trouble. FBI type trouble. Understand?"

"FBI?"

"Yes."

"What the …. I just pulled into your parking lot. There must be four different media vans here."

He's in my parking lot? Christ! "Patrick, I need you to listen to me. Leave. Now. Make a U-turn. Do *not* get out of the car! You're only going to make the situation worse. If the press sees you, they will pounce!"

"Yeah, okay, okay, I get it. Keep your panties on. I'm turning around now."

I blew out the breath I'd been holding.

"I don't think anyone noticed me. It looks like they're interviewing that crazy old lady with the cat. Muffintop, or…"

"Thundermuffin."

"Yeah, that's the one."

"I think it's best if you keep your distance."

"Karina, if I can help…"

"You can't. You'll only make it worse. Just … stay away … please."

He sighed. "Fine, if that's what you want."

"Thank you."

I pushed away from the dining table and paced around it half a dozen times, trying to decide which number to call next. "To hell with it." It rang twice before he picked up.

"Agent Patterson."

"You wanted to speak with me?"

"I'm hearing some interesting things in the news."

"Uh-huh. News you leaked. You gave them my name and showed up at my office to feed the animal. Didn't you?"

"Why don't we meet?"

"We're talking now. What do you want?"

"Why don't you tell me how Martin Dunne acquired the painting."

"If I am his lawyer, you know damn well I couldn't tell you anything."

"I could have you brought in."

"Under what charges?"

"I don't need to charge you to bring you in for questioning."

"Okay, this conversation is over."

I pressed my fingers against my temples. The next number I dialed was the one I should have dialed first—the lawyer Mike recommended.

Chapter Thirty-two

The curtains were drawn, and the flickering television was the only light in my apartment. Flipping from one station to another, I watched the news. The painting remained along the bottom crawl. However, luck favored me; Russian and US relations were heating up over two more consulate closures and alleged threats about illegal spying. On any other day, this news would give me heartburn. Today, it brought relief. I clicked over to the seven o'clock nightly news to see what Lester Holt announced as today's top stories—Russia, an officer shooting in L.A., a major earthquake in South America, and the painting. I sat forward when Lester announced they would go live to NBC Boston for a press conference following the first commercial break.

I could have sworn the three-minute break took thirty minutes as I paced the floor like a caged animal, yelling at the TV to shut up about erectile dysfunction medication. Finally, Lester's solemn face returned and sent us to their NBC Boston station.

On the steps of the Isabella Stewart Gardner Museum, in front of a brightly lit podium, stood a striking black-haired woman, dressed in a long navy overcoat and red scarf. The NBC tag identified her as Ava Rukovski, Museum Director. "I have a statement and then I will take some questions. A few days ago, the museum obtained a painting that we believe to be one of the pieces of artwork stolen from the museum in 1990. The art in question is known as *The Concert* by Johannes Vermeer. Preliminary reports indicate it is the original masterpiece, and it is in good condition. I will now take questions."

The press pool went nuts, and a woman to the left of Ava

pointed to a reporter.

"Who returned the painting?"

"As I stated, it was returned anonymously."

"*The Boston Globe* indicated the painting was returned by a lawyer named Cardinal, can you confirm the name of the lawyer and the law firm used to return the painting?"

"I'm not sure where *The Globe* got its information. No one with the museum spoke to them. I cannot confirm the name of the lawyer nor the law firm."

The press corps went up in a furor.

"Who received the painting?"

"Our security director, Mr. Bradigan."

"Will he be making a statement? Can we talk to him?"

"Not at this time. No."

"Will the donor receive part of the reward money?"

"As it was returned anonymously, no one is seeking remuneration for the artwork."

"Does Mr. Bradigan believe there is more where it came from?"

"I can't comment on that."

"So, you believe this donor has access to more paintings?"

"That is not what I said. I do not believe the donor has more of the artwork."

"There are theories that the paintings have mafia ties. Do you believe the donor is connected to one of those mafia families?"

"Uh…" She paused for a minute, pressing a finger against her left ear as if listening to directions. "No, we do not believe the donor is connected to the mafia. Our theory is that a good Samaritan, who didn't initially realize what he had in his possession, stepped up to do the right thing."

"How do you know?"

"I won't comment further."

"Will the FBI be pursuing the donor?"

"I don't speak for the FBI. You'd have to ask them. I can tell you the museum is grateful to the Samaritan and we will not be pursuing any further legal action. Also, we ask everyone watching to go on to our website where you can view pictures of the stolen works. Perhaps you've seen them in Grandma's attic, or at a castle in France. It has been over twenty-five years since the theft. They could be anywhere."

"Can you tell us about the tests you'll run to verify the authenticity of the painting?"

That's when NBC cut back to Lester Holt in New York. "We'll have more on this unfolding story on the eleven o'clock news. Next, when we return, tensions heat up with Russia. Are we headed for the next Cold War?"

I muted the commercial and flopped down onto the couch in relief. There were no guarantees the museum's statement would throw off the dogs, however, it was a good start.

****

The next morning, I didn't see any media vans through the glass doors of the complex's entryway, which I took to be a good sign. Relieved, I pressed the button for the fifth floor and rode the elevator back up. I'd made an appointment to meet the lawyer, Jessica Williams, at one thirty, so I had the morning to take care of emails and review some of the legislative materials Latesha sent to me. I considered going for a run to burn off my nervous energy. Then visions of a surprise attack from a reporter intruded, and I scrapped that idea. I had no interest in being on the front of some newspaper or blog site wearing sweaty workout gear and a grungy ponytail. Instead, I popped in an old Tae Bo DVD before hitting the shower.

The phone was ringing as I stepped out and my wet fingers fumbled with the screen before successfully swiping to answer.

"Hello."

"Karina? It's Martin." His voice sounded harried.

"What can I do for you?"

"There's an agent here."

"Where are you?"

"At the office. He's in reception."

I put the phone on speaker, so I could use both hands to wrap a towel around my torso. "What does he want?"

"He says he has some questions for me."

"Does he have a warrant?"

"Not that I've seen."

"Tell your staff to stall him. Keep him waiting in reception. I'm on my way and I'm going to see if I can bring another lawyer, a heavy hitter, with me."

"How do you suggest I stall him?" Martin asked.

"Have your staff tell him you'll talk to him. Get him a cup of coffee and a pastry. Do *not* let him wander around. Have someone to keep an eye on him. Tell them to be very attentive and apologetic for keeping him waiting."

"Okay, I get it. How long will you be?"

"Half an hour."

It ended up taking forty-five minutes to get there. Jessica Williams asked me to wait and arrived fifteen minutes later. Her strong, musky perfume filled the elevator as we rode up to Martin's floor. I guessed she was pushing six-two with her four-inch Manolo stilettos; she towered over me, and I idly wondered if she'd played basketball in school. Her stylish elegance reminded me of Michelle Obama.

Patterson was the only guest in the waiting area. "I should have known." He tossed aside his newspaper and rose. "What took you so long?"

"Agent Patterson, may I introduce Jessica Williams, perhaps you've heard of her."

"Indeed, I have." The smile could best be described as teeth baring.

"Good morning, Agent." Jessica didn't bother to remove her butter-yellow gloves as she held out her hand. "I understand you have some questions for my client."

"I wasn't aware Mr. Dunne was your client." It pleased me to see Agent Patterson forced to look up at Jessica. I imagine she owed part of her success, in this male dominated arena, to her glorious height.

"You are now. Do you have any sort of warrant?"

"No, ma'am."

Not to be outdone by my new colleague, I stepped forward. "What would you like to discuss with Mr. Dunne?"

"This and that."

"You'll have to be more specific," I said.

"I'd like to ask him about some artwork."

"Why don't you come back when you've got a warrant?" Jessica suggested.

"There's so much more civility in doing it this way. Don't you think?"

"I think you don't have enough to obtain a warrant, so you're harassing my client."

"I've got an internationally known fence attending Mr. Dunne's holiday party. I've had an interesting conversation with this young lady to verify that. I've got a stolen painting that's been returned to the Gardner Museum in a havey-cavey fashion."

"Miss Cardinal also represents Mr. Dunne. Unless you've got an affidavit or deposition under oath, her conversations about Mr. Dunne are privileged. The courts would never allow it."

"So, Miss Cardinal *does* represent Mr. Dunne."

"As I said, you've got nothing. I suggest you take your leave, Agent. If you'd like to harass someone, here's my card. Feel free to contact me. Don't try to speak to my client or Miss Cardinal again without me."

Once he'd gone, the young Asian male receptionist who'd

watched the exchange with wide eyes escorted us back to Martin's office.

"Martin, let me introduce Jessica Williams, the lawyer I told you about last night. She's a heavy hitter who's successfully gone up against the Justice department and won."

They shook hands, and we all took seats around the coffee table. Both of us signed some paperwork, then Jessica launched into a strategy that would bring Patterson's inquiries to a halt, which included obtaining an injunction by the end of the day. I had to admit, never having been a litigator, I felt out of my depth, and Jessica's calm planning of the next steps quieted my doubts.

Chapter Thirty-three

We left the office before noon, and returning alone to my apartment with only my thoughts to keep me company held little appeal. I decided to take my computer to the Panera at Crystal City to grab a bite and use their Wi-Fi. A pair of gorgeous red and white spectator pumps sitting in a shop window caught my eye when I strolled past. I made a mental note to stop in the shoe store before heading home.

A partly cloudy sky provided a sensational show of the sunset in pinks and oranges as I drove toward my complex a few hours later. Its tranquil beauty reflected my own mood. The stress of the past weeks had weighed heavily in my heart and on my brain. Bringing in Jessica relieved much of my own doubts, and the lack of visible reporters in front of my building only sought to deepen my serenity. Finally, my life was returning to normal. I could turn the page and begin the next chapter.

Even though I didn't see any reporters, I decided to play it safe. I drove around to the fire exit. This morning I'd taken the elevator down to the first floor and walked the stairs to the basement. I have no idea why it didn't occur to me to do the opposite the other day with Latesha. There'd really been no reason to climb the stairs all the way to the fifth floor. I waved my key fob in front of the pad. *Boy, Tesha would be furious if I told her.* I snickered at the thought of her reaction. The light turned green, and I pulled the handle.

The stairwell seemed gloomier than normal. The overhead

light by the door was out and I made a mental note to tell our maintenance guy about it. A movement from beneath the stairwell caught my eye. The shadow took human shape and came at me. Screaming, I wielded my bag of new shoes by slinging them at the form.

He was faster, swiping at the pitiful weapon with one hand and effectively cutting off my scream by backhanding me with the other. "Shut up!"

I stumbled backward against the stairs, flailing to catch my balance, but it was not to be. My left elbow and shoulder took the weight; I fell against the railing before landing hard. There was a grinding snap, and I cried out at the flash of pain.

It was the stuff of nightmares. He wore all black, including the ski mask and gloves, and my blood ran cold as he came at me again. I wasn't in a position to throw a punch; instead, using a Tae Bo move, I kicked with all my might at his kneecaps. My foot connected, digging in with the boot heel, and he grunted, stumbling back against the concrete wall. I released a shriek to rival the best horror movie scream queen as I scrambled to gain purchase on the stairs.

We both recovered our feet at the same time, but I figured I had the advantage now because I held the higher ground. I removed the handbag from beneath my armpit and held it with my right hand at my uninjured side. It was heavy enough to do some damage if I could clock him over the skull with it, and I might be able to outrun him and make it to the first floor where I could find help.

"I'll teach you a lesson, you little bitch."

I heard the flick of the opening blade before seeing the flash of its sharp, silver edge, and instead of being a weapon, my purse became my shield against the oncoming knife. He didn't seem to brandish it like a trained professional, more like a street fighter taking wild swings, which I dodged and batted away with the purse, inching backward up the stairs.

A banging against the heavy metal exterior door made him pause, and I took a few more steps upward and yelled for help. There were two pops and the door flew open. The exterior flood lights illuminated the stairwell. My attacker abandoned me and leaped down the risers to go after the new person.

"Watch out!" I hollered.

The door flew open so quickly it banged against the wall, and its backward swing whacked the gun out of the new guy's hand. Luckily, he twisted and was fast enough to defend himself against the deadly blade as it swished toward his chest. He grabbed the attacker's arm holding the weapon with one hand and threw a pair of quick kidney punches with the other. I watched in horror as the two tussled to gain control of the knife. The ski mask guy threw a knee. There was an "oof," and the new guy bent in pain, but remained holding on to the hand with the knife.

"Get the gun," he grunted.

His words galvanized me into action. Of course, the gun had flown into the dark recesses behind the stairwell. I stumbled down, only to be met with the two bodies reeling at me, locked in battle. Without their weight against the door, it swung shut, and the murkiness closed around us. The purse remained clutched in my hand and, when he got close enough, I walloped the knife guy upside the head with all my might. The impact must have rung his bell because he stumbled, dropping the knife. The new guy had a hold of the bad guy's ski mask, and as the bad guy went down on one knee, the mask popped off in my hero's hand. I scooted past both of them.

"Who are you working for?" The new guy snarled, and I heard a punch connect.

The corner was so dark that I desperately swung my right hand back and forth against the ground in search of the gun, my left arm numb and tingly, useless in my search. I couldn't seem to move it properly. Finally, my fingers skimmed across the heavy metal. I snatched up the gun, fumbling to get it in position. The two men were back at it, exchanging blows at close contact. My hand shook so much, there was no way I'd get a clean shot at the bad guy. In fact, the way they were positioned, there was a high likelihood I'd hit the new guy.

"Freeze! Don't move, I've got you covered."

Neither man heeded my warning.

The good guy tripped over my new shoes and stumbled to the side. I saw my opening and squeezed the trigger. I wasn't ready for the kickback; it tossed my arm aside like a ragdoll, and I'm pretty sure the shot went wide. I have no idea if I could have hit the bad guy with a second shot because, the next thing I knew, he threw open the door, briefly lighting up his blunt nosed profile, and ran out into the night. It slammed shut behind him.

The good guy pulled himself up using the bannister. "Are you okay?"

I swiped at the blood running from my cut lip. "I think so."

A car engine revved. My savior darted to the door and pulled it open. He looked back at me, as if trying to decide whether or not to pursue. The roaring noise dwindled as the car zipped around the complex. My hero groaned, placing a hand against his side while holding the door open with his hiking boot.

"Are *you* okay?"

"Cracked rib." He looked like a Marine, with close cropped dark hair, thick brows above stark cheekbones, and a dark sweater that fit tight against his muscled chest. I would guess he was in his mid-forties by the rugged lines etched around his eyes and forehead.

As I admired him, the adrenaline slowed and pain filtered in, and one-by-one, nerve endings identified each bump and bruise. My lower back, throbbing cheek, fat lip, painful tingle in my left arm. I looked over at my left shoulder, it seemed to hang funny.

"Hey, does this look right to you?"

He grimaced. "Looks like a dislocated shoulder."

"They're going to have to put that back into place. Right?"

"Uh-huh."

"Do you think that's going to hurt?"

He stared at me for a moment, as if contemplating his next words. "It'll hurt like hell."

I shifted and winced at the movement. "Sounds like you speak from experience."

"I do."

"Fabulous. Just when I thought my life was back on track." My swollen lip was making it hard for me to pronounce my f's and b's.

He grunted.

"I can tell you're a man of few words."

"Can I have my gun back?"

I stared at my right hand still clutching the pistol. "Oh, right. Sure." Pointing it at the ground, I held it out to him. "By the way, who are you?"

"Rick." He shoved the gun into a holster he wore on his hip and covered it up with his sweater.

"Do you live here, Rick?"

"Have you got a phone?"

"A phone? Uh, yeah, in my purse. If it didn't get broken when I used it to smack him over the head. I whacked him pretty good, don't you think?" That comment gained me a half smile and head shake. I sat on the steps with the handbag. It took a few tries for my unsteady fingers to unzip my purse and find the phone. "Yes, it still works."

"Call for an ambulance. You'll need to go to the hospital to get that fixed."

"Yeah, you too. You'll need those ribs x-rayed and taped, or whatever they do for broken ribs."

"Who's down there?" a high-pitched voice echoed from above.

I leaned my head over the railing and looked up. "Mrs. Thundermuffin?"

"Who is that?"

"It's me, Karina, your neighbor."

"Are you alright? Mr. Albert thought he heard a ruckus and called the police." Her heels slowly clicked down from the first floor.

Mr. Albert was our sixty-year-old maintenance man who lived on the first floor near the stairwell. He was also going deaf, so I guess I was lucky he'd heard anything at all. "Someone attacked me in the stairwell. If it weren't for Rick, here. I'd likely be dead."

"Who is Rick, dear? My goodness, Karina, you're bleeding. Why, you need an ambulance." She pulled a silver sparkly cell phone out of her caftan pocket. "Albert, tell them to send an ambulance too. Poor Karina's down here bleeding out. It looks like she's been mugged. I'm sure it will need to be cleaned up, but we'll worry about that later." Her attention returned to me. "Now, who is this Rick? Is he the one who attacked you?"

"Rick?" I looked to the doorway—now empty and held open with a concrete block. "That's odd."

"What's odd?"

"There was a man, he said his name was Rick. He heard my screams and busted open the door to help me."

"Who attacked you?"

"I don't know. He was wearing that ski mask over there. He'd been hiding behind the stairs. Waiting."

"Oh, my goodness! There was a man waiting to attack the next unsuspecting person to come through that door. Why would someone do that?"

"No idea."

Rick's voice snarling at the assailant rang in my head. *"Who are you working for?"* he'd asked. Not why. Who.

The distant siren wails soon arrived. Flashing blue and red lights bounced off the brick walls and trees. The fire engine came first, followed closely the ambulance and police, and then the fun really began.

One of the firemen came first with his bag. He gave me an ice pack for the face and was dabbing at the lip when the ambulance crew arrived. A nice looking dark-haired fellow with warm brown eyes hunched in front of me. "Let's see what we've got."

One look at the shoulder and the consensus determined dislocation.

"Well, can't you just jam it back into place?" I asked.

"No, we could damage it further, and you could have a fracture. We'll have to take you to the hospital to get that x-rayed before they put it in place."

I squinted at his name tag. "Tony? Is that your name?"

"That's me." He clicked on a tiny light and flashed it in my eyes.

I flinched at its brightness. "I don't have a concussion, I didn't hit my head. He just hit me on the cheek. Do you know a Jillian Cardinal?"

He put the flashlight back in his pocket and took hold of my left wrist. "As a matter of fact, I do."

"I'm Karina, her sister."

He paused his examination. "Well, now, it's nice to finally meet you, Karina."

"You too. Pardon the … uh … mess. I don't usually look this … disheveled."

"No problem." He grinned and took hold of my wrist again. You still have a pulse, which is good. We're going to give you something to make you more comfortable for the ride to the hospital, and let's hold your arm like this. Feel better?"

"Sort of."

"Someone shot the shit out of the lock," one of the police officers said to Mr. Albert, who'd come down to assess the damage.

I leaned around Tony. "Yeah, that was Rick."

"Who's Rick?"

"He's Batman."

"Did she hit her head?" The officer directed his question at Tony.

"No, I didn't hit my head," I howled indignantly. "Do you want to hear what happened or make conjecture?"

"I'd better hear the story, because the guys down at the station will laugh their asses off if I have to put out an APB on Batman."

So, I told him the story as the EMTs splinted my arm and loaded me into the ambulance. Then I told the story to my sister, who arrived at the hospital soon after I did, because Tony was kind enough to call her. I gave a shortened version to four different hospital staff, including the doctor who put my shoulder back in place. Rick was right; it hurt like hell.

And then I told the story once again to the bald detective who arrived while I waited for the dismissal paperwork to arrive. "And you didn't know either of these men?"

"Nope. Like I told the beat cop back at my apartment complex, he was Batman. Once he realized help was coming, he disappeared into the night." I failed to mention that Batman might be at one of the local hospitals seeking help for his cracked ribs. Although, his tough guy attitude may have had him stopping by the local drug store to get some tape and a bottle of aspirin to take care of the situation himself. I didn't know Rick from Adam, but intuition had me protecting his identity. No doubt, I owed him my life. The fact that he disappeared the way he did had me wondering if something in his past was buried somewhere in a police file.

"I'm interested in having you work with a sketch artist. Would you be amenable to that?"

"I'm not sure what I can tell you about my attacker. I only glimpsed his profile as he fled. As for Batman … he looked like a Marine. Like dozens of other jarheads in the area."

"Still, I'd like you to try."

"Fine," I sighed and shifted the ice on my shoulder into a different position.

"Do you have any enemies? Any reason someone would want to hurt you?"

"I'm a Capitol Hill lobbyist. What do you think?"

"Anything in particular? Any new enemies?"

While waiting for my x-rays, I'd contemplated those exact questions. Rick didn't ask why. He asked the perpetrator "who" he was working for. Somehow, I had a feeling both Rick and I knew the why. This was no random mugging. And the way Rick came out of nowhere—in my gut, I knew he didn't live in the building. So, what was he doing there at that exact moment? He carried a gun and knew how to fight. Every avenue my brain followed circled back to the threat on my voicemail and Martin. Was Rick a good Samaritan who happened by, or did Martin hire him to keep an eye on me? Is that what he meant when he said he'd "take care of it?" Was I being followed again, only this time by the good guys? The questions went round and round. They hurt my head.

"Miss Cardinal? Karina?"

My eyes snapped back to the detective. "Laurence Fishburne."

His brows puckered. "Laurence Fishburne is your enemy?"

I snorted. "No, I just figured it out, you look like Laurence Fishburne. Hasn't anyone told you?"

"Oh, yes." My sister pointed. "You're right. I see it."

"Right? When he shaved his head for *The Matrix*. C'mon, someone's pointed it out to you."

"I can't say as they have." His frown deepened.

"So, you want me to come to the station tomorrow to work with the sketch artist."

"I was hoping you could do it tonight."

"No can do, Morpheus. My back and face hurt, and the shoulder is killing me. I'm going to go home, take the pain pills these fine doctors have seen fit to bestow upon me, and I'm going to sleep for the next twelve hours. I'll meet with your sketch artist tomorrow and bring you a list of enemies. I think that nurse behind you has my discharge papers. Why don't you give me your card, Detective Fishburne, and I'll be in contact with you tomorrow?"

He took his dismissal well. I signed all the papers, promised doctors I'd take it easy, and Jillian drove me home.

Chapter Thirty-four
MARTIN

"He's a low-level enforcer for Monaldo."

"You're sure about that?" Marty paced behind his desk.

"Ninety-nine percent. He's been arrested twice for assaulting his girlfriend. I checked his mugshot. It's a match." Rick shifted and let out a grunt.

"Have you had that looked at?"

"One of my guys was a medic. He taped it up. Not much else I can do about it."

"Who's watching her now?"

"I've put a team on her. The medic is one of them."

"Was she hurt bad?"

"Cuts and bruises, dislocated shoulder. She'll be fine."

"Was she scared?"

"Actually, for a civilian with no training, she didn't do too bad. She clocked him pretty hard with her purse." He grinned. "And she kept her shit together afterward. Nine out of ten women would have lost it. Hell, nine out of ten guys would have crapped themselves."

"Thanks for the report. I'll be in touch."

Rick ponderously got to his feet. "Sir, they got past us ... me. I'm sorry, I thought she was okay once she entered her apartment building." He shook his head. "We'll be more vigilant next—"

Marty put his hands up. "Don't worry about it. You did good tonight. I'm working on a more permanent solution. Close my door on your way out."

"Very well. Goodnight, sir."

Marty waited for the snick of the tongue to slide into the door jamb before typing in his password and bringing up the document he'd been working on prior to Rick's arrival.

His cell phone rang, and he answered it without checking the caller ID. "Hi, honey, I'm still stuck at the office. I'll probably be another hour."

Chapter Thirty-five

"Rina. Hey, wake up."

My sister's concerned face hovered above me. "Jillian? What time is it? Are you still here?"

"It's six. I stayed the night."

"You didn't need to do that."

"I'm worried about you, but I've got to leave if I'm going to make it to work on time. I can use a sick day if you need me to stay."

"Don't be ridiculous." I knew sick days were like gold to teachers. "I'll be fine. Go to work."

"Can I borrow something out of your closet? Otherwise, I'll never make it on time if I have to go home first."

"Of course, use whatever you need. There's a spare toothbrush in the guest bathroom medicine cabinet. You know where I keep the towels."

"Okay, I'll swing by after school to check on you."

"Whatever." I pulled the covers up to my chin with my good hand and closed my eyes.

"And, Rina ..."

"Hm?"

"We're going to talk. I know you know something more than what you told Detective Fishburne last night."

"I know nothing," I mumbled and fell back to sleep.

I awoke a little while later; the pain meds having worn off. Showering, doing hair, and getting dressed was an exceptionally fun joy. I couldn't lift my left arm above chest level without crying out in pain. I couldn't even pull my hair into a ponytail, much less style it, so I ended up resorting to an old headband. It made me look like a parochial schoolgirl. Getting the sling into place provided its own adventure.

At nine thirty, I called Martin. He didn't answer, and I didn't leave a message. After Martin, I called Detective Fishburne. "Hey, Morpheus!"

"Miss Cardinal."

"Listen, do you still want me to come to the station today?"

"I'd appreciate it, yes."

"Well, you're going to have to send someone to come fetch me. 'Cause I'm going to take another one of these pain pills, and on the warning label, it says I shouldn't operate heavy machinery."

"How about an Uber?"

"Yeah … no. You want me to come in? Come get me. Otherwise, I'm crawling back into bed. Your choice."

"I'll be there in half an hour."

"Looking forward to it."

I tried Martin again while I waited. This time he picked up. "Martin, it's Karina. I don't know what kind of shit you're into, but it visited me last night … *at my home.*"

"I heard. How's the shoulder?"

"You heard? How did you 'hear?' Wait … don't tell me, Rick. He works for you."

"There's been a miscommunication."

"A *miscommunication?* What the hell does that mean? What are you into, Martin? Is this about that damn painting? Or some other dirty deed? I think you owe me answers, Martin."

"I promise it will all be cleared up within the next twenty-four hours. Nothing like this should *ever* happen again."

"What should I do for the next twenty-four hours? Hm? Hide

out in my apartment and hope no one firebombs it?"

"You can carry on with your business. I've got someone covering you."

"Who? Rick? He was pretty messed up last night. One punch to the ribs and that guy will be down for the count. I don't want to be responsible for that."

"No. Someone else."

"Great, a new able-bodied sucker. Where do you find these guys?"

"A security firm that was recommended to me."

"Well … you better tell Rick they were digging his bullets out of the concrete, and I'm supposed to go down to the police station to give a sketch artist his description. The police weren't too pleased with his disappearing act."

"Karina … I hate to ask …"

I rolled my eyes. "Don't worry, it'll be too generic to identify. Just tell him to keep a low profile in the next few weeks. But, there's only so much I can do. Your boy could have been caught on any number of security cameras in the area."

"Thanks … and, Karina, try not to lose your tail. He's on your side."

"I get it. Martin … talk to Jessica. She can help … far more than I."

"Is there anything I can do for you?"

"Fix this … as soon as you can. That damn painting has caused me more heartburn…"

"I know. I'm sorry … for all of it."

"Hold on, Jessica's buzzing my other line, stay there." I clicked over. "Hi, Jessica, did we get our injunction?"

"We sure did. We're good to go."

"I've got Martin on the other line. I'll let him know. Thank you."

"Just doing my job."

She hung up, and Martin came back online.

"Jessica got the injunction."

"Good news."

Another call rang in. "I'll talk to you later." I clicked over. "Hello."

"I'm in your parking lot."

"On my way, Detective."

An hour later, the Alexandria P.D. had themselves a sketch of some stranger. I'd had them lift Rick's forehead, put his eyes closer together, and elongate his chin. There was a vague resemblance, but nothing that would get picked up through facial recognition. Afterward, the detective asked me to look through some of the mugshots.

"Why do you think this guy would be in a mugshot?"

"He left the scene of a crime."

"But he didn't perpetrate the crime. He saved me."

"If he's innocent, why did he leave?"

"Maybe he was hungry and saw a passing taco truck."

That quip resulted in a sharp glower. "And what was he doing there to begin with?"

"Being my guardian angel."

The detective wheeled his chair in front of me. "Why are you protecting him?"

"I don't know what you mean. I gave your guy a description. He created it on his little tablet."

"Do you know him?" His black eyes drilled into me, and they weren't soft and kind like Tony's.

"Who? Batman?"

"You said his name was Rick."

"No, he told me his name was Rick."

"No last name?"

"He didn't elaborate. He was a man of few words."

"And the other man. The one who attacked you?"

"I told you, it was dark. He wore a mask. I only saw his profile; the light threw shadows on the side I did see. Your sketch artist created a nice silhouette. What more do you want?"

"Why was he hiding in *your* stairwell?"

"It's not *my* personal stairwell. I imagine he was there to mug the next unsuspecting tenant to walk in that door. I had the unfortunate luck to be that unsuspecting tenant."

"Not many people use that door."

"Some do. Especially those on the first floor."

"You live on the fifth floor. Why were you using it?"

"No good parking spots around front." I pulled my purse onto my lap. "My shoulder's hurting and I have a headache. I'd like to go home now." I pinched my lips shut and readied myself to stare him down.

It didn't take long. "Very well. I'll take you home."

"Thank you," I said grudgingly.

I'm fairly sure I identified my tail on the way home. He drove a silver Chevy SUV. Generic enough to fit in with the rest of traffic, he consistently stayed three cars back. I thought about taking him a glass of lemonade and a cookie, but once I plopped onto the sofa, exhaustion won out over my smartass gene, and I couldn't muster the energy to go back down.

Jillian called at two thirty, waking me from a too brief nap.

"Hey, Jilly, what are you doing calling? Don't you have a class?"

"It's my planning period. I can't come by until later. I forgot I've got journalism club after school. Why don't I bring dinner over around six?"

"You know, I spent half the day at the police station, and I'm kind of wiped out. Why don't you come by tomorrow?"

"Are you dodging me?"

"Not at all. I'm genuinely tired. It's been a long few days."

"Ok-ay. Fine. I'll leave you alone tonight. But tomorrow …

we're talking. Six. I'll bring dinner." She hung up before I said goodbye.

Afterward, I called Latesha to check in. She didn't answer and I left a message. I hadn't eaten lunch, so I made myself a peanut butter sandwich and flipped back and forth between the news networks. There was no mention of the attack on the local news, thank heaven, and coverage of the painting on the national news networks was nonexistent. There were bigger fish to fry, a high school shooting in California splashed across all the stations.

Patrick called around five, and I answered.

"I just got off the phone with my dad. He wanted to know how you were fairing. I assumed he was talking about our breakup, so I said you seemed to be handling it well. Then he asked how long it would take the shoulder to heal, and I realized I had no clue what he was talking about."

"You didn't tell him about our breakup?"

"No."

I assumed, since I hadn't heard back from Molly, that Patrick had broken the news. "What did you tell him?"

"That we were taking some time to work things out. Since you're so chummy these days, I figured you'd tell him."

"I didn't think it was my place to tell your parents."

"Have you told yours?"

I'd told Jillian last night. She'd shown no surprise, the little brat, adhering to her soulmate theory that Patrick was not the one for me. I'd yet to break it to my parents. "Not yet. I've had a lot going on. I plan to call them this weekend."

"It's not so easy, is it?"

"Patrick … we're not getting back together because it's hard to tell our parents."

He sighed. "So, you want to tell me what happened?"

"I got mugged in the stairwell."

"At your apartment complex?"

"Yes."

"My God, are you alright?"

"Some bruises, dislocated shoulder that will take a few weeks to heal. I'll be fine."

"Do you need me to bring you something?"

"Thank you, but no. My sister is playing mother hen. I'm being taken care of."

"Are you sure I can't do anything for you? Bring you dinner? Pick up some groceries?"

My cupboards were rather bare, but I didn't want to encourage Patrick. I feared if I gave him an opening, he'd take it to mean more than it was. "I'm fine. Jillian's got things well in hand, and I'm not bedridden. I can get to the store on my own."

"I miss you."

"Patrick … I miss you, too. Doesn't change anything."

Another windy sigh blew across the lines. "I saw the press conference about the painting."

"Yes, it seems *The Globe* misquoted a source. The press has bugged out of my life."

"Does our breakup have something to do with all of this? My father's involvement?"

"No."

"Well, then … I'd better go. If there's anything you need…"

"I'll let you know."

I dialed Chinese for dinner and was happily munching on Moo Goo while watching *Jeopardy!* when something slammed against my front door, followed by raised voices. I raced to peer through the peephole to find Mike and a bulgy blond guy with spiky hair holding each other at gunpoint.

"FBI, put your weapon down!" Mike barked.

"Let me see your badge," Blond guy demanded.

Uh-oh. I whipped open the door. "What is going on out here?"

"Return to your apartment, ma'am. *Now!*"

"I will not, and you'd better put that down! I know this man, and he *is* FBI."

Blond guy's gaze flicked to me, back to Mike, then he lowered his gun. With one hand, Mike pulled out his badge and held it up while keeping his weapon trained on the other man.

"I apologize, sir." Blond guy holstered his weapon. "There was a mugging here last night and we're a little on edge."

"Have you got a permit for that thing?" Mike returned the badge and weapon to their respective compartments.

"Yes, sir. Concealed carry in Virginia, D.C., and Maryland. I'm with Silverthorne Security." He dug into a side pocket of his khaki cargo pants and removed a business card.

My friend tucked it away. "Army spec ops?"

"Navy."

Mike nodded.

"How'd you get in?"

"Flashed the badge." Mike had the temerity to grin.

I rolled my eyes and checked the hall. Luckily, my neighbor across the way was a regional rep for some sort of tech company and traveled all the time. He was never home during the week. However, my buddy with the snakes and lizards always seemed to be wandering the halls and was as curious as Mrs. Thundermuffin.

"Mike, why don't you come in? I need to chat with Navy here. Help yourself to some Chinese." Mike slipped past me, and I pulled the door closed. The security guy wore heavy work boots, much like Rick's, a black T-shirt that conformed to his muscled chest and a black blazer that did a good job hiding the gun at his hip.

He eyed me, as if unsure what to say.

"So, you're the B-team?"

"I guess you could say that."

"Silver Chevy, SUV?"

His jaw muscles flexed.

"What's your name?"

"Joshua."

"And how did you get in the building, Josh? Because I know I didn't let you in."

He crossed his arms and stared at the floor. "The back door lock is still busted."

I pursed my lips at that. "How's Rick?"

"He's fine."

"And the ribs?"

"Sore." His green-gray gaze returned to mine.

"You want to elaborate on that?"

He shrugged.

"Is this something they teach you at the security company?"

"I'm not sure what you mean, ma'am."

"This yup-nope routine. Rick had it down pat."

This time an inclined brow accompanied the shrug.

"Okay, then. I'm feeling safe tonight, considering I've got an FBI agent in my apartment." I pointed at the door. "You can return to your silver SUV."

"If it's all the same to you, ma'am, I'll continue to monitor the perimeter around your apartment."

"Seriously? The neighbors are going to call the cops if they find some stranger wandering the halls."

"I've already informed a few that I'm hired security ... for the building."

"And how did that go over?"

"They were relieved. The prevailing belief is that it could have been anyone attacked in the stairwell last night."

"But you and I know better. Don't we?"

"As you say." His expression remained noncommittal.

"Fine. Just try to keep the gun in your pants."

His brows rose.

"You know what I mean!" The door snapped shut behind me.

I found Mike, in his shirt sleeves, slurping up a noodle from one of the Chinese boxes littering my coffee table. "Leave some Lo Mein for me, I haven't had any yet," I told him.

"You must have been hungry." He indicated the half dozen takeout containers with his chopsticks.

"I wanted leftovers." I sat cross-legged on the couch and retrieved my Moo Goo.

"The Greek Isles."

"Ah, ah, you forgot to put it in the form of a question," I admonished.

"I got it right."

"South Africa." "Liberia!" we both said at the same time.

"No, I'm sorry, the correct answer is Liberia," Alex Trebek said with his trademark condescending faux sympathy.

"Ha!" Mike triumphantly scooped another pile of noodles into his cakehole.

"You were always good at geography. Why is that?"

He swallowed. "I used to study maps as a kid. They fascinated me. This reminds me of our college days. Chinese food and cramming for finals."

I clicked the television off and tossed the remote aside. "What are you doing here, Mike?"

"How's the shoulder?"

"Painful."

"Want to tell me what happened?"

"I was mugged in the stairwell."

"And some stranger came to your rescue and disappeared again."

"How did you know?"

"There's a BOLO out for him. The detective I spoke to said you called him Batman and doesn't feel you're doing much to help them find the guy."

"Ah, you spoke to Morpheus."

"Who?"

"Forget it. Look, I gave a description and what I knew. The guy didn't do anything wrong. I don't know what the big deal is."

"He policed his brass."

"What does that mean?"

"He gathered the shell casings before disappearing. Do you think Mr. Navy out there knows this guy?"

I couldn't hold his gaze, so I returned to the Moo Goo. "I have no idea."

"Was it a random mugging? Or was he waiting for *you*?"

"Why would he be waiting for me?"

He slammed the box down, jabbed the chopsticks inside, and pushed to his feet. He pointed a long finger at me and opened his mouth. Expressions flickered across his face. "This is bullshit," he mumbled before stomping into my kitchen, around the island, and returning to stand in front of the TV with arms akimbo. "Something stinks, and you're into this up to your neck. I've got a hunch that it all stems from Martin Dunne, his son Patrick, and that painting. And, while you're running around trying to cover their asses, your name got onto someone's shit list. My guess would be some mobster, and that article from *The Globe* put you into their crosshairs."

I stared wide-eyed in guppy-like shock at how close to the truth Mike had gotten.

"Tell me, who hired Silverthorne Security?"

"Uh … the condo complex?"

"I don't think so."

"I just got mugged. What makes you think I didn't hire them?"

"Hiring Silverthorne is akin to hiring SEAL Team Six. Silverthorne Security is who you hire when you go to Iraq, or need high-level security for a diplomat, or are planning a small country coup d'état. They're full of ex-military mercenaries, and probably half are on the CIA payroll for wet work. In other words, you couldn't afford them."

"Wow. Silverthorne hires bad asses." I smirked and wiggled my brows.

"Damnit, Karina! This isn't a joke! You are in some serious shit, and it's going to get you killed."

Mike had never yelled at me before. His face blazed in anger, and, for the first time, I saw past my old college buddy for what he was now. A super-smart, trained FBI agent who was barely holding it together because he knew I'd lied to him, was still lying to him, and realized the information I withheld could get me killed.

The worst part … I didn't want him to be angry with me. I didn't want to lie to him.

I realized, I wanted him to hold me.

I wanted him to kiss me again.

We stared at each other, him with his chest puffing up and down, while I struggled to put on "interested neutrality." Maybe it was delayed reaction, or PTSD, or … something, but emotions welled up from deep down. Instead of defending myself, or firing back with a sarcastic quip, or maintaining "interested neutrality," to my dismay, my self-possession crumbled like a sandcastle under an ocean's wave. It started with a lump in my throat and wobbly lip, then Mike turned blurry as tears filled my vision. Rapidly, it morphed into a full-on sobbing inferno.

"I … I c-can't t-take it any m-more. Everyone is a-asking q-questions I c-can't a-answer or d-don't know the a-answer to. I'm t-trying my b-best h-here. M-my whole b-body hurts, and I c-can't h-handle y-you y-yelling at m-me t-too." The nose flooded, and I snatched up a handful of tissues.

"Ah, K.C., I'm sorry." He sat down next to me, and I leaned against him with my good shoulder as he rubbed my back. "I can't imagine what you've gone through."

In a romance novel, this is where I'd fall into his arms, and we'd start kissing, which would eventually lead to steamy sex. The reality of the situation precluded such ridiculousness. I was a disgusting mess of snot and tears, and having witnessed my face during a crying jag, there was nothing, I mean NO-THING, that would do less to rev up a man's libido. My face gets all pinched and red, and my mascara runs. Adding to that, the bruised cheek and half-swollen lip would probably drive even the most devoted lover to hit the road. And lest we forget, the injured shoulder; even the slightest jarring sent me into spasms and not the good kind of spasms.

Mike shushed, whispered inanities, and handed me clean tissues while I blubbered. He handled it well. Having a sister must have given him some training on dealing with weepy women. The tears dried up and my emotions turned to embarrassment. I excused myself to clean up. When I returned from the bathroom, the dirty Kleenexes were gone, and Mike was sitting on the couch with his elbows on his knees and his head hanging.

"Uh, sorry about that."

He looked up. "Lady, you're a hot mess."

I folded into the club chair and blew out a sigh. "You're telling me."

"I want to help you, but you're not letting me in."

"I know, and I want your help. But we're not in college anymore. I've got a client. You work for the FBI, and we can't talk about it."

"Even if he's putting you in danger? K.C., this is your life we're talking about. Look at you. I read the report. Tell me, do you really believe it was a random mugging?"

"Y-y…" His warm gaze held mine and I couldn't lie. "N-no."

"Key-rist." He rubbed his face.

"I have faith the situation is being dealt with, and that

Silverthorne Security can keep me safe until it is."

His mouth made a straight line. "What do you expect me to do in the meantime?"

I blinked and said in my most upper-crust British accent, "Keep calm and carry on."

He grunted. "Does the smartass gene run in the family?"

"I believe so." I produced my cheekiest grin.

Finally, his face softened. "You make it very hard for me to stay pissed at you."

"Must be my charming personality."

He reached for his coat. "Since you've got your own security team, I suppose I'd best make my way home."

Suddenly, I wasn't ready to face another lonely night with nothing but my thoughts to keep me company. "Wait. Why don't you stay and watch a movie, and we'll reminisce about the olden days? The cable company gifted me three free months of HBO."

"What's playing?"

"Dunno. There are about ten channels to choose from, bound to be something we can watch." I turned the TV on and pulled up the guide. "How about *The Breakfast Club*?"

"Does Barry Manilow know you raid his wardrobe?"

"Is that a yes?"

"You twisted my arm." He rummaged through the Chinese and picked up a box of beef and broccoli. "I'm in."

Chapter Thirty-six

He left around eleven. It was nice to feel secure and have my college friend back in my corner. I'll admit, Joshua's presence provided a sense of safety after Mike left and allowed me an easy night's sleep. The next morning, I had a follow-up appointment with a specialist the ER doctor recommended. I decided if Martin was paying big bucks for security, I might as well get some use out of them.

"Hello?" I peeped my head out the door. "Silverthorne guy, are you here?"

Joshua stepped out of an alcove where he could see my door, but not be seen.

"Good, there you are." I waved with my good hand. "Let me get my purse and we'll go. Be with you in two shakes."

I swear he cringed.

Moments later, he hovered a step behind me as we waited for the elevator. The doors swished open, and Mrs. Thundermuffin, wearing her coat of many colors and thigh high silver boots, exited carrying her cat.

"Good morning, Mrs. Thundermuffin."

"Well good morning, Karina. Ah, look at your face." I'd used cover-up, but there was still puffiness, and the makeup couldn't completely cover the damage. "You poor, poor thing. Don't worry, those bruises will be gone faster than a toupee in a hurricane, and you'll be as beautiful as before. How's the arm?"

"Feeling better already. I'm loving your boots, are they new?"

"How did you guess? Speaking of boots, I've got your shoes that were left in the stairwell." She leaned in, winked, and said sotto voce, "I picked them up before the police came, didn't want them left behind in some evidence locker never to be worn. A little staid for my taste, but they suit you perfectly. I'll drop them by this afternoon."

"Thanks, I appreciate that."

"Oh, hello, Mr. Joshua." She batted her eyes. "I see you're still roaming the halls, keeping us safe."

"Yes, ma'am." He followed me into the elevator, and Mrs. Thundermuffin eyed him as the doors closed.

"You changed your clothes."

Joshua wore a navy-blue pea coat, black jeans, and the same boots as yesterday. "Yes, ma'am."

"Does that mean you went home and got some sleep?"

"My shift ended at nine."

"So, who's on the … C-team?"

"Sanchez."

The elevator opened, and I proceeded Joshua out, but he walked ahead of me to open the foyer door. Once I stepped out, I looked around.

"I believe your car is still around back, ma'am."

"I'm not looking for my car. We can take yours."

He eyed me.

"Look, the jig is up. I know Martin hired you to keep an eye on me until he's fixed" —my hand flailed in the air— "whatever he needs to fix. You don't need to hide silently in the shadows like Batman anymore. Besides, even though I didn't take a painkiller this morning, I'll probably need one in an hour, and I can't drive after I've taken one. I've got a doctor's appointment. I'm going to make your job easy. We'll take your car, you can follow me around and be my bodyguard. Isn't that what you're supposed to do?"

"Yes, ma'am."

"So, where's the silver Chevy?"

He dug out his phone. "Jin, we're around front. Come pick us up." A moment later, the SUV pulled to a stop in front of us. Joshua held open the rear door for me.

"You know, you're a real gentleman, Josh. Don't let anyone tell you different." I patted his cheek and climbed in.

The driver wore a black Steelers baseball cap, black leather jacket, and black pants. He stared at Joshua as he climbed into the front passenger seat. "What are we doing?"

I leaned forward between the two front seats. "Hi, I'm Karina Cardinal. Who are you?"

"Jin."

"Just Jin?"

His black brows furrowed, and the scar on the left side of his face elongated the frown he gave me.

I had to smile. "It's the Jin and Josh show. Seriously, it can't get better than that."

"What's going on?"

Josh fought to hold back a smile.

"Jin, as I explained to Josh, the jig is up. You're my bodyguards, and right now I have a doctor's appointment to get to. Isn't this so much easier than following me around, three cars back? Like yesterday?"

If anything, Jin's frown deepened more. "The boss isn't going to like it," he said to Josh.

"Martin will have to deal with it. Now we'd best get moving, because we need to swing by a coffee shop on the way. I'm desperate for some caffeine."

Jin shifted into drive. "That's not the boss I'm talking about."

"Take a right out of the complex and a left on Duke Street, the office is in Falls Church. There's a Starbucks drive-thru on the way."

Jin's mood lifted slightly after I bought coffee for the boys, but it was still Josh who followed me into the doctor's office. My sister texted as I was filling out the paperwork in the waiting room.

> *I'm a bad sister! Forgot you had a doc appointment today. Did you need me to take you?*
> *No worries. I got a lift from a friend.*
> *Thank goodness. See you tonight. I'll bring dinner.*

I gave a thumbs-up emoji and turned to Joshua, who practically overflowed the chair next to me with his broad shoulders. "My sister's coming over for dinner tonight. Try not to shoot her. Okay?"

"Yes, ma'am."

There might have been the teensiest smile. I would have explored it further except a nurse called my name.

"I'll be back," I said in my best Arnold Schwarzenegger voice.

The specialist added nothing new to the diagnosis that the ER doc hadn't already determined. I was told to rest and come back in three weeks. Latesha called while we headed back to my apartment, and I gave her a sanitized version of the mugging.

"Jesus, Mary and Jehoshaphat! You are having the worst luck this week."

"Tell me about it. Although the press seems to have diverted on to other things, I'm going to continue to take leave. Doc says I need to rest up. I'll review the documents you emailed and get them back by close of business."

"Lordy-bee, don't come back yet. Do you need me to bring you something?"

"No, my sister is looking after me. I'm fine, thanks. I'll be back on Monday."

"See you then."

The phone rang as I hung up. I didn't recognize the number. "Hello."

"Ms. Cardinal? It's Detective …"

"Morpheus! What can I do for you?"

A sigh blew across the lines. "I was hoping you could come down to the station."

"What for?"

"We have a lineup."

"Lineup of what?"

"We think we may have found your Batman."

"Why would you put him in a lineup?"

"There are some damages sustained to your building, and leaving the scene of a crime."

I gulped. "When do you want me to come by?"

"As soon as possible. I'll send a squad car to come get you."

"No, that's not necessary. I'm already out and about. I'll swing by in about twenty minutes."

"That's fine. See you then." He hung up.

"Hey, J squared, we may have a problem." Josh shifted and turned to me. "That was our friendly neighborhood detective," I continued. "Says he found Rick, and I'm supposed to identify him in a lineup. You got a beat on your guy?"

He started working the phone as Jin made a U-turn and headed toward the station. It seemed no one had heard from Rick, and he wasn't answering his phone.

With trepidation, I trudged up the steps into the squat, brown brick building. The detective took me into a darkened room with a two-way mirror. On the opposite side, five guys lined up, of varying heights, all dark-haired, and tough looking. They stared back with bored expressions. Rick stood dead center, holding a placard with the number three. The detective had them each step forward for a few seconds and turn to the side.

"It could be number one, no wait, number f-four. Maybe … number … gee, detective," I dithered, "it must have been darker than I realized. I thought I'd be able to identify Batman in the light of day, but now I don't know. I'm sorry, none of these guys looks quite right."

"You're sure?" His eyes narrowed.

"Uh-huh." I held my purse tight. "Can I go now?"

"Yes, Officer Lee will see you out."

I speed-walked my way across the parking lot to the SUV and collapsed in the back seat with a whooshing breath.

Both the men turned to stare at me. "What happened?" Jin asked.

"Your precious Rick is safe."

The J brothers shared a look.

"Can we go home now?"

Jin started the car and pulled away. I stared out the window and chewed my lip. *When did I become such a crook and a liar?* I'd withheld information from friends, evaded the press, lied to the police, stole a painting from my ex-fiancé's father. *What's next on the roster? Grand theft auto? Who am I covering up for?* Mike said all these Silverthorne guys were mercenaries and assassins. What about Rick—he saved my life, but what if he'd been hired by the other guy? All this subterfuge turned my stomach, and the morning's coffee churned like lava.

"Are you okay?" Josh inquired. "You look pale. Is your shoulder hurting?"

"It's fine," I whispered.

"Are you sure?" He pulled his sunglasses down, his face drawn with concern.

I pinched the bridge of my nose. "Just ... take me home."

Nobody spoke the rest of the way, and I hopped out of the car before Joshua could come around to open the door. Once in the elevator, Josh pushed the button for the fifth floor for me. "Look, the Company appreciates your ... cooperation in this matter."

I snorted. "Do you guys do wet work?"

"Uh …"

"An honest answer please."

"No, I don't."

"But that Rick guy, he does?"

"Not that I know of."

"Yeah, right." I crossed my arms.

The doors opened but Josh's arm barred the way. "Hold on a sec." He paced left, then right. "You may proceed."

I stalked down to my apartment, keyed in, and pushed the door open. "Would you like to check it?"

Josh moved past me, but I didn't wait for him to give me the all clear before entering myself. He came back to the foyer as I was wrestling with my coat.

"Let me help you with that." He removed it, hung it in the closet, then cleared his throat. "You did a good thing today. Don't feel guilty. Rick's a good man."

"How can you be so sure? Did he save your life in Iraq or something?"

"No, Jin's."

The long scar across Jin's cheek and jaw came to mind. "What was it?"

"IED."

"Special Forces?"

He nodded.

"Jin, is that Vietnamese?"

"Korean."

I scrutinized him, trying to decide if he just fed me a load of crapola. His face remained as serious as ever.

"Can you get Rick on the phone for me?"

He pulled his cell out and dialed. "It's me. Yeah, we brought her there. She'd uh … like to speak with you." He listened for a moment, then held the phone toward me.

"Rick?"

"How can I help you, Ms. Cardinal?"

"How are the ribs?"

"Sore. How's the shoulder?"

"Sore. I wanted to talk to you because I thought, since you tore the guy's mask off, you might've gotten a better look than I did. I figured I could miraculously remember more details to give the police. Since it's clear you won't be speaking with them."

"It was too dark, and everything happened so fast, I didn't get a good look."

"Nothing?"

There was a slight pause before he answered. "Height and weight. He was white. Maybe mid-forties. Does that help?"

"Not really, I was able to provide that."

"I'm sorry."

"Yeah, me too. What would you have done if I'd identified you?"

"I would have dealt with it."

I remained silent.

After a moment, he filled the silence. "I admit it would have complicated things. Anything else?"

"Yeah, you owe me one."

"Yes, I do." He hung up, and I handed the phone back to Joshua.

"Give me one of those Silverthorne cards with your cell number on it. That way, I can ring you when I need to go out."

He withdrew a card from his back pocket, scribbled down his number, and placed it on the foyer table.

I opened the door. "Don't forget my sister is coming over tonight."

"I promise I won't shoot her."

I slanted my eyes at him as he passed by. "Did you just make a funny? That's a smile. Right? That little half-smirk thing you did. That's a smile?"

He shrugged and turned the corner.

I spent the rest of the afternoon working. My sister rang at 6:05 p.m. and I buzzed her into the complex. The scent of pizza entered the apartment before she did.

"Jilly, you are the best. Put it on the island and take off your coat. I'll pull out plates."

"I ran into this total hottie in the elevator."

"Oh, yeah? What did he look like?"

"Blond, built like a brick shithouse, pale eyes. Do you know him?"

"Yes, the condo complex hired him for security."

"Well, now that you're a free agent again, you should go for him. I wouldn't kick him out of my bed."

I rolled my eyes. "Let's give it some time. I just broke up with Patrick."

"I'm not saying you should *date* him. Just you know, have a quick fling, like in the janitor's closet or something."

"*Jillian!*" I flung an oven mitt at her.

"What? It'll help you get over Patrick." She pulled a slice of pizza onto her plate. "Which, by the way, is one of the reasons I'm here."

"Oh, really?"

"Yes, you haven't told me why you and Patrick broke up."

I poured Diet Pepsi for the two of us and handed one to her.

"Spill. What did he do? Cheat?"

"No. What makes you say that?"

"Just a guess."

"No, he didn't cheat on me. He put a tracking app on my phone."

Jillian paused mid-chew.

I sighed. "And he was basically spying on me because he was worried I would cheat on him."

She swallowed. "He … what? What kind of tracking app?"

"Spyware, like the one parents put on their teenagers' phones."

"How'd you figure it out?"

"He tracked me, and after I behaved like a fishwife, he confessed."

"Wow, that's … wow. Then you broke up with him."

"That's right."

"Do you think he hired this mugger to get back at you?"

I dropped the pizza slice onto my plate. "No!"

"Hm … I'm not so sure. Patrick seems like the vindictive type."

"Well, he's not. You can put that crazy idea out of your head. He called and was very concerned. He offered to bring food."

"Oh, then maybe he hired this guy to rough you up so he could come to the rescue."

If I didn't know what I knew, I'd actually be contemplating Jillian's theory. Especially considering Patrick didn't take the split too well. I shook my head. "I think not."

She delivered a disbelieving shrug and finished chewing. "Why don't you tell me what was in the box I shoved onto the metro platform?"

I should have known we'd come back around to this. It was one of the reasons I put her off yesterday. "Jilly … please … you promised. No questions. Besides, it's best—"

"—if I don't know. Fine. I have a fair idea of what it was anyway. What I don't understand is how *you* got involved." She held up her hand. "No, no, you don't have to explain or lie to me. Just know, one day, there will be a body that needs burying, and you're going to help. No questions asked." She rapped the counter with each syllable of her last sentence.

"Fine. But I'm not going over a cliff in a convertible with you, Thelma."

"No, I'm Louise, you're Thelma."

"Which one's Thelma?"

"Geena Davis. You're taller than me and have reddish hair, so you're Thelma," Jillian said.

"If you say so."

"How'd the doctor's appointment go?"

"No new information to tell. He reiterated what the ER doc said. I've got to go back in a few weeks for a follow-up. Why don't you tell me about Tony? What a sweetie."

She blushed and looked down at her plate. "He's fine."

"Fine? That's it? When is your next date?"

"We're having dinner on Friday."

"Are you excited?"

"Yeah…"

I grinned. "Good for you. Tell him I said hello, and thanks again for his excellent care."

My sister left around nine, and I decided it was time to break the news to my parents. Mom answered. I didn't tell her about the tracking app, but rather alluded to a fight and broken trust that couldn't be mended. She took it surprisingly well, assuring me that if it wasn't in my heart to love Patrick forever and ever, then we simply weren't meant to be. Then I broke the news about the mugging, again playing down my injuries and how frightened I was. Mom wanted to fly out immediately. The thought of her coming at a time like this, especially while I had J.J. and company following me around, had me cringing. It took a bit of convincing, but I assured her Jillian had everything well at hand, and I didn't need any more help.

I went to bed that night with fewer thoughts weighing on my conscience. My parents had been told about my un-engagement, my sister stopped asking the hard questions, and my friendship with Mike seemed to be in a decent place. Additionally, having Silverthorne outside my front door gave me a sense of security and peace of mind.

Chapter Thirty-seven
MARTIN

The sun disappeared from the horizon, and the evening gloom settled around Marty as he stared at the business card, its upper right edge now dirty and frayed, having been worried by his thumb and forefinger. It'd taken him a full forty-eight hours to put everything into motion, and now he knew it was time to convince Monaldo. He pressed each button with deliberation.

"Vincent speaking."

"This is Martin."

"Mr. Dunne." He clicked his tongue. "The news has been riveting."

"I need to speak with him."

"Mr. Monaldo is quite busy. Perhaps you could give me the message and I'll pass it along."

"I believe he'll want to hear what I have to say."

"And what would that be?"

"It's best if *I* speak to him. I wouldn't want my message to be misinterpreted or force him to take action that might ... endanger his own interests."

"How's that?"

"Tell him ... I've taken out an insurance policy. You know the number."

It took fewer than five minutes for the phone to ring. "Hello."

"Vincent tells me we should speak."

"First, you need to leave the girl alone. She knows nothing."

"And by nothing ... you're referring to..."

"I fed her a bunch of bullshit about how I acquired the item on a dark net auction site."

"I believe you were given specific instructions regarding the item."

"The situation changed. It was discovered by accident."

"I see ... and you're saying you lied about it."

"Yes. I lied to her. You need to leave her alone."

"I can hear the sincerity in your voice, Martin, but how can I be certain you're not lying to me now?"

"You can't. What you can be certain of is this—I have taken steps to document every transaction regarding the item, you, and a certain recording. All of which incriminates both of us. Should anything untoward happen to me, my wife, sons, or the girl, these materials would automatically be made public, and damn the consequences."

"I see."

"If you leave it alone, your name will never come up. If you force my hand ..."

"Touché, Mr. Dunne."

"Do I have your word?"

"I suppose ... we now have to trust each other."

"And the girl?"

"If she truly knows nothing, then she has nothing more to fear from me."

"No more late-night visits."

"That was ... poorly done. It wasn't my intention."

"I think it best if we sever our business connection once this contract is complete."

"Agreed. Goodbye, Martin."

The line went dead. Marty slugged back a finger's worth of whiskey, took aim, and threw the glass across the room. It hit one of the posts and shattered.

****

The darkness disconcerted Marty as he entered from the

garage. He banged his hand against the corner of the wall searching for the light switch. Usually, Molly turned the little hallway sconce on for him in the evenings, or the kitchen lights would throw enough illumination to light his way. Neither were on, and there was no scent of cooking dinner. He glanced back in the garage to assure himself that her car was there. Walking further into the house, he removed his coat.

"Molly?"

Past the kitchen, the family room remained in darkness as well, lit only by the little plug nightlights Molly had scattered through the house. He checked his phone for messages and then their joint calendar. No events were listed for tonight.

"Molly? Ivan?" His voice echoed in the silence as he stood waiting for the click of Ivan's nails to greet him. "Mols?" The hairs on the back of his neck stood on end, and his coat dropped to the floor.

Have I miscalculated my move with Monaldo?

He pounded up the backstairs, two at a time, his hands flicking on light switches as he passed. A hollow emptiness met his calls, as one-by-one the top floor rooms blazed to life: the den, the boys' rooms, the guest room, Molly's office/craft room, two guest bathrooms, the master bedroom. A wrinkled dress and pair of pantyhose lay draped across their king-sized bed, but otherwise everything seemed in order.

Frantic, Marty raced down the front stairs. He checked the front door and found it locked. The living room, dining room, and laundry room revealed nothing. He headed back to the kitchen for his phone when he noticed his office door was open a fraction, and a soft glow emanated through the crack. Slowly he pushed the heavy wood; it swung silently inward.

Marty's heart still pounded, but what met his eyes gave him pause. Ivan sat next to the tall wingback chair in front of the desk, his ears perked. He let out a whine and pawed at the floor, but didn't move forward because a tight fist restrained his collar. The empty crystal decanter sat on the desk next to a bulbous brandy glass full of whiskey.

"Molly?"

"Come in ... Martin."

Uh-oh. It was never a good sign when Molly called him Martin in that tone. She didn't bother to rise or look over the chair to greet him. All he saw was her perfectly manicured, clenched hand.

"Molly, what's going on? I've been calling your name for the past ten minutes." He patted Ivan on the head as he came around. "Didn't you..."

She wore an old sweatshirt and jeans, her hair was mussed and makeup smudged, giving her deep raccoon eyes. The rest of her face was pale, and the scowl she wore only sought to highlight her wrinkles. She looked older than her fifty-seven years. Martin froze, towering above her, as she gazed blankly past him at the French doors.

"I received a call today ... from Patrick. He and Karina have split." She released Ivan, and the dog sank to the floor, placing his head between his outstretched paws. "I knew they'd had a fight but..." She shook her head. "He started the conversation by telling me Karina was mugged the other night. Her shoulder's been injured. I asked what I should take her. Then he told me they were no longer seeing each other, and she gave him the ring back."

Marty sucked in a breath.

"I argued with him, telling him I simply couldn't believe it. Then he confessed he did something stupid and unforgivable, but he wouldn't tell me what. I told him to apologize, and as long as he hadn't cheated on her, which I knew he would never do considering the damage Chrystal did to him, Karina would eventually forgive him. He said, 'no, this family has already done enough, and we should just leave her in peace.'"

"Mol—"

"I thought about that statement for a long time. What on earth could this family have done to Karina that would make him say that? I thought about it as I drove to the nail salon and all the way home. It kept popping up in my head as I paid the bills. I thought about it as I came into your office to look for some stamps. And then … I found this." She reached down the side of the chair and pulled out the stack of 8X10 glossies, splaying them across her lap. The one with Karina rested on top.

"I can ex—"

"Something's wrong, Martin. Something has been very wrong. I've known it for months, and I've been waiting for you to talk to me. I expected it to be something about work. When you didn't come to me, I searched your coat pockets, smelled your shirt collars, reviewed the credit card statements, and even, on the days you claimed to be working late, checked on you at the office, searching for some sign that you were seeing another woman. I became ashamed of my suspicions when I found nothing. But this… This is something completely different. Do you know what this looks like to me?"

Marty opened his mouth to answer, but she cut him off before he could get a word out. "It looks like someone is trying to blackmail you, and they're using the safety of the family to do it."

"Molly, I don't know—"

"By the way, did you know there is a black Dodge Charger at the end of the street that, I believe, might have followed me home from the salon today? Would that have something to do with these?" She tossed the pictures onto the desk.

Rubbing a hand through his hair, Marty slumped into the accompanying chair.

"The truth, Martin. If you value our marriage and wish to celebrate our next anniversary *together*, you will tell me the truth.

All of it. Right. Now."

So he did. Everything. Going back to Jenkins' poor gambling choices all the way to tonight's conversation. He told her about the painting. How Karina had somehow discovered it and taken it. The meeting in D.C. and the lies he'd fed to Karina to keep her and the family safe. *The Boston Globe* article that put her in harm's way, and the subsequent attack. He even revealed Patrick's unforgivable mistake of putting a tracking app on her phone.

While he spoke, Molly gripped the brandy glass as if her life depended upon it, occasionally taking a drink to fortify her nerves.

"And the Charger is the security I've hired to watch over you." By the time he finished, Marty's spine and shoulders had slumped far down into the chair, making him look like a little boy waiting for the headmaster's punishment.

"That's quite a load you've been carrying around."

Marty nodded.

"You brandished a weapon at Karina?"

"I'm sorry. I allowed my passion for the artwork to cloud my judgement."

She took a long drink of the amber liquid. "That's quite a load you've put on that young lady's shoulders."

"I know," he sighed and scrubbed at the stubble on his chin.

"How much does Patrick know?"

"Not much. Considering what's happened, I imagine he's pieced some of it together."

"What on earth was he thinking, tracking her phone like that?"

"It stems from Chrystal."

"That little bitch. Her legacy is like a bad penny that turns up at the worst of times." Molly placed the snifter on the desk and held out her arms.

Marty sank to his knees in front of her, placed his head on

her lap, and wrapped an arm around her legs.

"Now what are you going to do?" she asked, stroking her fingers through his hair.

"I told you, I've created an insurance policy. I'll talk with the security company tomorrow."

"You are having all of us watched?"

"Except Jonathan. I figured it'd be pretty tough for them to track him down in Afghanistan."

"Explain more about this dark website."

Marty winced as he divulged his part in the black site auction last year.

"Do you think there may be other stolen paintings on there?"

"Maybe."

She stopped stroking his hair.

"Yes."

"You have to tell the FBI and that museum."

"But the Vermeer didn't come from the auction site."

"I understand. I want you to get on your encrypted email account and anonymously send that information to the FBI and the museum."

"Alright, I'll do it in the morning."

"No, now." She pushed his head off her lap, and he sat back on his heels. "You've been involved in a pile of pig shit, and I understand why you did what you did. But giving that website information to the FBI could help them. And I think it'll be good for your conscience. Since this is the avenue you've taken, it'll help Karina. Patrick's right, she's gotten the short end of the stick while trying to do what's best for this family. I don't blame her for running away from us. She could have easily made an anonymous tip, and we would have had a full-scale raid on our hands. Both of us could have been arrested if they'd found the painting. Don't wait for the confirmation. It's the real thing. You know it. Send them the address and your code key."

"The encryption key has expired. They can't use it to get on."

"They hire all sorts of professional hacker types. I'm sure with your information they'll make headway."

"You think this is the best idea?" Marty doubted his old key would break the site, but if it helped Molly forgive him for this mess, and maybe get him out of the doghouse, he'd do it.

"I really do. Now, I'm hungry." She pushed to her feet; Ivan and Marty rose with her. "I'm going to reheat some of that lasagna from the other night while you take care of this."

"Sounds like a plan." He slid his reading glasses on as the computer booted up.

"And, Martin" —She waited for him to look up from the screen— "don't ever keep something like this from me again. I'm not a child that needs your protection. We're a team. We work better together. Understood?"

"Yes, dear."

Marty watched the dog follow his wife out the door and thanked the lord she hadn't kicked him out of the house like he deserved. That woman was a saint. Much like Karina. It was too bad his son made a mull of it. He could have used a lady like that in his corner.

Chapter Thirty-eight

Two Months Later

"I'm surprised you came." A man's voice interrupted my contemplation of a letter by Percy Bysshe Shelley.

I turned to find Sam Bradigan, looking debonair in his tuxedo, at my shoulder. "I assumed you sent the invitation."

"I did. I'm surprised you accepted."

"And miss rubbing elbows with the relative Who's Who of Boston Society?"

He produced an arch expression.

"Okay, I'll admit, I was in the neighborhood."

Those eyes bored into me.

I sighed, "Curiosity won the day."

His face relaxed. "Have you seen it yet?"

I shook my head and held up a small square card. "I've been placed in group forty-six. I figured I'd take advantage of the free entry to view the rest of the museum."

A few weeks ago, I received an embossed invitation to the museum's event unveiling Vermeer's *The Concert*. Initially, I dismissed the notion, tossing the invitation straight into recycling. The next morning, due to a cancellation, I was invited to speak at a conference in Boston the exact weekend of the Gardner event. It seemed fate was knocking at my door. I accepted the speaking engagement and dug the museum's pretty communique out of the bin.

From the looks of those milling about in designer dresses and diamond necklaces, I deduced the invite list was restricted to wealthy current and potential patrons and other Boston VIPs. Upon arrival, we were each handed a card with a number on it. To maintain crowd control, museum staff took small groups in to view the return of its prodigal son. Every few minutes an announcement would come over the loudspeaker, broadcasting the next number like a deli counter line. In the meantime, free champagne and light appetizers were offered in the courtyard. I'd bypassed the light fare in favor of wandering the halls to view Isabella's exceptional collection.

Tomorrow morning, the museum would reopen to the public. Timed tickets to view the Vermeer had gone up on the museum website a week ago. They were sold out for the next three months.

An announcement came over the loudspeakers. "Group number twenty-one, please gather in The Rafael Room."

I looked at Sam and shrugged.

"Follow me."

My pumps tapped loudly against the wooden stairs as I struggled to keep up with his fast clip, bypassing dozens of other folks meandering through the various rooms. We reached a pair of security guards outside the Dutch Room. Bradigan shared a brief word with the shorter of the two men and motioned me past. Half a dozen people gathered around the painting. It was placed in the middle of the room, on a sturdy gilt pedestal, surrounded by stanchions and red velvet ropes. Lighting shone down from above, accenting the art piece.

"I thought it was supposed to live over the desk there," I whispered and pointed.

"In a year, it'll be rehung in its original location. Right now, it's easier to view and move the crowds through if we leave it here."

"Seems awfully easy for someone to just pick it up and walk out with it."

"It's surrounded by laser sensors."

"Haven't you ever seen *Ocean's Twelve?*"

The arch look returned. "Other security measures have also been taken."

I nodded. "Will you enclose it in glass again?"

"That has yet to be determined. Did you see the patch on the back?"

My eyes darted to him. It would be foolish of me to admit I'd handled the painting. I remained mute and raised a brow.

"We dated it within the past twenty years. The prevailing theory is that the painting was torn when they broke the glass."

"Is the patch done well?"

"Expertly."

"In other words, a professional saw to the painting while it was on the lamb."

"Cleaned it, too."

I drew in a breath. "Another avenue to follow in your investigation?"

"Indeed."

"How long did it really take before you knew?"

"Within the first twenty-four hours of its return."

"So all that waiting around? The experts? Tests?"

He didn't answer.

The crowd cleared. I approached the masterpiece, as close as the roping allowed. "He did beautiful work. There's something about the way the light reflects off the paints, giving it a luminescence."

"I didn't realize you were an art connoisseur."

"A dilettante only." The room began filling with the next group, and I moved on. To my surprise, Bradigan followed.

"We appreciated receiving the dark net site and encryption key. I'm surprised you didn't wait to hear the outcome."

"It wasn't my idea. My client acted on his own. Have you been able to get into the auction site?"

"We're working with the FBI. Interestingly, they received the same information we did … from a blind email account."

"Mm." Marty confessed what he'd done after it was a fait accompli. Neither Jessica nor I were pleased; we both felt it made him more vulnerable because he'd given away his bargaining chip. However, maybe his act of goodwill won him points, because the FBI laid off, and my life pretty much returned to normal.

Well, let's say a new normal. When Marty told me about the email, he also explained that the Silverthorne boys would be discharged at the end of the week. I kind of missed my linebacker-sized shadow and grouchy driver. The first few days after they were gone, I found myself jumpy and on constant alert. I didn't sleep well and checked the locks a dozen times before going to bed. I'd even had a handy man add a slide bolt into the floor for good measure.

A week after my bodyguards had been dismissed, I received a call from Detective Morpheus informing me that my stairwell attacker had been identified through a hair strand pulled from the balaclava Rick pulled off during the fight, and there was an APB out on the mafia connected enforcer. The knowledge that my assailant had been identified did nothing for my peace of mind until, three days later, Morpheus called back to tell me the man had been found … in the trunk of his car with a single gunshot through his head.

Needless to say, I didn't mourn his death. It was also the first good night's sleep I'd had in weeks. However, I decided, once the shoulder fully healed, to sign up for self-defense classes. In the meantime, I'd purchased a stun gun online. It was pink and fit handily in my purse.

We'd moved out of the Dutch room when my phone rang. "Would you excuse me?" I made my way to one of the balconies overlooking the courtyard. "Hello."

"Hey, you. How's Boston? How'd the lecture go?"

"I nailed it."

"Are you at the museum yet?"

"I am ... wearing Old Faithful and rubbing elbows with the Boston elite."

"I'm sure you fit right in."

I sniffed. "Well, at least I know the pearls I'm wearing are the real thing."

"When is your flight home tomorrow?"

"Almost noon. I get in just after one."

"How about I pick you up and take you to lunch? We can check out that new place that opened up on King Street."

"Sure, I'd love that."

"What's your flight number? I'll park and come in."

"Oh, Mike, that's sweet, but you don't need to do that. I'll text you the arrival time when I get back to the room. You can pick me up outside—in the loading zone."

"How's the shoulder feeling?"

"Fine. It was a little sore yesterday from hauling my bags around. But not today."

"Good, good…"

"How's your day been?"

"Boring. After the gym, I watched a *Back to the Future* marathon."

The conversation lulled.

"Well, I sh—" "I mi—" we both spoke at the same time.

"You go," I laughed.

"No, you first."

"I was just going to say goodnight and get back to the party."

"Right, then … um … have a good night."

"What were you about to say?"

"Nothing."

Silence.

"I'm getting a weird vibe," I prodded.

He sighed, "I was going to say … I miss you."

I'll admit, my heart warmed at his words. "I miss you, too. See you tomorrow."

"Looking forward to it."

I disconnected and watched the milling crowd below. A string quartet sat at one end, playing a lovely Bach concerto, conversations hummed, dishware clinked, and a few couples danced in the center. I took a moment to thank the powers that be that those tumultuous months were behind me and life was back on an even keel.

Guided Reading Questions

Available on Ellen's Website
EllenButler.net

Afterward

On March 18, 1990, in the wee hours of the morning, two men dressed as police officers obtained entry into the Isabella Stewart Gardner Museum. Holding the guards at gunpoint, the thieves marched them to the basement and proceeded to blindfold and handcuff them. Then the pair returned to the upper floors and, for the next eighty-one minutes, stole eleven paintings/drawings and two artifacts valued at $500 million. None of the stolen masterpieces were insured. The Gardner Museum robbery is considered one of the highest valued thefts of private property in history.

In the years following the heist, FBI, investigative reporters, professional art recovery specialists, and amateur detectives have spent hundreds of man hours trying to locate the paintings. As of this book's publication, all the artworks remain at large. The Gardner Museum has offered a $10 million reward for information leading to the recovery of the masterpieces.

According to *The Boston Globe*, "authorities said they believed some of the artwork changed hands through organized crime circles, and moved from Boston to Connecticut and Philadelphia, where the trail went cold." It is based on this article I created Monaldo, my Philadelphia mobster. Undoubtedly, the treasures are long gone from Philadelphia, shipped overseas, buried in nondescript warehouses, or possibly in the hands of unscrupulous private collectors—maybe hidden behind their fireplace wall.

Where is the art now? Well, that answer all depends upon which theory you subscribe to. There is a surfeit of theories on who perpetrated the theft, including connections to Mafia gangster James "Whitey" Bulger. The FBI has chased down numerous leads and though they believe they've identified the original thieves, there still seem to be more questions than answers about where the paintings disappeared. In March 2017, *The Globe* wrote an article titled, "Six Theories Behind the Stolen Gardner Museum Paintings." My research uncovered at least half a dozen more beyond the six in the article. However, among the varied theories, one overarching theme seems to remain at the forefront: Mafia connections. Whether domestic or international, organized crime plays a role throughout almost every storyline, including claims that the paintings were originally stolen to exchange them for Mafia capo, Vincent Ferrara, from prison. In my discussions with Robert Wittman, a former FBI agent who worked undercover on the case and co-authored the book *Priceless*, he believes the paintings are still out there, waiting to be recovered.

What's my theory? I agree with Wittman. The paintings have been split up, but they're still out there, maybe in the hands of organized crime members and being used as currency, e.g. paintings for drugs or weapons. I find it likely a private collector got hold of one or two. However, don't take *my* word for it. I recommend, dear reader, *you* take the time to visit the Isabella Stewart Gardner Museum website to view the stolen art (www.gardnermuseum.org). Do your own research. Who knows? Maybe you will look at the artwork and realize the pencil drawing on Aunt Martha's living room wall is a long-lost Degas from Isabella's museum.

In the meantime, I wish good luck to all the people involved in the search for the paintings. I had such fun incorporating *The Concert* into Karina's story and am hopeful, one day, the Vermeer finds its way home where I can visit it in person.

Acknowledgements

The inspiration for *Isabella's Painting* came to me when I caught a short documentary clip, while channel surfing, a few years before I began writing Karina's story. I started researching the heist for no other reason than fascination. The research began working its way into my dreams and random thoughts. Eventually, I determined to include the stolen artwork into a novel, and Karina's character began to develop. It was at this point that I began reaching out to my network to help me develop the storyline and characters. To those who provided their time and knowledge, I can't thank them enough.

Mimi, my ninety-four-year-old grandmother, still sharp as tack and a continuing patron, thank you for believing in me. To Emily at Lucky 13, my editor, *Isabella's Painting* wouldn't be the same without your awesome editing skills and sage advice. My former American Academy of Physician Assistants colleague, Sandy Harding, Karina's character would have been weaker without your knowledge of lobbying and Capitol Hill politics. Since Karina Cardinal will be an ongoing series, I appreciate your continued wisdom and time. My high school friend, Matt Fine, your introduction to a respected contributor was much appreciated. However, I believe your biggest contribution came from sharing your personal history with me, and describing how you came to be where you are in life. Your own confident and understated funny personality was an inspiration for one of the characters. Former FBI Agent, Robert Wittman, your knowledge of the case, undercover work, and advice was both fascinating and invaluable. It helped shape the storyline and a key plot points. Finally, Anthony Amore, at the Isabella Stewart Gardner Museum, thank you for answering my impertinent questions. To all my contributors, I ask that you forgive my fictional characters their flaws, over-exaggeration, and missteps. As we know from

Hollywood movies, sometimes we writers force plotlines to move in a direction opposite to real life simply because fiction makes for a better story. I like to call it, the magical hand of plot device.

Fatal Legislation

Chapter One

"Excuse me, Senator Kollingwoods," I interrupted, pausing the senator's tirade against one of her fellow colleagues for the pejorative comments he directed at her on the Senate floor. Her frustration was not out of line; however, my quarry, the reason I'd been skulking around the Capitol offices, exited the men's room and was walking away at a fast clip. "I see Senator Harper and must speak to him."

Senator Kollingwoods turned to follow my gaze as Harper turned the corner. "I'll just bet you do," she said with a smirk.

"Thanks for your time." I edged past. "I'll provide those research stats to Marianne tomorrow."

"Give him hell, Karina," she called as I strode around the corner.

Lucky for me, my target had been halted for a moment by a staffer, and I caught up with him as he entered the elevator labeled SENATORS ONLY.

"Senator Harper," I called out.

His milky blue gaze showed no surprise at my approach, and he waved me into the car. "Ms. Cardinal, I've been wondering when I'd hear from you. I'm headed over to the Russell building."

The doors closed behind me, and the elevator operator, an elderly African-American man dressed in the requisite navy-blue blazer and striped tie uniform, pressed the button that would take us to the basement.

"Did you have a nice weekend, Arnold?" Harper asked the

elevator operator.

"Yes, Senator. My oldest granddaughter came home for the weekend."

"She's a sophomore this year?" The senator's wheezing breaths filled the small car.

"Yes, sir."

"Remind me, what college is she attending?"

"University of Maryland."

We ended our descent with a slight bump. "Give my best to your wife."

"Will do, sir."

The elevator spit us out not far from the entrance to the underground passageways connecting the Capitol to the Russell, Dirksen and Hart Senate office buildings. For an overweight man in his early seventies, he walked at a relatively brisk pace, and my sensible heels clacked against the aged russet stone flooring. Fortunately, my height provided an advantage when walking with taller men and I could easily replicate their stride.

"How'd you get past security?"

"I came over from Dirksen with Senator Kollingwoods."

Either he preferred not to talk over my noisy heels or his own pace was too much for him, because he slackened his gait. The heavy breathing continued, and I was relieved he slowed us down. "You want to know why I voted against the bill," he stated.

"I don't understand. You voted for it in committee, and on the Senate floor the first time. Why?" We exited the drab putty-colored walls of the Capitol basement to enter the bright white halls of the tunnel system.

"You know why."

"The amendment?" I clarified.

"Amendment? Try amend*ments*."

"That happens with every bill as it passes back and forth between the two houses," I pointed out. "Everyone has to do a little give and take. We knew it wouldn't come back the same way it went over. Some negotiating has to be done."

"Negotiating?" He gave a dark laugh. "Is that what you call it? By the time it came to a vote on the Senate floor, there was so much pork added to it you could wrap the White House up in bacon and deep fat fry it like a Thanksgiving turkey." He indicated for me to proceed him down the short escalator.

"Granted, I wasn't thrilled with the ten million Texas package," I conceded as we rode down. "But, overall the bill retained its integrity. It would have helped the lower income families."

"The Texas package was the least of my concerns. Did you know Florida stuck on a fifty million grant to research chickens?"

"Wild fowl, migratory birds."

"Ducks, geese, chickens!" He coughed and pressed a hand against his chest. "What does it matter?"

One of the trams that carried passengers through the tunnel to the Russell building cruised around the curve and out of sight. The other tram sat empty with an OUT OF ORDER sign on its side.

"I believe it had something to do with research on aging."

"Fifty million! For fowl! Let's walk."

I squinted at Harper. Beads of sweat covered his upper lip and his coloring seemed to have paled. "Are you sure you don't want to wait for the tram?" I asked.

"My doc says I need to get more exercise." He lumbered past the tram stop to the walking path. "I'd have been willing to vote for it until the Uptown Trio gutted the incentives."

"I agree the incentives were a blow. But, when your support departed, you took your own trio along, Tottengott, Goldman, and Tucker. Surely the incentives were a minor blip that could have been righted through section seven, part c. I won't even mention the position you put me in with the Alliance or the damage it's done to my reputation and possibly my career."

"Pfft. Your reputation is fine," he said. "You can't tell me the

National Healthcare Advocacy Alliance is going to fire you over this. You're too well connected, and I'm sure they didn't like the changes either."

They didn't, but I wasn't about to let him get away that easily.

"Besides," he continued, "Tottengott, Goldman, and Tucker make their own decisions. You can't place their votes at my doorstep."

I gave him an arch glare. Harper had been in the Senate for over twenty-five years and was considered the leader of the few moderate republicans—a dying breed—left in the Legislature. Gloria Tottengott, Stephen Goldman, and Rhonda Tucker tended to stick together on votes, and often followed Harper's lead.

He flapped his hand. "Bah. You can direct that look elsewhere. I'm working on something even better. Something that will make S46 pale in comparison. Something that will put the fat cats in their place."

"Really? Tell me. How can I help?"

"You'll know when I'm good and ready for you to know. You lobbyists are all the same. Couldn't keep a secret if your life depended on it, and right now I'm working the back channels. I decided it's time to call in some chips . . . maybe all of them." His breath came out in pants and he stumbled.

"Senator!" I reached out to steady him.

He pulled a roll of Tums out of his coat pocket, but his hands were so unsteady that he fumbled to open the package.

"Here, let me help you." I used my thumbnail to slit the wrapper, and two antacid tablets fell into his palm.

He pressed his fist against his chest as he chewed. "Must have been the pastrami sandwich I had for lunch."

It was close to six. Lunch had been hours ago, and I didn't like the greenish tinge of his coloring. "Are you going to be okay? Do you want me to get help?" We'd reached the curve, the midpoint between the two buildings. The tram at the far end was empty of passengers and the operator.

"I'll be fine." He puffed past me.

"I'm not sure, Senator." I glanced over my shoulder to see if anyone was coming from the Capitol side. "I think I should—"

His right hand slapped against the wall, his knees buckled, and he pitched forward. I'll never forget the dull, smacking *thud* that reverberated through the tunnel as his skull hit the polished cement floor. In the movies, dramatic events often transpire in slow motion. Not so in real life. The collapse happened in nanoseconds.

"*Senator!*" I crouched down and heaved him onto his back. A bruise on his forehead was already purpling from where it impacted. "Holy shit! Senator Harper!" I shook his shoulder.

No response.

"Help! I need help!" My voice echoed against the glass separating the tram track and concrete block walls.

Visit your book retailer to get your copy of
Fatal Legislation,
A Capitol Hill Murder Mystery

About the Author

Ellen Butler is a bestselling novelist writing critically acclaimed suspense thrillers, and award-winning romance. Ellen holds a Master's Degree in Public Administration and Policy, and her history includes a long list of writing for dry, but illuminating, professional newsletters and windy papers on public policy. She lives in the Virginia suburbs of Washington, D.C. with her husband and two children.

You can find Ellen at:
Website ~ *www.EllenButler.net*
Facebook ~ *www.facebook.com/EllenButlerBooks*
Twitter ~ *@EButlerBooks*
Instagramn~@ebutlerbooks
Goodreads ~ *www.goodreads.com/EllenButlerBooks*

Novels by Ellen Butler
Karina Cardinal Mysteries
Isabella's Painting (book 1)
Fatal Legislation (book 2)
Diamonds & Deception (book 3)
Pharaoh's Forgery (book 4)
Swindler's Revenge (book 5)
Suspense/Thriller
Poplar Place
The Brass Compass
Contemporary Romance
Heart of Design (book 1)
Planning for Love (book 2)
Art of Affection (book 3)

Made in the USA
Middletown, DE
02 October 2022